SILVER CITY

A Novel

ANTHONY MCDONALD

Anchor Mill Publishing

Anthony McDonald

Anchor Mill Publishing
4/04 Anchor Mill
Paisley PA1 1JR
SCOTLAND
anchormillpublishing@gmail.com

Artwork on cover: Copyright   Netfalls Remy Musser. ©
Shutterstock. 'Three Young Men Relaxing On the Beach'.The
individuals depicted in this artwork are models. No inference
in regard to their sexual orientation may be drawn from the
content of the book. Also: Ralf Manteufel. Bristol
Superfreighter Mk 32. Cover design by Barry Creasy

.

For Uli Lenart

ONE

I was young. No, that won't do. I still am young. Young in the heart anyway. Which is the only place that matters. The only place where it's important to be young.

The fact is, I was *very young*. I had some experience of sex although not a great deal. But I had no experience of the bigger things that went along with sex. Love especially. Though all of that was about to change, in the course of one magical summer. It was a summer of the bluest skies and the warmest, freshest air. I spent much of that summer up in those blue skies: beneath, among or above the small fair-weather clouds. As for air... I spent much of that summer walking on it.

The year was nineteen-sixty-three. I was twenty-one. You can call me Jack if you like. That is, if you want to call me anything at all.

***

Nineteen sixty-three. Late May...

I asked in the pub. It was a short walk from the station where I'd arrived. 'Do you have a room for the night? I've got a job interview in the morning. I've had to come down the night before.' I was hopeful because the place was called the Railway Hotel and its frontage was big and impressive: three big-windowed storeys.

'We haven't. Sorry,' said the woman. 'We don't do accommodation.' She had just opened the doors for the evening. I was her first customer. 'But a lot of my

1

regulars let rooms. If you want to stay around for a bit I'll point you towards them. You don't need to worry. You'll get in somewhere.'

I thanked her, but with some misgivings. Railway Hotels in tiny provincial towns were clearly no longer what they'd been a generation or two ago. I hadn't planned to spend the evening downing pints in a public bar. Because it wasn't just an interview I had in the morning. More like an audition. I was going to have to fly an aeroplane.

I asked for a half of Whitbread Trophy. I'd make it last all evening if necessary. I sat at a small table in a corner of the empty, linoleum-floored bar and waited for customers to come in. Customers who might have rooms to let.

The first arrival was an elderly man with a cloth cap on his head and with a spaniel on a lead. He took a seat at a table a few yards away from me, facing in my direction. His dog sat down on the floor next to him and stared at me. I nodded minimally to the man. He returned the greeting equally minimally. The spaniel just went on staring.

The next customer to come in caught my attention instantly. He looked about two years older than my twenty-one. He struck me at once because I found him immediately attractive to look at. The word that came into my mind was *stunning*.

I watched him order a pint. I saw the landlady talking to him as she poured it for him. Then I saw her point me out.

Unhurriedly he walked towards me and my table, his pint of Trophy or Tankard in his hand. It was a warm evening and he had come out without a jacket. The sleeves of his open-necked shirt were rolled up to his elbows. He had wonderfully capable, reassuringly muscled, forearms. His blond hair was cut short and his fair-skinned face was reddened by the sun. His eyes shone out from it like flashes off the sea. I thought, Army boy. I especially liked his cushiony lips and his snubby nose.

Standing beside my table he addressed me. 'Evening.' His eyes flicked towards the landlady, some distance behind him, behind the bar. 'They said you were looking for a room for the night.'

'Yep,' I said. 'I am.'

'I might be able to help.'

'That would be nice.' We'd both been gruff, unsmiling up to now. Army boy, he; Air Force boy, me. But now I smiled. 'Want to sit down?'

'Ta,' he said. He put his pint glass down on the table then pulled out a chair. He sat on it and drew it in under him. Then he smiled at me. 'Name's Will.'

'Jack.' We shook hands across the table.

'I've got a spare room in my bungalow, just minutes away from here. The room's rented to another chap, but he's away tonight. Up in town. If you wanted to make use of it... Just the one night...'

'That would be super,' I said. 'Um... How much...?'

Will looked me up and down – looked up and down as much of me as he could see above the table top, that is – and evidently liked what he saw.

'No. Buy me a pint and we're square.'

'That's very kind of you. I'll put one in.' I began to stand up to go to the bar but Will stopped me. By putting his hand on the back of my hand. The contact was unexpectedly intimate. It gave me a slight shock. Though not an unpleasant one.

'As and when. Unless you've got...'

'No,' I said quickly. 'Not going anywhere. Though I've got to be a bit careful how much I drink. I have to fly a plane in the morning.'

Will's eyes widened slightly. 'Really? Over at the airport? You've got a job there?'

'No. I mean, not yet. It's just an interview. But it is at the airport….'

Will said, 'I work there too. Not as a pilot… I'll explain. Meanwhile…' He raised his glass. 'Here's to you getting the job. You must tell me about it. But I'll be careful of you. Won't let you drink more than's good for you.'

'I've just come out of the Air Force,' I started to say.

'Me too,' interrupted Will. So he wasn't Army, but Air Force, like me. 'Finished my National Service six months ago…'

'Me a week ago… I saw this advert… I used to come to Lydd as a child…'

Will said more quietly, 'Me too. I used to come to Lydd. To watch the aircraft.'

TWO

Lydd. It had a pretty, historic High Street, of houses that were Georgian and Tudor, and there was a church whose size and perpendicular grandeur reminded you of the town's naval importance in the far-off days of the Cinque Ports. Though now the sea lay a couple of miles away. The town was raised just a few feet above the wide flat sea-level corner of Kent that formed the Romney Marsh. The Marsh was shaped like a guitarist's plectrum and Lydd lay close to the pointed tip that reached into the sea towards France. Part of the nearby shoreline was a military firing range and training ground. Big guns were trained on the Channel and were fired out to sea. There was a barracks. Lydd was an Army town these days.

But then had come the reason for my being here, and for Will being here also. Lydd airport. Also known as Ferryfield, constructed in 1954, it was the first purpose-built civilian airport to be created in Britain after the end of the Second World War. It was commissioned by the up-and-coming airline Silver City, and was intended mainly to serve as a terminal for ferrying cars and other vehicles across the Channel in specially adapted freighter planes, in competition with the boat ferries that plied between Dover and Calais, or Folkestone and Boulogne, just a few miles away.

The other end of the air route was the French holiday resort of Le Touquet, little more than forty miles across the sea. It already had an airport of its own, as well as good road links to Paris and beyond. France was an exotic destination in those days, but Lydd was a bare dozen miles from the village I'd grown up in. When the airport opened I was just twelve. I was as interested in aeroplanes as any boy of my age, and so my parents took me there.

I'd never seen a plane close up before. I knew what they looked like. They flew high overhead like silver-winged needles threading the blue, no bigger than stars against the sky. And I was familiar with them in films. (In common with most people then we didn't have TV.) But now, on my first trip to Lydd, winding across the flat distances of the Romney Marsh, I came face to face with aeroplanes for the first time.

Face to face quite literally. As my father drove into the car park the terminal building stood before us. Most of it was just one storey high and the planes – a row of perhaps six of them lined up on the tarmac on the other side – seemed to peer over the roof at me, their pairs of cockpit windows like inscrutable pairs of glassy eyes set in the white paintwork of their upper fuselages.

Two kinds of plane made up this reception line. A couple were Douglas DC3s (familiar to everyone as Dakotas – military transport and parachute-drop planes – from the War.) But most, some four or five of them in today's line-up, were the planes that carried the cars to and from Le Touquet. They were of a type called Bristol Superfreighter Mark 32. And they were very odd looking indeed.

They would have been a deep disappointment to me as a young air-struck boy, if it hadn't been for the novelty and the wonder of the whole experience of being there with them, watching them from just a plate-glass window away.

The planes I knew from books and films were sleek, aerodynamic tubes with swept-back wings, into which film stars disappeared waving, after climbing a flight of a dozen or more stairs. Or they were the wonderful, dashing Spitfires and Hurricanes of the War years. But these, the planes I now looked at through the window, were a very different kettle of bird. They looked as aerodynamic as bumblebees. (Though we have to bear in mind that bumblebees do actually fly: something we might not believe if we didn't regularly see them do it.) Their fuselages were square in section, not circular. This made sense when you saw that they were designed for garaging three cars apiece, but still... And the small passenger cabin at the back was approached by a flight of a mere three steps such as you might find in a public library.

The Superfreighters sat back on their tail wheels, their noses pointed very slightly up in the air. Their wings were set high up, with fuselage, engines and wheels effectively hanging beneath them. Only the cockpit craned up above the wings, like a cobra's head above its hood, its front windows – those two letter-box-shaped eyes – peering forward above the clamshell doors of a nose as thick and blunt as Moby-Dick's.

But as I sat in the airport lounge that first afternoon, taking tea with my parents among the departing passengers, and able to walk out through the windows onto the tarmac itself, where only a waist-high chain-link fence came between me and the shiny machines two dozen yards away, they enchanted me, and I fell under their spell.

I watched as boiler-suited men climbed athletically onto the wings from the roof of a fuel tanker and ran pipes into the wing tanks. I watched the company drivers run cars up the ramps, very quickly, three per aeroplane. I watched the pilots walk up the same ramp in caps and braid, then miraculously appear inside the cockpit high above, now wearing dark glasses, donning headsets and fiddling with unseen knobs and dials. I saw the passengers embark and the nose doors close; saw a tractor attach itself to the tail wheel and haul the monster backwards; and the two engines come to life, one by one. The four-bladed propellors, fourteen feet in diameter, slowly turned, then quickened with a clatter like a football rattle, as puffs of dense silver smoke issued from the exhausts beneath their cowlings. Then you couldn't see the blades, the football rattle changed to deafening machine-gun fire and, by some optical trick, the blur of blades appeared to reverse and turn the other way.

The plane began to move: to tiptoe away into the distance, growing small and silent as the minutes passed before it turned to face us, at the end of the runway, outlined in miniature against the sky, two thirds of a mile away. Then nothing seemed to happen for a while. At last the sound of its quickening engines reached us, and then it began to move slowly towards us with a lion-like roar. When it was again big in front of us its tail wheel rose lightly into the air like a toy and a moment later the whole huge contraption simply flew off the runway before our eyes like a piece of magic. How did it do that? I knew, of course, about lift and drag, and aerodynamic surfaces. But it was magic all the same.

There was one landing and one take-off every ten minutes. And after little more than an hour the first plane that I'd watched as it disappeared into the sky, France bound, was back again, a homecoming speck against the blue…

'I wanted to know everything,' said Will. 'Didn't you?'

'Of course.' It turned out that Will's experience of watching the planes at Lydd as a boy had been the same as mine. It was almost a surprise that we hadn't met at the time. 'I asked my father about the little things attached to the plane. The little aerials and antennae. The wire that ran from the top of the cockpit to the tip of the tail fin. He told me what he knew…'

'Same here,' said Will. There was a pause. We'd been talking for an hour. I'd bought Will the pint I'd promised him and he was drinking it slowly, respectful of my need to restrict myself to a single half in view of what the next morning held in store for me. Now Will shifted on his chair and asked, 'What are you doing about eating?' There was a look in his blue eyes that spoke to me. But I was too inexperienced to make out the words. I liked the look anyway.

'I hadn't thought,' I said.

'I've got some shepherd's pie…' he said a bit diffidently. 'It's left over, but there'd be enough for two.'

'Sounds good. If you're really sure…' I didn't tell him that my heart had leapt crazily. Sharing leftover shepherd's pie with Will, sitting opposite those blue eyes, those sexy lips and that snub nose, seemed as close to heaven as I could dare to imagine.

Will said, 'Of course I'm sure.'

A few minutes later we were in Will's Mini and rattling along the flat but winding lane towards his bungalow.

The flatness of the land… It had to be seen to be believed. The Romney Marsh merged here with the shingle spit that is called Dungeness. The sea lay just a mile or two away to east and south and west. You couldn't see it because of the flatness of the terrain, but it had to be there. Most of what you could see was sky. The great blue dome of it, cloud-flecked this evening, filled the eye.

And then we were there. Will's bungalow was small, built of wooden planks and roofed with synthetic tiles. But it was his own. How he came to have a house of his own at the age of … what, twenty-two? … was an intriguing question. I might ask him at some stage, though not now.

I had fallen in love with flying as a direct result of my childhood trips to Lydd. So had Will. I'd made a point, when it came to National Service time, to try and get into the RAF and I'd managed it. I'd learned to fly on old transport planes. Will had done the same. But I'd been the luckier of us two. I'd flown the number of hours required to get my Wings; Will had flown too few. That was why I was on my way to an interview to be a Bristol Superfreighter pilot, while Will had the job of driver and loader of passengers' cars.

Will lit the Calor-gas oven and popped in the shepherd's pie. He said, 'Sea-kale with it?' which slightly startled me. 'It grows wild here among the stones. We can get some while the pie heats up.'

The sea-kale grew almost outside Will's door. Huge ragged cabbages the size of lavender bushes, pushing up through the shingle that stood in for soil. 'Only pick the tenderest shoots,' Will said. 'We don't want to chew through the outside leaves.' And so I picked those tender inside leaves and so did Will. When we got back inside we boiled them up and by the time they were cooked the pie had warmed through. We ate our simple meal in Will's shabby living room, with Kia-Ora orange squash to wash it down, like two members of the Famous Five.

'The chap whose room you're having tonight's a pilot too,' Will told me casually. 'First Officer, anyway. Like you'll be…'

'Only if…' I cautioned.

'Don't worry. You will.' From across the plain table Will gave me a blue lightning-flash smile. 'Michael his name is. The chap whose room you're…'

'Yeah, yeah.' Suddenly I'd stopped wanting tomorrow. I'd stopped wanting to fly. I just wanted Will. I wanted to stay with him for ever. Here, in a shabby bungalow on a bleak peninsula, drinking orange squash full of cyclamates, and eating warmed-up shepherd's pie. For the rest of my life.

'Sometimes I go night fishing,' Will said when we'd finished our meal. 'I'd say, let's go down and do some tonight, but we've both got early starts…'

'Perhaps we could just drive down, though, and look at the sea?' I might have sounded peculiar, but the sea wasn't something I saw every day.

I was relieved to see that Will was taken by the idea. 'Yeah,' he said. 'Let's go.'

Down to the sea was hardly the right way to put it. Lydd airport had an elevation of precisely three metres above mean sea level, and so did Will's bungalow – as well as everywhere else round here. We drove across the flat for a mile or so and then the shingle stopped abruptly, and so did we, just before the pebbles shelved down into the sea.

We'd stopped near an inn that was called The Pilot. It stood almost alone on the shore. Just a few shacks and cottages kept it company. They all looked as though they'd blown here on the wind. We didn't go into The Pilot. That morning interview…

We sat on the sloping beach together and looked at the breaking waves. It was late evening now but still very light. It was the last week in May. The sea seemed endless, the way it does when you're in a small boat. In the far distance, looking leftward – looking north – Dover cliffs were catching the pinkish evening light. Then Will said, 'Hey, look there. Dead ahead. The hump.'

I looked. It might have been a heavily laden container ship that I was staring at. But it wasn't a ship. I knew my local geography. There was only one thing it could have been. I checked with Will. 'That's France?'

'Yep.'

'I didn't know you could see it from here,' I said. 'We're so low down. And it must be…'

'Thirty miles. We're too low to see the cliffs. And it's not the bit you see from Dover anyway. It's some high ground behind Boulogne. Known to us locals as the hump. But it doesn't appear very often. Usually when it does it's in dull weather, not on a bright evening like this.'

I said, 'It's an odd sight.' I thought of Brigadoon.

'In days gone by the local fishermen used it to navigate their way across,' Will said. The words struck me forcefully. If I got the job I wanted, that's what I would do: *navigate my way across.* Le Touquet lay hidden beyond the horizon, just ten miles to the right of the hump. If I got the job… If I got the job I'd see Will again. We could be friends. Come down here at night and fish for sea-bass, and plaice, and Dover sole…

We were sitting facing each other, cross-legged on the stones. I found myself admiring Will's chunky thighs through his cord trousers. And the considerable mound of his crotch. I wondered eagerly what he would look like with his trousers off. The light sank towards the west behind The Pilot. Eastward the sea became a sheet of glass between us and France. On the darkening 'hump' the tiny light of a car or lorry appeared, seeming tentative as it made its way across the lonely top of that distant hill. I wanted to reach out and touch Will's hand. As he had touched mine, across the table in the pub. But I couldn't find any plausible excuse to do so.

THREE

We were driving back to the bungalow. With headlights. 'I heard that centuries ago the fishermen of Dungeness sailed off to Boulogne when they wanted a wife or a bit of sex,' Will said. 'It was easier than to walk across the shingle to Rye. Back then.'

'I suppose it was,' I said. 'No roads to speak of.'

'Not much land either. Dungeness was an island, shaped like a boomerang. Lydd was another, lying in the curved shelter of Dungeness. Rye too…'

'I knew that,' I said. 'Rye's kind of where I grew up.'

'So where, exactly?' Will sounded interested, not just polite.

'Wittersham. On the road from Rye to…'

'To Tenterden,' said Will. 'Which is where I grew up.'

There was a moment's silence as we both contemplated the fact that we'd been born a mere five miles apart.

'We moved away when I was…'

'I went to London…'

'Before I joined the RAF…'

The conversation lasted till we reached the bungalow. I'd have been happy to let it go on all night.

'OK,' Will said, opening a door off the hallway. 'This is Michael's room. Yours for tonight. The bed's…'

'That's fine,' I said in a quickly reassuring voice. I wanted him to know that I wasn't expecting clean sheets for the price of a pint.

'Bathroom's…'

'Yes. If you remember I used it earlier.'

'Of course.' Then we seemed to hang in the hallway, suspended in place and time. We looked at each other. Will's eyes had become very big, though in the dull light of the hallway they looked less blue now. 'I suppose it'd be OK if you had a very small nightcap? Whisky? I mean a seriously small one?'

'Yes,' I said. 'If it was a very seriously small one I suppose it would.'

We sat opposite each other in the spartan living room. The curtains remained open to the night. Again I wanted to reach across to Will and touch him. Again I ached with the knowledge that I couldn't possibly do that. We talked of small things while we drained our thimble glasses. Then Will said. 'I'll drive you in tomorrow. I'm in for eight.'

'My interview's at nine,' I said. 'It doesn't matter. I can hang about. I'd be grateful for the lift.'

'I won't be able to help you get back to the station afterwards…'

'Of course not. I understand. It's only a mile or so. I can walk.'

Then Will gave me a look for which I can't find an adjective. 'If you do get the job… I mean, I'm hoping you get the job… I mean, we'd get to meet again.'

Will's words shook me like an earthquake. What he'd just said was better than anything else on earth he could have.

'I'd better get the job then,' I said, with more sang-froid than I'd ever thought I could muster. 'Because I'd like to see you again.' More than anything else on earth. But I didn't say that, of course.

We looked across the room at each other for one of those long moments in which the whole world unravels and you are too incompetent, or just too young, to deal with it.

'Right then,' said Will. He was the older of the pair of us. It was for him to handle the moment. 'I suppose it's time we turned in for the night.' He didn't mean together. I did know that. Whatever he might have wished. Though that I did not know.

We stood. We parted in the hallway. Stiffly. Without a handshake. 'See you in the morning,' we both said. Will said, 'I'll give you a knock at seven.'

I said, 'I think I'll be awake by then.'

I went into Michael's room and shut the door. I heard Will go into the bathroom, then come out again and go into his own room. Sure that I wouldn't bump into him in the hallway I headed for the bathroom myself, barefoot and naked to the waist. Ablutions over I returned to my temporary bedroom, took my trousers and pants off and hopped into Michael's double bed.

I had a hard-on of course. I usually did when I climbed into bed naked. And at this point I would normally have masturbated. That night I certainly wanted to. The company of Will, his physical beauty, and the fact of his presence in bed just the other side of the flimsy wall that separated us for the night, had stirred me up. But I held off as a matter of courtesy to the unknown Michael. I didn't want to get my spunk all over his sheets. This wasn't entirely a matter of polite selflessness. I didn't want the embarrassment. Even if Michael and I never came face to face I knew that he would forever remember the unknown interview candidate who'd left an unmistakable patch of dried semen in his bed.

Not wanking, though, trying to ignore the craving of the rock-hard thing between my legs, posed problems of its own. With what I had to face in the morning it was going to be difficult enough to get to sleep even if I did wank. Let alone if I didn't. And the other thing was the very real risk of a wet dream in the night. Which would have an even more devastating effect.

I could have reduced the risk of damage by putting my underpants back on, but I knew from experience that that would make very little difference. Not only was I capable of projecting my spunk through quite thick fabric but my dick was rather a long one and if it got stiff in my underpants would often poke its nose out of the top. And anyway, I preferred the feeling of sleeping in the buff, whether sleep was preceded by a wank or not.

I didn't do it. I didn't put on my underpants. And it did take me an age to get to sleep. As if the not-wanking thing and thoughts of tomorrow's interview were not enough to keep me awake, I also had to contend with the flashes of the Dungeness lighthouse, just down the beach from the Pilot Inn, which lit my thin curtains precisely once every ten seconds and would continue to do so throughout the night whether I was awake or asleep.

But I did go to sleep at last. I realised I'd gone to sleep when I was awoken quite soon afterwards by a different light. It was the light from the hallway, coming through the bedroom door, which was being quietly opened. By someone.

Someone I could only see in silhouette. Will? It wasn't Will. The figure was taller and had a differently shaped head. The silhouette was carrying a mug of tea or coffee, also in silhouette, and it proceeded to sit down on the bottom corner of the bed I was lying in, to drink the contents of the mug.

Because the bed was a double one the new arrival – it had to be Michael, I guessed – managed by a fluke to sit on the corner that was not occupied by my feet. I wasn't sure what the etiquette of this unusual situation was. I knew that I would have to announce my presence at some point. But if I did it now, while Michael had a full mug of something in his hand, his surprise might cause him to spill it on the bed. I decided I'd need to wait until he'd drunk most of it at least.

But Michael foiled my little plan by quite suddenly getting up off the bed and disappearing out into the hallway with his mug. I heard him go into the kitchen.

Then I heard him go into the bathroom. I could have, perhaps should have, got up at that point, put my clothes back on and headed into the living room to spend the rest of the night on the sofa. But I didn't. I didn't know how long Michael would spend in the bathroom and, all things being equal, I would have preferred him to find me tucked up in his bed rather than hopping about beside it, struggling into my pants.

After a while Michael did come back. This time his silhouette was naked. He carried his clothes over his arm but at once dropped them onto the chair on which I'd put my own. His hand must have brushed against my garments then: I saw him stop in his tracks and feel them with his fingers. Then he walked back to the door and switched on the light.

So I had my first proper sight of Michael. He was a tallish, handsome man of about thirty. Dark hair, finely shaped face, good muscles, nicely in proportion. A light suntan. A wonderful, dangling, big, uncircumcised cock. It was time to introduce myself, I thought. 'Hallo,' I said, sitting up in the bed. 'I'm Jack.'

Michael, who had turned to look at the clothes chair as soon as the light came on, now turned towards me and my bare chest with a start. A look of total astonishment was on his face.

'I'm so sorry,' I said. 'Will said you weren't coming back tonight...'

Michael's astonishment disappeared. He grinned and laughed. 'I'm sorry too,' he said. 'I wasn't coming back. But change of plan at last minute...'

'Look,' I said. 'I'll move into the living room. Just give me a mo to...' I began to pull the blankets back.

'No, no,' Michael said. 'No need for that. Stay where you are. Bed's big enough for us both. Unless...'

'No. I'm fine with that. But...'

'Don't worry about it,' Michael said. 'I'm fine with it myself.'

I muttered, 'You're very generous,' (I heard myself sounding very formal) and lay back down in the bed.

Now it was Michael's turn to pull the covers back. I thought even at the time that he pulled them back a bit further than was strictly necessary. Enough to give him a view of my loins and now flaccid cock. Well, I was getting an eyeful of his nakedness; arguably it was only fair that the score should be even. And he certainly did take a good, if quick, look at my endowment before he climbed in beside me and pulled the covers up.

'Well, sorry if I woke you up,' Michael said, turning to look into my face.

'It's OK. I'm just here for tonight. I've got an interview tomorrow at the airport.'

'Oh, wow. That's where I work. Though Will's probably told you that. And my name's Michael, by the way. No doubt Will's also told you that. Though you, please, call me Mike.'

We talked for a further couple of minutes, pillow to pillow, then Michael said abruptly, 'Right. I must let you sleep. Big day for you tomorrow. Lights going out.' There was a two-way switch, I realised, as Michael reached out an arm and dealt with it.

And so I found myself naked in bed with a man I'd never met before. A man called Mike. I wondered if Will also called him Mike.

FOUR

I fell asleep. I dreamt.

I was in bed with a big, handsome man. I wasn't sure who it was. Will? Mike? In a way it didn't matter. To be so intimate with another man, any other man, was wonderful enough. We reached round and embraced each other. I felt my penis gorge with spunk. I started to shoot it out. One, two, three, four spurts. The spurting died away. I woke. I was lying on my back. My tummy, and the sheet above me, were sopped with spunk. I used my hand, instinctively, to ease the last drops out. Mike lay naked on his back beside me. I was mortified. To think I might have wet him with my ejaculate. Tentatively I touched his tummy with a finger. Like my own tummy it was swimming wet. Could I have done all that? I wondered how I could have got it all over him like that. Had I rolled onto him in my sleep? Surely that would have woken at least one of us, if not both. Very carefully I moved my exploring finger downwards. Barely had it made contact with Mike's curly pubic forest than it encountered the tip of his big dick. It was hard. So extended in fact that its foreskin had slid back. The tip of it was slippery and wet. I didn't think I could have been responsible for that. I began to consider the possibility that I was trailing my finger not in my own, but in Mike's, spunk.

Mike made a noise at that moment. 'Mmmm.' Was he asleep or awake? He made no movement, and no further sound escaped his closed lips. I withdrew my finger and pulled my two arms against my sides. I lay there possum-like. So did Mike. Complete stillness. Physical stillness only, though. My mind was in an uproar.

As I said back at the beginning, I wasn't a total innocent in matters sexual. I had had sexual encounters with men in the Air Force and with boys at school. I knew which way my sexual instincts lay. But I also knew it was a way that society frowned on. It was actually banned by law. Now here I was, ejaculating in my sleep alongside a handsome naked male with whom I'd only exchanged a few words. The only thing that might save the situation was the possibility – it was only a possibility – that Mike too had ejaculated in his sleep. Because of me? I could hardly dare to imagine that that might be. My thoughts turned in alarming circles, somersaulting through my brain. But mercifully I was tired by now. After a period of anxious and unproductive reflection I eventually fell back to sleep.

Loud knocking at the door. Will's voice. 'Seven o'clock.' I opened my eyes at the same moment as Will opened the door and looked in through it. Mike stirred into wakefulness at the same moment.

'Oh gosh,' said Will, his eyes wide with surprise. He was fully clothed. 'Both of you…'

'It's OK,' Mike said sleepily. 'We've introduced ourselves. It worked out fine.' I listened with huge relief to Mike's calm words, though I couldn't guess exactly what he meant by *worked out fine*.

'You need to get up if you're coming in with me, Jack,' Will said.

'Of course.' I started to roll the covers back and sit up. 'Give me five minutes…'

'It's OK,' Will said reassuringly. 'There's time. Coffee and Corn Flakes in the kitchen if you're interested.'

Mike, still lying flat beside me, said to Will, 'I'm on the later shift. I'll make my own way in. Don't make Corn Flakes for me.'

Will chuckled and withdrew, closing the door behind him. I threw the covers back on my side of the bed and saw the very big grey stain I'd made on the top sheet. I was alarmed, though, to see that Mike clocked it too. But half a second later he startled me again, though in a different way. He pulled down the covers on his side of the bed too, exposing both of us down to the thighs. We both had big erections; that was the first thing I saw. But I also saw that Mike had made a stain on the sheet, identical in size to mine, but quite separate from it. Before I could decide whether to say anything or not (though what on earth would I have found to say?) Mike spoke. 'Well, well. It looks like we've both been naughty boys.'

I giggled my relief. 'Yes. Yes it does.' I started to lever myself out of bed.

Mike touched my upper arm. 'It was nice to meet you. Come back and say goodbye before you go.'

I had to pick most of Mike's clothes up off the chair before I could get at mine. I found it strangely exciting to be handling them.

Will was full of apology when we met in the kitchen a few minutes later. Over the promised coffee and bowl of cereal. 'I'd no idea he might change his plan. It must have been very embarrassing for both of you.'

'It was at first, but don't be sorry. It was all fine. Michael's very ... well, you know him better than I do. I'm still very grateful to you for putting me up for the night. Grateful to both of you...' I told him the story of our encounter in the darkness: the mug of tea, the light going on... It sounded very funny now I was telling it to Will. It made him laugh anyway. And that was nice to see. His blue eyes sparkled again. Like cornflowers in the sun and rain.

'Before we go...' I told Will, 'Michael wanted me to look in and say goodbye.'

'Fine,' said Will, quite unsurprised. 'I'll see you by the car.'

Mike was still lying flat in the bed when I went in – I gave a polite knock as I did so – but he sat up, showing off his fine chest, when he saw me. I clocked the nice little whorls of hair around his nipples and the fine line of them that disappeared beneath the sheet in the region of his navel. I also clocked the lustrous sheen of his brown eyes. I'd spent the night, quite by chance, in a house that was lived in by two wonderful looking men. A thought crossed my mind at that moment for the first time. Did Will and Mike find each other beautiful? Did they…?

'Come here,' I heard Mike say. 'We met in rather unusual circumstances. We haven't actually shaken hands.'

I moved towards Mike. We both held out our right hands. Mike took firm charge of the handshake that ensued. He held mine tightly in his slightly larger one. Then he looked me in the eye and said, 'Good luck for today. I hope you'll get the job. I'm sure you will. Not least because that'll mean we meet again. As colleagues.' He stopped and his gaze at me intensified. 'Also as friends.' Then he let my hand go.

'Certainly as friends.' Something inside me seemed to be bursting upwards like a rocket. 'Certainly as friends.' I wanted to hug Mike. To roll exuberantly onto him, and wrestle my way back into his bed.

He must have caught my enthusiastic tone. Otherwise I don't think he'd have said what he said next 'If you're still around this evening and need somewhere to stay… Well, you're welcome here again. Same sleeping arrangements as before.'

The astonishing, almost unbelievable offer went ricocheting round my brain. 'Yes … wow … yes,' I answered incoherently. Though my eagerness as well as my astonishment was more than evident in my tone. 'I'll talk to Will.'

I told Will about Mike's invitation as soon as I joined him in the car. It was now or never. Before I could think too much and get cold feet about it.

Will listened gravely and nodded as he drove. If he was surprised or startled by my news he did his best not to show it. 'Of course you can stay. But you'll have to make your own amusements during the day. I won't be able to take you home after the interview.'

'I'll be fine.' An idea came to me suddenly. 'What time do you finish?'

'Four o'clock.'

'This is going to sound very cheeky, I know,' I said. 'But if you let me have the keys to your car I could do some shopping and cook us an evening meal. The three of us. I'd come and pick you up at four. Pick Michael up too…'

'He'll be going on till nine,' said Will. 'And he's got his own car.' He paused a second. 'The rest of the plan sounds good, though.'

'We could have a late meal if that's OK… Is there anything you don't eat, either of you?'

A part of me managed to reflect that this was a very unusual conversation to be having on the way to a job interview.

By now the hangars and terminal buildings of the airport were looming across the landscape, almost rushing towards us. And the Superfreighters and Dakotas were peering at us over the low rooftop with difficult-to-read expressions on their faces, just as I remembered them doing when I was a child. Will drove into the staff section of the car park and stopped the car. We got out and locked the doors. Then Will came round to my side of the car. He pointed first towards the terminal entrance, then to the car loading tunnel. 'You go that way when the time comes. There's a reception desk inside.

Meanwhile, I go over there.' He handed me his car keys. 'House keys are on there too. You'll need those.'

I put them in my pocket. 'Thanks.'

'Good luck, mate,' he said. 'I hope you'll get the job. If you want somewhere to stay when you first arrive…'

'Oh wow,' I said. 'And see you this evening anyway…'

Will said, 'I'll be running into Mike at some point, if you don't see him when you go back. I'll tell him about dinner tonight.' Will gave me his hand. I shook it firmly, and he placed his other hand over the back of it. Not to be outdone in friendliness I added my second hand to the pile as though playing some children's game. Will leaned towards me for a second as if he wanted to kiss me. He didn't kiss me. He leaned back again, and we disengaged our hands. I knew bloody well that I wanted to kiss him.

'Come and find me when you're done,' Will said. 'Either out here among the cars or in there. In the tunnel.' He pointed again to the covered way that led between the passenger car park and the tarmac beyond.

I said cheers and we walked off on our separate ways. Among all the thoughts that clamoured for my attention was one very minor one: that Will too called Michael Mike. It had registered strongly.

I walked towards the passenger entrance of the terminal in a daze, finding it difficult to focus on the interview ahead of me, my thoughts pulled three ways. Towards Will, with whom something seemed to be happening; I didn't think it was just my wishful imagination; he seemed to be as attracted to me as I was to him. Towards Mike – to whom all of the above also applied. And towards the interview and flying trial I was to face within an hour. If I were to pass that I would be able to see Mike and Will again. That was good. But… Both of them? The complications posed by that *both of them* would mount up if we found ourselves all living in the same house and would almost certainly cause trouble in the long run. I couldn't see any possible outcome that would be good for all three of us, only a messy situation that would bring unhappiness and hurt all round.

Perhaps it would be better if I didn't get the job. Then, after tonight, I could walk away from the bungalow, take the train out of Lydd and never see the place, or Will or Mike, again.

I walked anxiously towards the terminal building, and as I did so, cars began to arrive in the car park, others already waiting there were driven through the customs post towards the tunnel, ready for loading aboard the first outbound flight. The inscrutable eyes of the aeroplanes that peered over the roof at me began slowly to dip down and hide behind the building as I got nearer to it, as if playing peek-a-boo.

'You're nearly an hour early,' said the receptionist at the desk when I walked inside the place that had been familiar to me as a child. She smiled at me. 'Why don't you go for a walk in the sunshine to steady your nerves?' I took her advice and walked around the nearby fields, listening to larks in the sky overhead, and startling a hare. Meanwhile, in the space of thirty minutes or so, the first three freighters of the morning roared deafeningly into the air a couple of fields away.

Wing Commander Davies regarded me beadily across the desk from beneath shaggy eyebrows. We still addressed those who had served during the War by the rank they had attained. Even – perhaps especially – if they were now the head of a civil airline. 'You've flown transport craft both as pilot and co-pilot,' he said. 'Which came first?'

'Co-pilot,' I said. I found myself smiling. 'I was never demoted. I did it the right way round.' To my relief the Wing Commander smiled in return.

'Flown passengers before?'

'No,' I admitted.

'It's not a big deal,' Davies said. His fingers touched his uniform cap, which lay on the desk in front of him. I could imagine him frustrated by his desk work and fidgeting to get into the air. 'On the car ferries you don't get to meet the passengers. They're tucked away at the back behind the cars. So no worries there. On the other hand, don't upset them by steep turns and rolls. They may not be able to complain to you but they will to me. We can't go seeking after thrills for ourselves. Sedate is the order of the day.'

Through the window behind Davies's head I could see a half each of two Superfreighters. From the look of the lumbering things it seemed that sedate would quite necessarily be the order of the day. I tried to picture them doing loops or other aerobatic stunts but my imagination failed me. Instead I found myself seeing the dancing hippos in Fantasia, dressed in tutus. I said, 'I take your point, sir.'

The Wing Commander got to his feet and picked up his cap from the desk, as his fingers had been itching to do. In full uniform he was an impressive sight; he was about six inches taller than I was. He said, 'You present yourself well, young man. All good so far. But let's get up in the air now. Then you can show me what you're actually capable of up there.'

FIVE

We were driven along the apron, under the noses of the lined up planes, their clamshell nose doors gaping and giving views into their holds that resembled the interiors of biscuit tins. Our driver was not Will. I was relieved about that, for reasons too obvious to need setting out here.

We turned the corner and headed towards the maintenance hangar. In front of it stood yet another Bristol Superfreighter, its doors closed and its wheel chocks already removed. It wouldn't need pulling backwards away from buildings: there was space in front of it for it to turn towards the runway under its own power. For *it* to turn... Someone in the cockpit would be turning it. I swallowed hard as we got out of the car.

And then I smiled. I read its registration sign, G-ANWK, in large proud letters on its huge tail fin. I remembered the plane from when I was a boy. The obvious anagram of those last four letters had made me chuckle as a twelve-year-old. Eleven years on it was making me smile now.

I noticed as we walked towards it that since I first knew it the plane had been given a name. In French and English. *Le Quatorze Juillet,* The Fourteenth of July.

We hopped up through the passenger door. No library steps for us. The small cabin with its twenty seats was like the interior of a pre-war bus. There was a large light set in the centre of the front wall for the passengers to focus on as they crossed the sea. *DITCHING WARNING* was written above it. We walked through the door beside that ominous warning light into the empty vehicle hold, then climbed the metal ladder into the cockpit that was set above the ceiling, accessed through a hole in its floor.

Davies motioned me to sit in the pilot's seat. He took the first officer's. As we fastened our safety harnesses he said, 'I'll fly us on a nine-minute circuit, talking you through it as we go. Then I'll let you have the aeroplane as we repeat the circuit.' He saw the look on my face. 'Don't worry; I'll talk you through that one too.' He took dark glasses from his top pocket and put them on. Like a good apprentice I followed suit.

Davies started the right (starboard) engine and then the left. The props turned slowly for ages, cranked by protesting electric starters, before each one fired up in turn. My eyes darted around the cockpit as Davies introduced me to the instruments and controls. If you could compare the cockpits of most passenger aircraft to the front section of a saloon car, then you had to compare this one to a Land Rover. But happily it wasn't unlike the transport planes I'd already flown in the RAF.

We had headphones on by now. Otherwise I wouldn't have heard Davies talking me through everything as we began to taxi out towards the runway. At last we reached the holding point at the runway's foot, two thirds of a mile from the terminal, and turned into the wind. Then we waited while the engines laboriously, deafeningly, spooled their way up to full power, ready for take-off.

'At this point,' I heard Davies's voice, deadpan in my headphones, 'don't forget to release the footbrakes.' He did that as he spoke, and off we roared, slow and wobbling at first, then smoothing out as the air began to take our weight while we gained speed. 'Throttles,' Davies said. 'Keep your hand on them. Keep pushing forward. Don't let them shake back.' I did as he said. Then Davies eased the yoke, the control column, gently forward, and we pitched forward equally gently … as behind us the tail wheel lifted off. For five seconds nothing more happened and then we were airborne. By some wonderful trick of physics that until recently only the birds and bats and insects had known about, our twenty-ton steed was now lighter than the air that supported it.

The up-tilted nose now blocked our view of the way ahead. I could, however see what lay just to our left. There was the point of Dungeness, foreshortened and rounded by our low altitude, surrounded by the blue sea. The lighthouse on the Ness's tip, black and white striped like a football shirt. I looked for the 'hump' of France in the distance beyond the Ness but it was hidden in the haze.

'Climb to a thousand then level off,' Davies's voice crackled in my phones. 'It's one thousand all the way to Le Touquet. On the return trip two.' That made sense. I already knew there was a separation of a thousand feet between civil aircraft flying the same route in opposite directions. For obvious reasons. Eastbound you flew an odd number of thousands of feet. You flew the even thousands going west.

'By coincidence you'll hit one thousand at the same moment you cross the beach,' Davies said. 'Makes it easy for you.' A second later we left the shingle spit of Dungeness behind us and were suddenly above the waves. Simultaneously Davies halted our climb by pushing forward on the yoke. The horizon came into view above the nose. Then, because we weren't flying to France but back to Lydd, Davies put the plane into a leisurely left turn, a turn that would take a full minute, of 180 degrees. Now we were heading northwards, a mile or two out to sea. The beach came into view again, the town of Lydd a couple of miles inland, and just north of it Lydd Ferryfield, the airport we had just left and would shortly be returning to. I had time to think for a second about Will, down there, loading cars into the freighters that I could clearly see at three miles' distance. I thought for a second too about Mike, having his lie-in in a bungalow I couldn't pick out but that was down there somewhere on the edge of the shingle spit. Was he asleep? Awake? Thinking about me? Having a G-ANWK?

'Turn when you're abreast of New Romney church tower,' Davies told me through the headphones. 'If the weather's good. Rely on Decca if you're in cloud. Are we there?'

'Any second now,' I said, spotting the church in the centre of New Romney a mile or so from the beach. It was on my side of the plane, the left-hand side, and not so easy for Davies, on the outer side of the turn, to see.

We made our second unhurried 180 degree turn and after a minute Lydd's runway appeared ahead of us, foreshortening as it lined itself up for our arrival. Davies spoke to the control tower, straightened out, then lowered the flaps as calmly as a tractor driver lowering the blades of his plough. Two minutes more and we were down. Davies pulled off the runway onto a taxiway just before we reached its end. 'And now,' he said, smiling at me, 'it's your turn. Ask permission from tower to taxi back to the other end.'

'Do you want me to turn off the engines and re-start?' I asked.

'Oh God no,' said the Wing Commander. 'We can't be doing with all that again.'

I swallowed hard, took a firm hold of the yoke in front of me and said, 'I have control, sir.'

My legs felt wobbly when, twenty minutes later, I lowered them to the ground. A car was waiting for us. Again, thank heaven, the driver wasn't Will. But I already knew the outcome of the test. As soon as the engines had clattered to a stop and we'd taken off our headphones, Davies had turned to me and said, 'Well, that went all right, I thought. Can you start on Monday?' There remained only a bit of paperwork to do in the office. I had to provide a signature or two. And be measured for a uniform.

Will had told me to come and look for him when I was done. He proved very easy to find. He was in the car park, among the passengers' cars. 'I've got the job,' I called to him as soon as I was close enough for him to hear. 'I start on Monday.'

'That's wonderful,' he said. We looked at each other. Another difficult-to-interpret look appeared suddenly on his face as he said, 'I saw you take off. Twice. I waved both times.'

'That was nice. I wish I'd seen. I'd have waved back. But I was on the other side.'

'I realised.' At that moment I knew for certain that he was longing to hug me but dared not. I knew that because I felt the same towards him. 'But you've got the job. That needs celebrating,' he said. He unzipped a bit of his boiler suit and took his wallet out. From it he took a pound note and handed it to me. 'When you're doing the shopping for this evening, get us a bottle of wine.'

'You're still sure about me borrowing your car?' I checked.

Will grinned. 'Of course I'm sure.' Then, 'Better get back to work now.'

'Of course,' I said. 'I'll pick you up at four.'

'Cheers,' said Will. 'Right here.'

I made a noise with his keys inside my pocket to show that I still had them, then turned and headed for his car.

I stopped off in the station yard and walked to the phone box outside the station. I called my parents and told them I'd got the job. I told my mother at any rate. My father was out at work. My mother was delighted enough for them both. I also told her I'd stayed the previous night with two of my future colleagues and they'd asked me to stay on another night. And that I'd be staying with them for a bit when I started my new job. Until I found a place of my own. My mother sounded happy enough about that, which I was relieved about. I said, 'See you tomorrow,' and hung up.

As I walked back to the car I thought about what *a place of my own* might mean in practice. What it might mean in my mother's mind. What it might mean for myself. It would only be a room in someone else's house, or at best a shared flat above a shop in Lydd High Street. I thought about that invitation to stay at the bungalow. Will had left it vague and open-ended. But there were only two bedrooms in the place. I wondered how it would work out. I put the thought behind me. Time alone would sort it out.

I didn't drive back to the bungalow. I guessed that Mike might still be there. If he was... I wasn't sure how I'd deal with him, or what I'd say to him. I wasn't sure what I felt about him. And I wasn't ready for how he might deal with me, what he might say to me. I also knew that, ironically, I'd be disappointed if he wasn't there.

All in all, I realised, it would be easier to handle Mike if I was in the company of Will when I met him next. As would happen soon after nine o'clock tonight.

I drove to the beach, to the place near the Pilot Inn where I had gone with Will last night. I even took a slightly circuitous route there so as not to pass the bungalow and be spotted by Mike and cause him to wonder why Will's car was driving past without stopping while its owner was out at work.

I lay on the shingle slope, almost alone, on my back beneath the great blue sky. I listened to the gentle crash of the summer waves a ridge of stones away. And every ten minutes would come the din of an approaching, climbing plane. Then it would come into my upward field of view: flat silver belly and engines, sturdy black wheels, grey wings and tail planes. Then it would grow small and disappear against the blue, en route for France. And if I chanced to look in the right direction – eastward – at the right moment I would see the silent silhouettes of the returning planes, flying the downwind leg – as I had flown it just an hour or two ago: flying northward along the coast a couple of miles out to sea before turning inland. Both those sights, the outgoing and the inbound planes, awakened feelings of both nervous anticipation and eager excitement. This time next week … some of those flights would be co-piloted by me.

I knew when it was twelve o'clock without needing to look at my watch. Cars, and walkers, began to arrive at the Pilot Inn. After a while I followed them. I treated myself to a pint of bitter and a cheese roll, then went back and lay on the beach again. I remembered how, just a few hours ago, I'd thought it might be better for everyone if I didn't get the job, and wouldn't have to meet either Will or Mike again. Well, it was too late for that now. I'd got the job, and was very pleased I had, though it looked as if, for better or worse, my life would now remain tangled up with Mike's and Will's for a little while yet. Ah well, life was made to be dealt with, and deal with it I would. Somehow. Meanwhile there was shopping to do. And I was too elated at having got a wonderful new job to be cast down for very long by thoughts of the complicated things in the world.

I stood up and teetered for a second as I got my balance on the shelving stones. The main ingredients for the meal I was going to cook were within sight already, a hundred yards away. On a trestle table set up beside a boat that had just been winched up the shingle on its return from a night at sea.

I bought a large turbot that was still flapping and panting in its tray, and prawns that jerked, clicked and clattered in a wooden box nearby. The precious sea-fresh treasures cost just pence.

Then I drove into Lydd proper, and did most of the rest of my shopping in a greengrocer's shop in the High Street. I didn't forget the wine that Will had insisted on giving me the money for. I found an off-licence a little further down the High Street, and spent nearly the whole of his pound on a bottle of Chablis.

SIX

I drove back to the airport, arriving in the car park on the dot of four. Almost at once there was Will walking towards me. I got out of the car. 'No, get back in,' he said.

I said, 'Don't you want...?'

'No,' he said. He smiled roguishly. 'You can drive me.' I got back into the driver's seat. As Will took his place next to me he patted my leg lightly across the gear lever. 'Take me home,' he said. 'Air-ferry pilot now. You should be able to manage one of these.' He meant the Mini. I patted his leg lightly in a return of the compliment.

As we made the short journey back to the bungalow I told Will what I'd bought for our late meal and what I planned to do with it. 'Bit of a cook, you are,' he said approvingly.

'Wait,' I said. 'Proof of the pudding... You know.'

Will said, 'I have the utmost faith in you,' and again he patted my thigh.

When we got out of the car Will said, 'It's hot.' He stretched his arms and legs in a released-from-work movement. 'I'll make us a cup of tea and we can sit outside. Might put a pair of shorts on first, though.'

'Wish I'd brought a pair myself. But coming here for an interview...'

'I'll find you a pair.' He looked me up and down as if glad of the excuse. 'We're about the same size.'

We went indoors. Will darted across the hall and into his room. Though he left the door open I didn't follow him inside. A second later he appeared in the doorway. 'Catch,' he said. I caught the pair of shorts he threw me. Then he disappeared inside his room again and this time he did shut the door. I took the shorts he'd given me into Mike's room.

I'd been in Mike's room only half an hour ago. Returning from my shopping expedition I'd come back to the bungalow and put the fish and wine in the little fridge. Mike had gone off to work by then. I'd lain down on his double bed – my bed last night and, it seemed, for the night to come – and rested for half an hour. I hadn't wanked. Ever hopeful I'd decided I ought to save myself for what was to happen tonight. Whatever that might be.

Now, standing beside that bed of Mike's I took my trousers off, and my socks and shoes. Then, after a moment's indecision, my underpants too. I thought it might be nice to spend some time in Will's company in the sunshine, wearing his shorts with nothing between them and my skin, my naked prick and balls. I pulled his shorts on. They were tight on me. I guessed they would have been even tighter on him. They were white and very brief and thin. I presumed they were the ones he'd worn for gym at school. They gave me a sexy feeling and inside them I felt my cock thicken and stir. If Will were to notice that… Too bad, I told myself, and felt a smirk flit across my face.

I walked back out into the hall barefoot, in Will's shorts and my cheekily unbuttoned white interview shirt – which I hadn't bothered to tuck in. Will was in the kitchen, putting the kettle on and spooning tea into a teapot. He was dressed much the same as I was. No shoes or socks. Just a pair of white shorts and a light blue Aertex top that barely met the waistband of the shorts, and certainly would not do if he bent down or reached up. I saw him from the back at first. I couldn't tell if he was wearing underpants beneath the shorts. Though from the clearly defined look of his buttocks through the white fabric I was able to imagine that he was as under-dressed as I was. He had sturdy thighs and beautifully sculpted calves. The skin on his legs was very fair, and fuzzed with thistledown hair. He looked utterly superb, and my cock twitched at the sight of him.

He turned round as he heard me come in. We faced each other and took in the sight of each other's front view. If I liked what I saw, then Will was making no effort to hide the fact that he felt the same about me. 'Hey, you look ... relaxed,' I heard him say.

'You too.'

Will indicated a stack of trays with his eyes. 'Could you just pick up one of those?'

A minute later we were sitting facing each other on uncomfortable garden chairs, sipping mugs of tea. Our legs were spread in front of us as if insouciantly, yet outrageously wide.

In a casual tone Will said, 'You obviously scored a hit with Mike.'

'Evidently.' I tried to sound equally neutral about the idea.

'Him inviting you back tonight... Same sleeping arrangements as before...' Will twinkled me a smile that was half cautious, half expectant. It said: you can tell me about it if you want to but you don't have to.

'How long's he lived here?' I asked. It was a delaying tactic. While I decided how much I wanted to tell.

'About six weeks. Not very long.'

'He's very nice,' I said banally. 'Handsome too.' I paused for a second. 'Like you.'

There was a further second's silence during which Will and I gazed each other in the eye, while our peripheral view haloed each other's crotches. Then Will said, 'And you.'

'Thank you. But Mike... Umm, is he... that way?'

'Umm... He might be.'

Rowing back I said, 'I mean, nothing of that sort happened... We didn't...'

'No,' said Will. His face had become inscrutable.

Again we looked at each other during a two-second's silence that seemed to go on and on. This time I definitely saw a movement in Will's shorts. It seemed even more probable that, like me, he wasn't wearing underpants. The position of his dick, fat and lying half upright against his left groin, was very apparent, which it hadn't been before. I said, 'Well actually…'

'Hmmm?' enquired Will, though his face still gave nothing away.

'I don't know if I ought to…'

'Go on.' Will's face now wore a faint smile – encouraging but also cautious.

'Well, we slept lying next to each other. I mean we didn't touch or anything…'

'Of course,' said Will, his face again an inscrutable mask.

'But we were both naked. And…'

'And…?' Will was only just managing to keep up his pretence of nonchalance. I could see from his cock that he was absolutely dying to know.

'And we both had wet dreams.'

Will couldn't help himself. He guffawed aloud. In my relief I guffawed too. For some seconds we couldn't speak, but only laugh. And each time one of us tried to say something we both roared again.

Eventually the crazy laughter died away. 'What? All over the sheet? Together?'

'Yes,' I said. 'It wasn't till this morning that we actually saw…'

'Your stuff all over…?' Will's eyes were wide. I could imagine him imagining the scene.

'Yeah,' I said. 'We'd plastered the bed with spunk.'

We both laughed again, but briefly this time. That one of us had used that word – or any vernacular word to do with sex, male sex – had peeled away yet one more layer of reserve from between us. It had been a rite-of-passage moment. Things were different between us now. I said, 'If Mike's a little bit … you know … inclined that way, that's fine with me. Because actually…'

'Actually,' I heard Will say, 'I sometimes think I might be a little bit that way too.'

'So might I,' I said. 'I mean, just a little bit that way. Sometimes…'

(A little bit? Sometimes? I wasn't any other way. Not even a little bit. But we all had to be cautious in those days. The wrong word in the wrong person's ear – if, for example, you'd misunderstood someone's interest in you – might be broadcast around your whole social circle and turn you into an outcast or a laughing stock overnight. At worst it could land you in trouble with the police.)

I watched as Will very slowly and deliberately moved one hand onto his crotch and touched his penis through the white fabric as if absently dealing with a slight itch. Feigning an equal nonchalance I did the same to mine.

'I don't think you've seen my bedroom yet, have you?' Will said. I could hear his voice striving for casualness as his words tiptoed over eggshells.

'Not properly. Up to now, only Mike's.'

'When we've finished our tea I'll show you,' Will said.

Then we finished our tea as quickly as was seemly, gulping it down as fast as its lingering heat would allow. Even so it seemed to take an age.

We stood up and walked indoors rather awkwardly. Neither of us tried to touch the other. We deposited our empty mugs on the wooden draining board next to the kitchen sink. Then Will looked into my eyes a bit doubtfully. I gave him an encouraging smile and it seemed to work because he said, 'Come on,' then beckoned me with his head and led me into his bedroom.

Once there we squared up to each other. After a second's pause I put my hands on his shoulders. Then he put his hands around my waist and squeezed me against him till I could feel our cocks mashing against each other through our shorts. 'You smell nice,' Will said.

'Thank you.' I'd pinched a splash of his aftershave – or Michael's, I wasn't sure which – before driving out to meet him an hour earlier. 'So do you,' I said. He simply smelt of himself, a healthy young man after a day's work. I thought it lovely.

'You're lovely,' said Will, telepathically borrowing my unspoken adjective.

'So are you.' By now we were locked in a tight, dick-squashing embrace. Then Will released me just enough for him to pull my unbuttoned shirt right off. I took the opportunity to pull his top off over his head. Then we looked at each other; experimentally tweaked a mutual nipple and looked into each other's eyes in search of further instructions.

I ran my hand down Will's smooth chest and tummy and into his shorts. It met his upward-pointing cock – which was hot and wet. I grabbed it tightly.

Will tried to copy the manoeuvre but found his old gym shorts too snug a fit on me. I helped him by undoing the waistband clip. He immediately tugged down the zip and my own cock obligingly sprang out. 'Wow, you're big,' Will said.

'Not as big as Mike,' I said incautiously.

'Oh, I don't know,' said Will, in a tone of voice that announced that he did know. But it wasn't the moment to pursue that. I pulled his shorts right down instead. And then we were on his double bed.

Will was the same height as I was, but a fraction more developed in terms of muscle. Slightly broader at shoulders and hips. His dick, which like mine was uncircumcised, was a half size smaller, but it had the identical tapering shape: thick-based and pointy tipped. I lost no time in starting to play with it. His balls, like mine, were hefty: the size of bantams' eggs.

We lay clasped together, masturbating each other's hugely excited dicks. Experimentally we kissed each other's lips. Will said, 'I love doing this.'

I said, 'I love it too.' Sometimes the word love, like a trapped bird inside you, rises unbidden to your lips in this situation, even in a disguised context. Sometimes it doesn't. Today it did. For both of us. It depends who you're with.

'I think I'm coming,' I said.

'I know you are,' Will said.

I gasped, 'I always shoot too quickly.'

'It's nice,' Will said, and my cock immediately squirted its load all up his chest.

That set Will off instantly. I felt him tense and buck and a moment later it was all over. All over me, that is.

We lay together hugging wetly for half a minute, then we released each other and lay back, side by side on top of the bed, like effigies on a tomb but less decently clad. After another minute Will reached round, away from me, and grabbed a towel from his locker. He proceeded to mop us both up with it. Then we cuddled each other for a while without speaking...

Will was looking into my eyes when I opened them. 'We've both been to sleep,' he said.

'What time is it?' I asked anxiously. I thought urgently of Mike's return and about cooking the fish.

'It's all right. It's not yet six. The sun's still shining. Do you want to go for a walk?'

We took the car the mile or two to the beach. Except for plimsolls we were dressed in nothing but our shorts. After all, it was the beach.

The waves were rolling more gently than they'd been that morning. Again there was no sign on the horizon of the hump. We walked along the edge of the water. The car ferries were still flying overhead.

'I wonder if that one's Mike's,' I said, pointing up at the underbelly of one of them.

'Could be,' said Will, looking at his watch. 'Not quite seven. Time for him to get over one more time and back again before he knocks off work.'

It was funny to think that the person who was going to join us for dinner in a little over an hour would be going to France and back before he turned up on the doorstep. 'I suppose you've done it with Mike,' I said.

'Done what?'

'You know,' I said, a touch impatiently. 'Done what we just did. Or something of the sort.'

'Well, yes and no,' Will said. I knew what he meant. There were degrees and degrees of sexual contact.

'You don't need to explain if you don't want.' A line of black ducks flew low over the waves a few yards from where we walked.

'We both knew we were attracted to each other from the moment we met,' Will said. 'But we were cautious, like everybody is. We got in the habit of touching each other as we moved around the house. Just shoulder pats at first. Then little pats on the bum or strokes down the back. One night at bed time we felt each other through our trousers. Both of us were stiff...'

'Yes,' I said in a do-go-on tone of voice.

'That was just a few nights ago actually. The next night we got into bed together. Naked. That's how I know the size of his dick. We started to ... you know...'

'Wank each other,' I supplied.

'Exactly. But we were both too nervous. It didn't work. After a while we agreed to split for the night. We kissed each other and I went back to my own bed. We'd been in his.'

'Of course.'

'Next day he went away to see his parents. He came back last night. By which time you'd turned up.'

'I see.' I looked away from the sea to get my bearings. We were almost abreast The Pilot. 'Fancy a pint before we head back?'

'Yes,' said Will very positively, perhaps glad to be able to get away from the complex subject of Mike, and we turned and headed up the shifting pebble beach towards the pub.

But there was one more thing that we needed to agree on before we dropped the awkward subject. I asked Will, 'Do we tell Mike what happened earlier – I mean between us?'

Will stopped and stared at me. 'I don't think that's in our hands. Mike's going to know as soon as he looks at us.' We resumed our climb up the beach.

SEVEN

We bought our pints at the counter and took them to a table beneath a huge window that overlooked the shingle beach. Not that either of us looked at the beach. 'So,' I asked, 'how do you come to own a bungalow of your own at the age of…?'

'Twenty-two,' Will said.

'I'm twenty-one,' I said for the sake of tidiness, but Will ignored that.

'It was my grandparents' holiday home before the War,' he said. 'When Grandma died my parents came in for it. By then it was a bit derelict. The whole area had been off-limits during the…'

'I know.' I nodded to Will across the table. Nodded my head and nodded my heart.

'They were about to sell it, then six months ago I got this job and…'

'They're letting you use it,' I said.

'It's good of them. They're not paupers but they're not rich either. They don't charge me rent. I pay the bills, of course.'

I nodded my appreciation of Will's uprightness.

'I charge Mike a bit of rent.' He sounded a bit doubtful about this. 'Do you think that's…?'

'Wrong? Hypocritical? No, of course I don't.'

'It's not that much…'

'Who cares?' I smiled an abandoned smile across the table at Will. We'd just had sex. I liked him very much. He smiled back at me, blue eyes flashing in the pub-light. He was on the brink of falling for me, I realised.

Like a baby duckling imprinting on the first thing it sees. Perhaps he didn't have much experience of sex or love.

But who was I to talk? I was in the same boat. And I was on the brink of falling for him too. 'Have you had other blokes before?' I boldly asked.

'One. What about you?'

'Three, I think. Or four. It depends what you include and what you don't.' We shared a quiet chuckle at that. We had bonded. At least I thought we had. And then I felt the touch of Will's hand on my knee beneath the table and I knew that we had.

Back at the bungalow Will showed me round the place. Dusty knick-knacks I wouldn't have noticed. He pointed out a small needlework sampler in a frame in the hallway. It was a view of St Michael's Mount. I knew that because it said so underneath. 'My grandmother did that,' he said. Then, in his bedroom, 'My mother gave me this.' He had picked up a small cheap trinket and was holding it in the palm of his hand. It was a deeply intimate moment. He might have been holding out his heart for me to look at.

'Do you like the Beatles? he asked.

'Of course.' It was 1963. There was no other answer to give.

Will looked at me in a way that is difficult to describe. 'Have you got the Please Please Me LP?' he asked. It was as though he was exposing his nakedness in a deeper way than when, a few hours ago, he'd taken all his clothes off.

'Yes, I have. It's fabulous.'

'Would you like to hear it now?' he asked with childlike diffidence. The moment was fragile. I had the feeling that If I'd said no he'd have shrivelled like a winter leaf and that would have been the end of us. I said yes.

When Mike returned from France and work I was straining the just boiled prawns in a colander and Will was rubbing the skins off the very new potatoes we were going to have with the turbot. We both turned as Mike entered the kitchen. I felt very uncomfortable. It wasn't as though I belonged to Mike, but we had enjoyed an odd kind of intimacy last night and it was he who had invited me back to share his bed tonight.

Mike grinned at Will and me. 'Ha. Very domestic. Quite the little couple already.'

'How do you mean?' I asked, trying to maintain a poker face.

Mike's grin became a sort of broad smirk – if such a thing exists. But it was a nice smirk. 'It's written all over your faces. Don't worry. Life's like that.'

'Sometimes it catches us out,' I said primly.

Mike said, 'And sometimes when it does it's nice.' He stopped and scrutinised my face. 'Don't look so worried. It's all right.'

Will turned to me with a sheepish smile on his face. 'I told you he'd rumble us at once.' He looked back at Mike. 'There's beer in the larder. And there's wine to go with the fish.'

'Good.' Mike turned back to me. 'I'm slow with my congratulations, though. Well done for getting the job.' He went over to the larder and took three bottles of Carlsberg Pilsner out. 'Gives us an excuse to celebrate.' Then he moved to the kitchen table and fished a bottle opener from the drawer in it. 'Will told me. He also told me you were definitely staying the night.'

'I hope that's still…' I began awkwardly.

'Of course it is,' said Mike. 'I've been looking forward to it.' He looked at Will. I couldn't interpret the expression on his face.

Will said, 'I've also told Jack he can stay with us when he gets the job. I hope that's all right.'

'Very much all right, I should think,' Mike said. 'I should think everyone'll be happy about that.'

I found myself having to think about where things were going at that point.

Mike handed me an open bottle of Carlsberg, and another one to Will. We raised them to our lips and all said cheers. The other two said, 'Here's to the new job, Jack.'

Either Mike was a very accommodating sort of fellow or he was feeling hurt by my behaviour with Will and trying to hide the fact. It was too soon to tell yet, and I certainly wasn't going to ask.

We drank our beers as we cooked. The prawns were ready. I left them in the colander on the sill of the open window to cool down in the faint breeze. We would simply dip them in salt and pepper, butter and lemon juice. The potatoes were on, boiling away with mint. There was more mint, and parsley, finely chopped, to sprinkle on them when they were on our plates. I had bought a bunch of samphire to add something green and astringent to the dish. It would need a minute only in boiling water, just before the fish was cooked.

I'd got four good-sized fillets from the turbot. Luckily Will had two big frying pans. I put a load of butter in them in readiness. Will set the table. Mike opened the wine and poured it out. Then we sat down at the kitchen table and ate the prawns, wonderfully fresh, while the potatoes cooked.

'They're gorgeous,' Mike said to me. The prawns, he meant. But then he said, jerking his head towards Will, 'He's got a nice cock, don't you think?'

I was startled but determined not to show it. I decided to join in with the banter. I just hoped I could carry it off. 'It's beautiful. Not as big as yours, maybe, but…'

'Size doesn't matter,' said Mike.

'Nobody's got a bigger one than Mike has,' Will put in generously. He looked at me. 'And yours is also very nice.'

'I'll drink to that,' said Mike, raising his wineglass. 'Here's to young Jack's beautiful dick.' We somehow managed to both laugh and drink without spilling a drop of the precious Chablis. But then Mike dropped the subject of our penile adornments and I was a bit relieved about that.

The turbot took just a few minutes. I floured it and fried it in the butter, while Will and Mike dealt with the veg. The fish, having been alive till very recently, was a bit unruly and kept wanting to curl up in the pans. I had to plonk a sieve on top of one of the pans and the empty colander on the other, to keep the fillets flat. While I was busy with the fish and Will was putting the water to boil for the samphire I felt Mike's hand easing its way down the back of my shorts. I looked half round and saw that his other hand was down the back of Will's shorts.

'Well, well,' said Mike. 'You naughty boys. Neither of you wearing pants.'

'Sit down,' said Will with mock severity. But he giggled after he'd said it. He sounded as happy as I felt.

The dinner was a great success. Though the wine ran out disappointingly soon. Well, actually it didn't. Mike got up from the table. 'Hang on a minute,' he said. He disappeared but a moment later came back with a dark green bottle. 'I had a few minutes inside the terminal in France,' he said. 'Beaujolais. I know it's red but it's supposed to go well with fish. Well, that's what everyone says. I thought if we were going to celebrate Jack's good fortune then I should make some contribution to the feast.'

The Beaujolais went beautifully with the last of the fish. It also went extremely well with the raspberries and cream I'd got for dessert. (Beaujolais does. Everyone should try it.)

We did the washing up together, the three of us. Will washed, I dried, and Mike put away. He also pulled my shorts right off, and Will's too, while we were doing this. Will made no protest, though he did giggle, and I followed him in both. Complicitly we lifted up our feet one after the other at the correct moment so Mike could get our shorts right off. I looked sideways at Will and caught him looking at my exposed hips and dick. We both had hard-ons (hards-on?) as we stood side by side at the sink.

'That's not fair, Mike,' I said a moment later. 'You're still fully dressed.'

'Well,' Mike said broadmindedly, 'there's something you could do about that.'

I put down the pan I was drying and did it. Unsurprisingly the cock that was revealed when I'd taken Mike's uniform trousers and non-uniform pants down was also erect.

It was a hot, end-of-May night. When we'd finished tidying the place we went into the living room and closed the curtains. Then we removed our last vestiges of decency: our shirts. We got into a three-way clinch, standing up, enjoying the delicious feeling of our three cocks all nuzzling up together.

'There's a bit of Cognac in the cupboard,' Will said. 'Anyone fancy a drop of that?' It turned out that we all did.

Will put on the second side of Please Please Me and we sat and sipped our brandies, facing one another across the room, each in a separate armchair, and admiring one another's nakedness. I'd never before done anything that involved two other people. I wondered if either of the others had.

Our dicks didn't stay hard all the time. They went up and down from time to time, like electric lights with an intermittent fault. But they took their cues from each other. Whenever one of our cocks re-hardened then the other two would follow suit. This was not only amazingly sexy; it was also amusing to watch. It was clear that the evening would end with the three of us having some sort of sex together. It only remained to be discovered where, and how, and what.

'We're lucky,' said Mike when the LP had finished, and after a short silence during which we'd simply watched each other like cats. 'I mean finding one another like this.'

'Needles in a haystack,' I said.

'Like buses,' said Will, muddying the metaphor. 'You wait an age for one and then two come along at once.'

It was true. In those underground and secret days it was difficult to find your way towards others who shared your illegal, abominated, sexual orientation. Difficult but not impossible. Country lads often felt by instinct that it would be easier if they moved into a town – and away from the curious eyes of their parents and those they'd been at school with. Some people moved into professions in which homosexuals were tolerated at least, and even understood. Hairdressing. Interior design. The theatre and other arts. But for others life could be an emotional and sexual desert. There might be oases in the middle of it. Periods at boarding school. In prison. In the armed forces. The Navy in particular... But outside those oases, not all of which were happy places anyway, life still remained a barren place. As Mike said, we three were lucky. Civil airlines were not hotbeds of man-to-man lust in those days. As yet there were few male cabin crew about. And in a tiny outpost like Lydd... It was not as if, like glow-worms, we carried bright tail-lights. Yes, it was a piece of luck.

Well, that's what I would have said if there had been two of us. But right now we were three. I had no practical experience of such a situation. There weren't many obvious precedents to follow. I wondered how the others felt. However, here we were. We had the night ahead of us. I determined to look no further into the future but to pick up my moment's nugget of good fortune and run with it.

Mike finished his brandy and put down his glass. He stood up. He walked towards Will's chair and took his hand, pulling him out of it. Though Will wasn't difficult to pull: he used his own power to help. Almost without pausing Mike moved towards the chair in which I sat, towing Will alongside him. He reached out his other hand towards my now upraised one and then I too was on my feet. A second later we were back in our three-way clinch. It was warmer this time round, less tentative. Increased familiarity with the situation? With each other? Perhaps the warming Cognac helped.

We nuzzled our three heads together, and our three cocks followed suit. Then Mike spoke. 'As they say in the pictures, "Your place or mine?"' The question was aimed mainly at Will. I didn't have a place. Yet.

Will said, 'I think Jack should decide, don't you? As he's the guest.'

'Oh hell, I don't know,' I said. 'I suppose we could toss for it.' I said that in the hope of raising a snigger from the others and I was successful in that. 'All right, then,' I said when the snigger was finished and it seemed that I really did have to take the decision myself. 'Let's say … er … let's go to Mike's.' And so we did.

As we were completely undressed there was nothing left to do except to tumble gently together onto the bed. A moment before we did this I saw a large drop of pre-come emerge from the tip of Mike's bowsprit cock and sink slowly downwards on an extending glistening thread. It was as if a plumb-line were unwinding itself from somewhere inside him. I pointed it out to Will just before it landed on the carpet. That made Mike look down at himself, at which the thread of course broke. 'More where that came from,' Mike said. 'Scout's honour I haven't come since the middle of last night.' He gave me a mock-severe look. 'And Jack knows all about that.' Then he shared his gaze between Will and myself. 'Whereas you two…'

'We'll just have to see,' Will said.

'That was hours ago,' I objected. 'Faint heart…' At that moment Will became the second of us to spill a long thread of clear fluid. His went onto the bed because he was standing right beside it and his dick projecting above. We all laughed at the sight and then collapsed together onto the bed, nosing into one another and wrapping around one another, like a litter of lively puppies.

After a minute I found myself sucking someone's penis. I couldn't tell whose. I tried to guess from the taste but I couldn't, as I hadn't had either of them in my mouth before and was unable to compare. Nor could I easily ask just then.

And then, deliciously, someone was sucking on mine…

An hour later Will and I had both come twice and Mike – though much more heavily – once. None of us had fucked, though there had been moments when Mike had come close to it, both with Will and me. He'd had his cock between both our pairs of thighs at different moments and I'd felt it nosing a bit indecisively at the pucker of my anus once or twice, like a nibbling goldfish. That had made the whole of that area, and the insides of my thighs, delightfully wet. I'd seen Mike try the same tentative experiment with Will's arse. Myself,

I'd gone no further in that direction than to insert a finger in both my new friends' rear entries – after Will had done the same thing first. When we all came eventually, each time, it was into someone else's fist.

At last, all three of us completely spent, we lay together on our backs on Mike's bed, Mike in the middle, with our arms around one another's shoulders. We'd mopped ourselves up with a towel as best we could, but we could do little for Mike's bedspread, which we'd managed to wet with huge quantities of spunk.

After a while, Mike said, 'We now have to decide where we all sleep.' Will and I made non-committal grunts. This looked like being a difficult one for me. How could I choose the nocturnal company of one of the two without giving offence to the other? Or without short-changing myself?

I had a sudden inspiration. If a decision to defer a decision can count as an inspiration. (Ask Hamlet.) I said, 'There was a bit of brandy left. Anyone fancy a final nightcap while we think about it?'

I wasn't sure the others would jump at this, but to my happy surprise they both did. A minute later we were back in the living room (though this time wrapped in dressing gowns) and playing for time with the last small drops of Cognac in our brandy glasses. When at last the decision about bedtime could no longer be put off it was Will, to my surprise, who proposed it. 'Why don't we all get into my bed?' he said. 'At least it's dry now.' Polite chuckles from Mike and myself. 'And if anyone's uncomfortable or too hot in the night they can simply move into Mike's, without any hard feelings.' Mike and I were as full of praise for Will's idea as if he'd been Solomon, and a few minutes later we'd adopted it. We all went to the bathroom first. After what we'd done together we felt no need to be coy about this. One would clean his teeth as another pissed and the third waited in the doorway, casually chatting as he watched. And turn and turn about.

We all fell asleep eventually, Mike and I the two guests in Will's bed. And to the surprise of all of us, I think, we were all still there in the morning when Will's alarm clock went off at seven o'clock.

EIGHT

We hadn't really planned this morning: our thoughts had been occupied elsewhere. Now it all turned into a bit of a scramble.

'I can give you a lift to the station on my way in,' Will said, hopping into his pants and trousers.

'Do you need to go so early?' Mike asked sleepily from the pillow beside my head.

'Mmm, no,' I murmured in reply.

'I can drop you off later. Say, eleven o'clock. I'm on the late shift again. Though earlier if you want…'

'That sounds much better,' I said. 'Eleven o'clock.' I felt Mike wrap his legs and arms around me from behind. I also felt the pressure of his erect cock in the small of my back.

'Talk before I go,' Will said. He reached beneath the covers and gave my dick a squeeze. It too was stiff.

The same went for Will's of course, which I immediately groped through his trousers. 'Ah, what a pity,' I said.

'Can't be helped,' Will said briskly. 'Work is work. You can have a wank with Mike after I've gone.'

'That's very decent of you,' I said. 'And you can have one with him tonight. Which I can't.'

'You'll be back on Sunday, Jack?' Mike asked.

'If you'll have me,' I said.

Mike gave my legs a python squeeze with his. 'I think there's no doubt about that.'

'Come in time for lunch,' said Will. 'If you can.' He left the room. We heard him go into the kitchen – presumably to put the kettle on – then come out and briefly use the bathroom, and go back again into the kitchen. As we listened, Mike's hand stole down my tummy and clasped my stiff dick.

'Better not just yet,' I said. 'With Will still in the house…'

'I know what you mean,' Mike said, letting go of my cock – with some reluctance, I thought. 'It would seem a bit … disrespectful. Wait till he's gone, like he said.'

'Exactly.' I reached behind me, searched out Mike's dick and gave it a momentary squeeze to show that I meant what I said. So, while Will ate his Corn Flakes in the kitchen Mike and I just spooned and cuddled each other, and the feeling of that was unbelievably delicious, the anticipation of what we were going to be doing in fifteen minutes almost as wonderful as the thing itself.

Will popped back into the room, still finishing the dregs of his tea. With his free hand he reached down into the bed and felt my cock again. This time he also felt Mike's. We were both still stiff. And, Will informed us, both wet. 'Ah, you haven't done it yet,' he announced.

'Well done, Holmes,' Mike said. 'We agreed we'd do the decent thing and wait till you'd gone. Like you said.'

'I'll think about you both in the car,' Will said. 'Won't be able to keep my hand off myself.'

'Mind you don't crash on the bridge,' Mike said.

'See you tonight,' Will said to Mike. 'I'll shop.'

'No you won't,' said Mike. 'I'll do it when I take Jack to the station. When you come home you'll want a nap.'

'Thanks.' Will bent down and gave Mike a quick kiss. I was afraid he'd lose control of his tea mug in the process but he didn't. Then he kissed me. 'See you on Sunday. Lunch at one o'clock.'

'I'll phone you the night before,' I said. I realised I didn't know the phone number – or even the address. 'I'll get the number from Mike.'

Will disengaged from us then, and waved humorously from the door before he disappeared through it. A minute later we heard the Mini start up and then drive off. Mike turned me towards him and began to kiss me seriously on – and in – the mouth.

I found there was something seriously wonderful about sharing a lie-in, and mutually masturbating, with someone you found extremely handsome and whom you liked and could trust. It wasn't an experience I'd often had. Most of my previous sexual experiences had been furtive and quick. But it was mine to enjoy this blue-skied May morning. And Mike was enjoying it just as much as I was. To judge from the look of him, the feel of him, the things he said, the quantity of his spunk.

'I hope Will'll forgive us,' I said when we'd both finished ejaculating. 'All over his sheets…'

'I'm sure he will,' said Mike, companionably ruffling my wet pubes. 'He gave us the go-ahead to get on with it.'

'And you'll probably make even more of a mess of the bed when the two of you get it together tonight,' I said, in a self-justifying tone of voice.

'Probably,' said Mike. He lay back then between the sheets, and so did I, and we both dozed for a bit.

I didn't put Will's shorts on when we at last got up. If I had done I suspect I would never have got away from the place, and Mike would have been late for work. But we had our morning tea and Corn Flakes sitting in what passed for the garden, sitting opposite each other, fully dressed. It was still heavenly enough.

'Will told me,' I said, 'that the two of you had gone to bed together once before but that it didn't work.' I felt myself blushing hotly as I realised I'd been very indiscreet. 'Sorry. I shouldn't have brought that up. It was just something Will said… Or I thought he said…'

'No, no.' Mike saw my embarrassment and stepped in quickly to put an end to it. 'It's true. That first time it didn't work for either of us. Don't know why. It happens sometimes the first time…'

'I know.' I wasn't very experienced but I certainly knew that. 'But the chemistry was pretty good between the two of you last night.'

'It certainly was…'

I added, 'And it'll be pretty good when you get together again tonight.' Mike gave a confident, satisfied nod. I went on, 'Do you think you'll make a long-term thing of it, you two? I've heard that some men do. Some actually become partners for life…'

Mike stopped me with the faintest of frowns. 'Yes, but now there's you in the mix.'

'Gosh.' I knew that was true, but I'd shied away from the implications of that thought. Last night had been such a spectacular, and unforeseeable success. The odds against it being so had been enormous. Even so, I'd assumed it was a one-off. A unique event.

'You're moving in with us on Sunday,' Mike said.

'Until I get myself fixed up, Will said.'

Mike looked at me searchingly. 'Do you want to fix yourself up somewhere else?'

'No, not really, but…'

'When Will made that offer he hadn't had sex with you. None of us had lived through last night. None of us could have guessed… I'm sure that when Will has a chance to re-shape the invitation he'll say it's permanent. I mean, for the foreseeable future. As long as our jobs down here last.'

'Do you really think that?' I asked, awe-struck.

'Isn't that what you'd like?' Mike asked quietly. 'It's what I'd like.'

I felt something tugging inside me. The thing that used to tug when I was a child and I'd know that tears were coming next. They didn't come now, of course. I was twenty-one and grown up. I said, and was astonished to hear my voice come quiet and rasping, 'It's what I'd like.'

Mike smiled a big smile of relaxation and relief. 'Good. I'm glad we've sorted that out.' It seemed a rather major thing to have sorted out in four and a half sentences but I didn't share that thought with Mike.

'Well,' I said instead, trying to turn businesslike. 'There is a bit of a practical difficulty. Three people. Two bedrooms. Two beds.'

'True,' said Mike, as though he hadn't considered that. 'But if you suddenly found you didn't want to share a bed with me for any reason you could simply move into Will's bed. I'm sure he'd be more than happy with that.'

'Supposing he wasn't? Supposing he and I fell out?' I added, 'I don't mean out of bed.'

Mike grinned wickedly. 'Then you'd come back to sleeping with me. And if we all fell out, as you put it, then you could sleep on the sofa in the living room. And if it got really bad, one of us would move out, like in any other situation where young people share a house or flat.' He smiled at me fondly. 'But it won't happen like that. Trust me. It'll work out.'

I'd never heard of a case in human history where such an arrangement had worked out. But height-ho, perhaps there was going to be a first one day, and we were going to be it. I laughed. 'I trust you,' I said. 'Give it a go. But you'll need to talk to Will over the next couple of days. See what he thinks.'

'I know what he thinks,' Mike said, his voice full of calm confidence. Then he got up from his chair, came over to me and gave me a kiss. Then he went back to his own chair and sat on it, gazing at me. In wonder? Did I dare think that?

I said, 'Have you had experience of … of three … what do they call it? … I mean, before last night?'

'I've heard the word "threesome",' Mike said. 'But I've never done anything like that. Last night was a first in that respect.'

'For me too,' I said slowly. 'Will too, I think.' I looked carefully at Mike. I still thought him handsome. Perhaps even more so this morning than last night. Straight nose, fine cheekbones and strong mouth. His brown eyes had a strong look about them too. But when you looked into their depths they seemed to melt. At least that was what happened when I looked. 'Where do you come from?' I asked.

'A village called Odiham in Hampshire,' he said. I nodded, though I'd never heard of it. 'It's where I was born. My parents still live there.' He looked awkward suddenly. 'They've got … um … quite a big house.'

The English are so genetically programmed with understatement ("We have a little place in the country") that when someone admits that their parents' house is big that means it's absolutely enormous. I now formed the impression that Mike had been born in a palace. I said, 'Will and I were born just five miles apart.'

'I know,' Mike said. 'He told me that yesterday at work.' So I'd been talked about. I decided to think that was something good and positive. 'Our two schools played each other at Rugby and cricket. It's surprising we never met.'

'Well, you've made up for that now,' Mike said with a poker face.

There was silence for a moment. Then I said, 'I suppose you've had sex with men before.' He was ten years older than me. It was a reasonable guess.

'Yes,' he said. 'But given my great antiquity, probably not as much as you might think.' His chin jutted towards me, ready for my next question, whatever it might be.

'Women?' I asked. He shook his head and looked almost sheepish.

'Nor me,' I said quickly, to make him feel less bad about it. Then I said … and I didn't mean to say it, the words just tumbled out… 'You're wonderful.'

'You're wonderful too,' Mike said. And I knew that he hadn't intended to say it either. Then he got up from his chair again. 'Time I got you to the station.'

My parents' home, a semi-detached in Bromley on the edge of London, seemed a different place when I got back to it that Thursday afternoon. It had grown smaller for a start. It had done that the first time I came home on leave from the Air Force and had got used to buildings, events and people being big. Yet this time I'd only been away two nights. But my life had changed utterly during those two nights and the day that had been sandwiched between them. I'd been given a fabulous job. I'd flown a Bristol Superfreighter; I'd got it off the ground and landed it. I'd had sex with two wonderful men, together and separately. They had both thought I was equally wonderful. They had invited me to join their household in what looked like being a way-of-life experiment. Every time I thought about that I went dizzy with astonishment… Yet only the first two of these life-changing experiences was I able to talk about with my parents.

My father was mightily impressed that I'd been taken on as a First Officer by Silver City. At that time it was the most talked-about independent airline in the country. And my father knew something about air transport. He was also, I guessed, a little envious.

Dad had served in the RAF during the war. He had been a mechanic on Lancaster bombers, those mythic steeds of the Dam Buster raids – among the many less famous sorties that were embarked on without fuss night after terrible night. Even as a mechanic his responsibility had been enormous. The dice were loaded high against those brave Lancaster crews. There was rarely a night when all of them came back. To make the odds against them even worse by careless repairs or sloppy routine maintenance would have been criminally negligent and morally abhorrent. My father might not have gone into combat as a pilot, but his responsibilities weighed heavily enough on him even so; and the war aged him, greying his hair to silver-white.

But he didn't have to endure the whole of the War without flying experience. He flew in Lancasters on training flights and had taken the controls, under supervision, on several occasions. When I had told him I was flying a York during my own RAF days (the Avro York was simply a peacetime adaptation of the Lancaster as a freight aircraft) he knew exactly what I was talking about. He knew enough to question me with interest about the Superfreighter I had flown. Horsepower? (4,000 against the Lancaster's 6,500.) How did it handle? Not as nippy as a York, I said. Though you got used to it, I said. It was a bit like driving a Jeep. My father nodded comprehendingly. That was also something we'd both done in the RAF. I didn't tell him that the aircraft I'd flown at Lydd, *Le Quatorze Juillet,* had a reg. sign that was an anagram of wank.

My mother was far less interested in the statistics and the boy stuff. She wanted to know more about the place I would be living in and the men I'd be sharing it with. This was much more difficult terrain to tread through than details of pistons and undercarriage. I did my best, censoring myself as I went.

'The bungalow belongs to a chap called Will. He's my age. Actually it belongs to his parents. It used to be his grandparents' holiday home before the War. His parents were going to sell it, but then Will got his job down there...'

'Lucky Will,' put in my father, who was listening from behind the evening newspaper.

'He's really nice. Friendly.' I half saw my father looking a bit anxious when I said that. 'Ex-RAF.' My father visibly relaxed. 'The other chap's his lodger. First Officer, like me. Also ex-Air Force.' I put this in for my father's benefit, since the phrase had had such a happy effect on him the first time I'd used it. 'A few years older than Will and me. He'll very soon be a full Captain. The bungalow's big,' I told my mother. 'We have a room each, of course.'

Oh God, why had I said that? What would happen if she ever came down and saw the place? We'd have to build a lean-to, or a full extension! I felt a sigh escape my chest. 'What are we having for supper?' I asked.

'It's a pity you aren't staying for lunch,' my mother said on Sunday morning as we loaded my things into the car. Dad was driving me to the station. I'd be met at Lydd by either Will or Mike. That had been arranged over the phone on Friday night, during a call I'd taken care to make when it was cheapest, after six o'clock.

'I know,' I said. 'But Will's invited me, which was very nice. And I need time to settle in. There'll be things to sort out before I start work.'

Some mothers would have sniffed and bristled and said, 'What sort of things?' challengingly. My mother wasn't one of those, thank God. 'Well, I hope he cooks nicely for you,' she said instead.

'I'll be back in a fortnight,' I assured her. 'With sixty more flying hours under my belt. And hungry. And I promise I'll stay for Sunday lunch.' My mother smiled, and we kissed each other. Then I got into the car with my father. He started the engine and we drove off towards Bromley South station and into my new life.

NINE

I got off the train at Ashford and changed onto the branch line service to Lydd. To give an idea of how remote a spot Lydd was – well, this branch line was a branch of a branch: more like a twig. The main branch ran south from Ashford to Rye and Hastings. My train diverged at Appledore en route. It was pulled by a small black tank engine with a tall funnel and lots of sparks. There were not many such engines left on the network. We stopped for a time outside Appledore signal box. I watched from the open carriage window as the signalman leaned out and handed the fireman a metal object the shape and size of an un-strung tennis racquet. This 'token' was the authority to proceed along the single track that lay ahead, forking away to Lydd. Only one of these tokens existed per single-line stretch. If your train driver didn't have it that meant that someone else's train driver did and you would meet head on with predictable results.

From Appledore onward the terrain was pancake flat. It was the Romney Marsh, populated by the occasional farmstead, a few windblown willow trees, and uncountable sheep. Nine un-hurrying minutes brought us to Lydd.

For a second I didn't spot Mike. It was one of those long seconds in which you realise that your life is permanently on the brink of total collapse, that you are always an eye-blink, no more, from disaster, ruin or death. What if they had changed their minds about having me to stay with them? If the whole experience of last week had been a dream or a mistake? And I was now stranded on Lydd Town station, with my luggage, and would have to rebuild my whole life and expectations from scratch? And there would be no lunch.

'I'm here,' said a voice. I turned. Mike was walking towards me from out of a patch of shade that the bright sun had made impenetrably dark. 'Are you OK? You look a bit...'

'It's nothing,' I said. 'I just didn't see you at first...'

'Let me take one of those.' Mike bent down and picked up one of my cases. 'Car's across the yard. I left Will at home preparing lunch.' Had we been man and woman, I thought, or even two girl friends, we would have hugged or kissed and thought nothing of it. But we were two men and it was 1963. There was no question of our doing that in a public place. A place like Lydd station, with all of three other people about. Though it was an effort to restrain ourselves. Mike was wearing dazzling white shorts. He looked gorgeous. I had made a point of wearing shorts too – my own this time, which I'd brought from home. I was hoping that my appearance would have the same impact on Mike as his did on me. Reading his face now I discovered that it had.

Mike drove me to the pub a few hundred yards away, the Railway Hotel, in which I'd first met Will five days ago – by happy chance. After a few minutes Will joined us. Also looking wonderful and athletic in his shorts. 'It's in the oven,' he said. 'Keep an eye on the time.' We had time for a pint.

There was still an air of novelty, of something out of the ordinary, about having chicken for Sunday lunch. Although the price of chicken had tumbled during the last two years – it cost little more, these days, than lamb or pork – we were still not quite used to it. For most of our lives chicken had appeared once a year, at Easter – or twice at best. (Turkey meant Christmas.) So the smell of roasting chicken that hit me as we walked into the bungalow carried the whiff of celebration with it.

None of us had touched one another in the pub. We hadn't even shaken hands. Ironically it would have seemed an odd way to greet people you'd already had sex with. I'd clocked the signs, though, from the easy and cosy manner in which Mike and Will behaved towards each other that they had been getting along very happily, sex-wise, in my absence. But now, in the privacy of the kitchen, I placed an arm around the shoulder of each of my housemates, and they both gave me a quick peck on the cheek. Then they broke away. Will to boil a kettle so the chopped sea-kale could cook quickly, and Mike to get a large, sharing-size, bottle of beer from the larder.

'You'll want to know what's happening tomorrow,' Mike said as we started lunch. 'You're in at nine, and you're spending the morning learning the ropes. Two round trips to Le Tooks in the afternoon, under the watchful eye of a very senior captain, then you're finished for the day. They're being gentle with you. On Tuesday you get the full whack. Six round trips.'

'You're very well informed,' I told Mike. 'How do you...?'

Will answered. 'It's he who's been picked to show you the ropes. Someone was asking if anyone knew where you were going to live. Mike said you were staying with us...'

'It sort of slotted into place. Made sense.'

'It makes brilliant sense.' I was more than happy with the arrangement.

After lunch we washed up together. We began to touch each other lightly as we did so, then as we grew excited the touching became more intense and intimate. When the last items had been put away we immediately got into the kind of three-way hug that I remembered being the prelude to our first sexual explorations as a trio four days back. In the middle of this tri-partite cuddle Mike asked me humorously how many times I'd wanked while I'd been away.

'Twice,' I answered truthfully. 'Friday morning and Saturday morning.' Then I added light-heartedly, 'I suppose you two have been at it like knives ever since I left.'

Neither of them spoke immediately. But I felt their answer as a sort of tremor between their two bodies. Clearly they had been having sex together in my absence. And why not, after all? I'd already half assumed it and not been bothered by the thought. Yet somehow the act of voicing it, along with their wordless answer, made a huge difference, one that I felt on my skin and through my bones. An extraordinary, unexpected pang of jealousy shot through me. I suddenly found I wanted to know all about it. How often had they done it? What exactly had they done? Had one of them fucked the other? Had they both done that – without waiting for me to come back? Which bed had they used? And how recently? Had they been in bed together this morning, enjoying a long lie-in, and only getting up when it was time to put the oven on and prepare the chicken and potatoes?

I felt an answering tremor go through me now, a little mini-moment of rage. But I fought it down. I realised I had to. There could be no place for jealous anger in any of us if the arrangement we seemed to be embarking on stood any chance of success.

The others felt the tremor. Will said, 'You OK, Jack?'

I decided to be honest. 'I felt jealous for a moment. You two doing things without me. But it's passed. You were at home together. It's natural that you'd have sex.'

I felt Mike's strong arm tighten around me. 'Thank you. And sorry if you were upset.'

'I'm really not,' I said. By now that was true. By now, somehow I wasn't.

'We'll make it up to you,' I heard Will say, his breath warm in my ear.

Mike said, 'We haven't done anything we didn't do with you last week.' He sounded for a second like a child trying to play down a misdemeanour after his parents had caught him out.

To my own surprise I heard myself say, 'You're lovely, Mike. You both are.' A sudden wave of affection for each of them choked me up.

Will said softly, 'Let's all get into bed.' I felt his fingers tucking themselves down into my shorts as he spoke.

A minute later, with Mike's bedroom curtains prudently drawn, we were naked and kneeling together on the bed. We had slipped one another's foreskins back and were lightly massaging stiff cocks. But doubts kept nagging me. I asked, trying to keep my voice steady, 'You said you didn't do anything over the last few days you hadn't done with me. You didn't fuck each other?' I tried to make the question less pointed by not adding *while I was away*.

'N-no,' Will said. 'We haven't done that yet.'

'Waiting for you to come back,' Mike said kindly, though I suspected that wasn't quite the truth.

'Have either of you, with anybody?' I asked conversationally, stroking Will's cock. (Mike was stroking mine and Will was stroking Mike's.)

'Actually no,' said Will.

Mike said quietly, 'Yes, I have.'

I thought it would be nice to have the details, though perhaps this wasn't the right moment. We dropped that conversation then and all got horizontal on the bed. And we didn't try and fuck each other then. This was a healing moment, a return to the comfort of familiar interaction after my three-day absence: not a time for new experiments. We all climaxed happily in one another's fists and came heavily over tummies and chests.

As we lay relaxing afterwards Will said, staring up at the ceiling, 'Jack, Mike told me about your conversation before you left on Thursday. That we seemed to be turning into a thing together, if you see what I mean. Because we all get along so well... and because this part of things is so good with the three of us. Mike said he hoped you'd stay with us... Not just until you found somewhere else...'

'I think what Will means,' said Mike, 'is that he doesn't want you to find somewhere else. Just like I don't.'

'I want you to stay here,' Will said. 'For as long as...'

I said, 'I want to stay for ever if things go on as well as this.'

Will's answer was to roll on top of me and give me a kiss.

There were hours of daylight still remaining. We walked together along the beach, then took our shorts off for the second time that afternoon, waded into the water and swam and splashed around for a bit. We had taken the precaution of bringing towels and swimming trunks. Will said, 'One night soon we'll come down here and fish. Sea-bass, sole and plaice. I'll let you both have a go with my rods.'

Mike said, 'You're always saying that, Will. We never get round to it.'

'We will one day,' said Will. 'I promise.'

When we were dry and dressed again we bought prawns and cockles at a beach stall. The next best thing to catching our own fish. They became our simple Sunday supper. Our first.

At some point I was going to need a car of my own, I realised, or at the very least a bike. I couldn't expect always to be working the same hours as either Will or Mike. But for the moment everything fitted very nicely. I would be working the early shift for the first fortnight – and so would Mike. He would drive me to work every morning, then drive me back.

As he had promised we spent my first morning at work together, Mike showing me around the place. 'We need to be a formal with each other,' he warned me as we pulled up in the car park.

'Obviously,' I said. 'It wouldn't do to look like a pair of chaps who've spent most of the last twelve hours together in bed.'

'And some of the twelve hours before that,' Mike said with a poker face. So we walked rather stiffly together and spoke unsmilingly to each other as we entered the crew room. We spent some time in there, going through the library of maps and charts. On these Mike pointed out our routes. The principal one was the forty-three mile crossing to Le Touquet. But Silver City also ran car-ferry services from Ferryfield to Ostend and Calais, though these were much less frequent. And the fleet of three Dakotas had their own agendas, doing charter trips to Holland, Germany, and deeper into France.

Mike told me that yet another car-ferry route would shortly be opening up. From Lydd Ferryfield, to Geneva. In comparison with the Le Touquet run that four hundred mile journey sounded like a positively long-haul flight. 'Where am I going this afternoon?' I asked.

'Le Touquet,' Mike told me. 'Twice.' We both knew he'd already told me this. The formality of our exchanges in the presence of other people made me want to giggle. I wondered how long I – or Mike, or Will – would be able to keep the pretence up.

The morning passed in a fog of new information. There was a visit to the control tower. Though tower rather overstated the case. Housed in an upward extension to the one-story building that comprised terminal, crew room and office block, the all-seeing windows of the tower were at little more than bedroom height. But they were high enough to give a clear view of the whole runway and aerial approaches, over the backs of the Superfreighters and Dakotas that looked back at us from slightly below, like wolves or dogs.

There were introductions to other pilots and to cabin crew. A brief chat with the Wing Commander. An introduction to my First Officer's uniform, with braided jacket and cap. It had arrived just that morning from the stores. To my surprise it fitted me nicely. Even the cap.

There was a sandwich lunch. Soft drinks only, of course. Then Mike and I parted company. He had a flight to Ostend to prepare for. I had a new Captain to meet.

Captain Evans was, like Wing Commander Davies, a pilot of the old school. I suppose that means that he was heavily into his forties or fifties and had flown in combat during the War. I wasn't sure if protocol required me to call him Sir. I just did it anyway – it was a reflex honed in my Air Force days – and he didn't protest. When we'd introduced ourselves we studied the weather report for the afternoon. It was going to stay fine and clear-skied for the rest of the day, the charts said. We were to take off on runway 22… No, there weren't twenty-two runways at Lydd. Its number was the first two digits of its compass heading. We would be taking off towards the south west, into the wind; it was the same departure I had already flown last week. Arriving over Le Touquet we would have to fly past the airport and turn back in order to land into the wind on their runway 31. We would use the same runway heading for our departure back to Lydd and land again on 22, just as I had done on my trial flight. Captain Evans talked me through all this, pointing out the route that was already marked, as if graven in stone, on the chart. Then he looked at me and said in a fatherly tone, 'Have a slash before you go. It might be a while before you get another chance.' I thanked him for his thoughtful words and took his suggestion up.

We walked out to the plane, did a circuit of the outside of it while Evans checked the plane's externally visible parts, then made our way up the car-loading ramp. We climbed the ladder inside the hold and emerged into the cockpit. This time I sat on the right, in the co-pilot's seat. In front of the windscreen I could see our payload of three cars emerging from the vehicle tunnel and following us on board. Through the windscreen of the second car, as it emerged from the tunnel, I saw Will's face for a second. We gave each other a polite nod.

I picked up the list of pre-start-up checks and called them out. Together Captain Evans and I went through the controls and instruments. The stewardess emerged from a door in the terminal with her dozen or so passengers behind her; they followed her as a brood of ducklings follow a mother duck.

Permission to start engines came from the control tower, and the tractor towed us back. We set off on our slow progress towards the runway's foot, two thirds of a mile away. It felt a surprisingly familiar experience, now that I'd already done it twice.

We lifted off right opposite the apron and the terminal building on the far side of it. Seated on the right this time, yes, I did glance down towards the apron as we rose into the air. A small figure was standing between the planes on the tarmac. It waved to me. I waved back to it, barely able to believe that I was doing this.

Evans noticed. 'Friends come to see you off?' he asked as, together, we hauled back on our yokes.

'It was one of the drivers. Will, his name is. I rent a room in his house.'

'Somebody said you were staying with another young First Officer. Mark... Mike.'

'That's right,' I said. 'We both rent rooms in Will's house.' Necessity is the mother of most inventions, lies included.

'Lucky Will,' said Evans. 'Collecting two sets of rent.' I wasn't sure whether there was something a little snide or knowing in the way he said it. Then, 'Keep an eye on the altimeter. And the Decca.'

'We usually hit a thousand as we cross the beach,' I said naughtily. 'Right now we're at six hundred. Heading two two six.' The red brick railway station where Mike had met me yesterday came and went beneath our right wing tip. The town of Lydd with its tall church tower peeled off towards the west, and then we were over the mile and a half of shingle that brought us to the beach.

'One thousand,' I called out. Evans pushed gently forward on the yoke. I shared the movement in my own, right-seat, yoke. We levelled off. The sea and the horizon came into view ahead.

'Gentle left turn at this point,' said Evans. He touched the rudder with his left foot and turned the yoke left to bank. The yokes, the control columns, were like the steering wheels on a dual-control Land Rover or Jeep. Though the top bit of the rim – from ten o'clock till two – was absent. But they moved in several planes, and you could do a lot more with them than you could with the steering wheel of a Jeep.

As we turned, the horizon filled with a great swathe of westward-facing French coast. Prominent was Boulogne harbour and the high ground behind it that Will had taught me to call the hump. We were still turning, rounding the tip of Dungeness Point. The moving map of the Decca navigation system, placed where a car would have its rear-view mirror, told us rather superfluously that we were three miles east of the airport. A direct line ran across the map between the radio beacon at Lydd and the one at Le Touquet. In a minute our slow turn would intersect it. It was Evans's job to reverse the direction of our turn a moment before we crossed that line on the sea and, like a car joining a motorway, merge our course with it.

The coast south of Boulogne came into focus after another minute. 'See the estuary?' Evans asked me. 'That's our landmark.'

'The River Canache,' I said. 'The runway lies right alongside it, exactly parallel with it. Which makes it easy to spot.'

Evans might have been pleased that I'd done my homework so thoroughly. Or simply irritated. I suspected the latter. But he gave no sign that that was the case. He didn't hit me at any rate.

TEN

For a few minutes the estuary stayed in front of us, apparently not getting any closer, and there was nothing much to do except keep a lookout. Captain Evans took his farewell from Lydd tower and started talking to Le Touquet. They replied in impeccable English, in very strong French accents.

Then the estuary was somehow big and close. If we went on following our heading, guided by the beacon that lay between the beach and the airport, we would fly straight onto the runway – but downwind, which would have been the opposite of our planned upwind approach. So a couple of miles before we crossed the coast Evans turned the plane away from the beacon heading, slightly to the left. 'Keep a mile to the left of the river,' Evans said. 'Or thereabouts. See the town ahead?'

'Étaples,' I said. That too came from doing my homework. The town lay across the river from Le Touquet airport and a couple of miles inland from the beach town of Le Touquet itself.

'Eat-apples, that's right,' said Evans, correcting my French pronunciation. 'Use it to guide your approach. Think of the town as a wheel, and you circle round the rim of it. When we've done our one-eighty we'll be on track for final approach.'

By now we had crossed the coast. The river lay to our right, parallel to our track, and immediately the other side of it ran the airport runway, parallel to both. On the apron beyond it I could see five of our Superfreighters, lined up like tiny toys too small to be manufactured even by Fabergé. Then they, and the runway, disappeared behind us and we carried on to Étaples.

Evans made the slow right turn around the town, which cart-wheeled beneath us. When we straightened up I saw that Evans had got it exactly right. The sea lay ahead of us, and before that the estuary lay conspicuous in our path; the runway, a little more difficult to spot, was lined up helpfully slap-bang next to it. Not only that. The beacon line returned to our Decca map. We were heading towards it from the landward side now. Dead centre. Evans's turn had been perfect. With just over two miles to run we began our brief descent from a thousand feet.

We crossed the railway line. Ahead of us was a small pine forest. A swathe had been cut though this along the line of the runway approach. We followed it. At a hundred feet we flew over the Le Touquet to Étaples road near where it crossed the river bridge. I could see the faces of the lorry drivers looking up at us. Then we kissed the tarmac and I had completed my first international flight.

Though not all the duties associated with it. As Evans steered us towards the terminal it was my job to descend the ladder into the vehicle hold and start to unlatch the clamshell nose doors. The final latch was left closed until I heard the engines stop. Then I undid that too, and switched on the hydraulic door opener. As soon as the gap was wide enough the ground crew pushed the loading ramp up to it and I scrambled back up the ladder to the cockpit.

'Need to get out?' Evans asked. It was probably his way of asking if I needed another slash.

'No.'

'Good,' Evans said, and we set to and did our brief paperwork.

The cars rolled off. The passengers walked off. The dispatcher came on board, took our paperwork from us and gave us a new lot. New cars rolled aboard. New passengers. We did our pre-flight checks. Less than twenty minutes after Evans had stopped the engines he started them back up.

It was clear all the way back. Kent lay emerald green ahead of us in the early summer light. The white cliffs of Dover sparkled like a necklace, way off to the right. Dungeness Point sprawled in the sun ahead of us like a tawny, stretching cat.

'Head for the lighthouse,' Evans instructed. 'Can you see it yet?'

'Decca takes us straight to it,' I pointed out ill-advisedly.

'Imagine the day,' said Evans in a steely tone, 'when Decca for whatever reason goes on the blink. You'll be glad of the lighthouse. Get out the binos and look for it.'

'Yes sir,' I said. I fished in one of the many small equipment pockets and pulled out the binoculars. I peered through them, and a moment later, there the lighthouse was.

But before we reached it Evans steered us northwards, up the coast. 'New Romney church tower,' I offered contritely, although I couldn't see it from my side of the plane. But I knew that Evans could.

'Well done,' Evans said, and turned inland. A minute later we were lined up with Lydd's runway 22 ahead of us and starting our descent. And twenty minutes after that we were taking off again and repeating the whole operation.

But by this time a veil of haze had come up over the sea between England and France. We followed Decca all the way across. The first sign of France I saw outside the cockpit this time was the town of Étaples directly underneath. It cart-wheeled reassuringly as Evans calmly made his turn onto the approach.

Again we accomplished the turnaround in under twenty minutes. As we lifted off a few minutes later, heading towards the sea, I could see that the light sea haze had vanished as quickly as it had appeared. By the time we had coasted out, a mile from the airport and at about eight hundred feet, the English coast was already in sight ahead of us – a long dark line that ran from Dungeness to Dover cliffs. Soon the Dungeness lighthouse, our homing landmark, would come into focus. I couldn't help remembering Evans's warning about the day Decca might go on the blink. There would always be the basic compass to look at. But I still found myself hoping it would be a day on which there wasn't a sea fret.

As we turned off the runway, following our second return to Lydd, I scanned the tails of the aircraft lined up on the apron. There were G-AMWE (the City of York), G-AHUI (City of Bath) and G-ANWK (Le Quatorze Juillet and still my favourite.) But Mike's – G-AMWD, City of Leicester – wasn't back from its last trip to Ostend yet.

I headed down the ladder as Evans rolled our plane (G-AMWF, City of Edinburgh) towards the line-up. Unlocking the nose doors from the inside, latch by latch, I thought of the opening of the Wooden Horse of Troy by city insiders, and wondered what, or who, would be the first thing I saw when the hydraulic arm pushed them open.

To my surprise I came face to face with Will, one of two drivers manoeuvring the motorised ramp into place almost beneath my feet. 'Hey!' I said.

Will grinned up at me. 'Hey there,' he said. The look on his smiling face was a palette of many colours. I saw some admiration, pride in me, and great affection. A look of envy too, that had something almost sad about it. But also I realised that Will wanted to hug me: that was plainly evident.

I wanted to hug him too, and shower him with triumphant kisses. It was impossible, of course. We were both at work. There was a fast turnaround to do. Evans and I had to hand the plane onto the next shift of pilots. And we were in company. The other two drivers were swarming up the ramp already, all fired up to drive the inbound cars off. I told Will, 'It was all great. Tell you about it later.' Then I had to scamper back up the ladder to finish shutting down the aeroplane with Captain Evans and preparing it for handover.

Two minutes later Evans dismissed me. 'Well done,' he said. 'You did well on your first two trips. See you tomorrow. Nine o'clock.'

'On the dot, sir,' I said. I sensed a crazy grin on my face and felt light-headed. I hopped down the ladder again. The vehicle hold was already empty; the oncoming cars were not approaching yet. There was no sign of Will. But pulling into the space next to our aeroplane came slowly clattering the City of Edinburgh, the plane on which Mike had been today's co-pilot. He was on the wrong side of the cockpit for me to see him or for him to see me. But I waved exuberantly up to his Captain instead.

I made my way indoors to the crew room. The clock on the wall said five minutes to four o'clock. A few minutes later in walked Mike, tall and elegant in his uniform of braided jacket and peaked cap. He grinned broadly at me. 'Well, how was it?' he asked.

'It was amazing,' I said. 'I've been to France twice.'

'You'll go there six times tomorrow,' he reminded me.

'That's not the point,' I told him. 'Before this afternoon I'd never been outside England in my life.'

My RAF experience in transport planes had involved flights around England, air base to air base, as a co-pilot. As pilot I'd done short hops, though always with a more experienced flier in the co-pilot's seat. I told Mike and Will about some of my experiences as we ate together later that evening. Mike in his turn had some news for us.

'They've offered me promotion to Captain,' he said.

'Why didn't you say before?' I asked.

Mike gave me a smile I couldn't have described easily. 'It's your big day,' he said. 'Not mine. We wanted to hear your stories first.'

I looked at Will a bit uncertainly, but his face seemed to be sharing Mike's sentiment. I began to ask Mike, 'So when...?'

'In two weeks. It's a busy summer schedule. Extra flights. They've taken on a new First Officer...'

'Who?' I interrupted, genuinely surprised.

'You, I think,' Will told me with a straight face.

Mike resumed his much interrupted story. 'I've clocked up the flying hours already. And I notch up the right number of landings and take-offs some time tomorrow.'

You needed to accumulate a certain number of landings to qualify for captain. It was easier to accumulate them working on the Silver City air ferry than it would have been with most other airlines. Flights to Le Touquet, the distance little more than forty miles, meant you could clock up twelve in a single day if your captain let you 'have control'. A potential sixty in a single week.

'Congratulations,' I said. Then, uncertainly, 'Are we allowed to...?'

'Drink to that?' Will finished my sentence for me.

Mike looked at his watch. 'It's not eight o'clock yet, so ... yes.' He and I were both flying at around nine-thirty the next morning. The golden rule was "Twelve hours between bottle and throttle". It was becoming clear, as the three of us felt our way hesitantly around our new three-way set-up that Mike, nine or ten years older than Will and me, was very much in charge of it.

And I was learning my role too: I got up and fetched three bottles of beer from the larder.

During that milestone day, my first day as a First Officer with a civil airline, the day of my first two trips out of Great Britain, I had given almost no thought to sex. On the rare occasions I had done it had been to guess that I wouldn't be interested in any such activity when evening came. I would be too exhausted, my mind and feelings otherwise engaged, and I would let the other two get on with it between themselves if they wanted to, while I went to bed in the other room.

How wrong I was.

By the time we had eaten, and drunk our modest ration of beer, I found myself appraising the others, instinctively looking for the subtle signs that they were in the mood to have sex with me, and I found them looking at me with the same animal keenness. We didn't even delay things by doing the washing up; we went straight into Mike's bedroom and took one another's clothes off. Once we were clustered together, embracing and playing, caressing cocks together on the bed, Mike said, 'Neither of you has ever fucked another chap, right?' We grunted our acknowledgements of the fact with a bit of embarrassment. 'Maybe it's time you had a go,' Mike said casually. He sounded like a flying instructor giving us the controls on take-off for the first time.

'Yeah,' I heard Will say, with the same excited but apprehensive determination in his voice that I had heard in my own on the occasion of my own first take-off. Before I had time to echo his answer Will squeezed me and said, 'Can I do you, Jack?'

I said, 'Yes.' Will was a year older than me. It seemed only right and proper that he should go first.

'It won't hurt, Jack,' I heard Mike say. 'Provided you really relax.'

'Which way…?' Will asked uncertainly.

'Lie on your back, Jack,' Mike instructed. 'Will, lift his legs. Get them over your shoulders…' But Mike's instructions were becoming superfluous. Like bright apprentices we were getting the thing right even before he told us. 'Use plenty of spit,' he told Will. 'And get him used to it with a finger. Gently at first. Will, loosen up…'

And so I got fucked for the first time in my life, lying beneath a grunting, smiling, thrusting Will, while Mike lay alongside us, his body turned towards us. He was no longer talking, giving instructions, and he didn't need to encourage us with words. Instead he excitedly wanked my dick with one hand and his own with the other, though he occasionally interrupted himself (and me) to rub Will's heaving back or to tickle my tummy or stroke my forehead.

Yes, it did hurt a bit. There were split seconds when Will pushed awkwardly and it hurt a lot. But for the most part I was loving it. It was like sailing, like flying… And yet it wasn't. It was like being sailed, or being flown – if that makes sense.

I felt Will's cock swell and empty itself inside me. It hadn't taken him long to get there. 'I'm coming,' he said as his body bucked in his ecstasy.

'You don't say,' said Mike laconically. Though the news, or more probably the sight of Will's naked body in spasm, made him accelerate the stroking of his own, and my own, distended penis with an excitement that was anything but laconic.

Still, I came before Mike did. I felt as though it would have happened anyway, with or without Mike's attentions to my dick. And once Mike had seen the outward signs of my orgasm, the flying streams of my semen arcing up my chest to land on my chin and collar bone, there was no holding back on his cock's part. It shot his sperm everywhere. All three of us were slippery and awash. Then we relaxed and rested together on the bed, still all wet. Will remained plugged into me and I found I really liked that. But after a while I felt his cock grow small inside me and then it sort of fell out. Mike found his bedside towel and gave us all a wipe. Then he sent Will and me off to the bathroom together to clean up properly. 'You'll know what to do when you get there,' Mike advised me. 'It'll become sort of obvious.' It did become obvious as Will and I waddled together across the hallway. Our very intimate minute in the bathroom together became a weirdly bonding experience. Almost as seismic as the other moment of bonding we'd recently experienced.

I tried to calculate, as I briefly sat on the toilet seat, how many permutations of what had just happened were mathematically possible among the three of us. But without a pencil I couldn't work it out. By the time we emerged from the bathroom Mike was in the kitchen, clad in a very minimal pair of shorts and nothing else. Dutifully he was embarking on the washing up.

ELEVEN

We didn't have any more sex that night. Though the three of us slept all together again. And though I was in the middle this time and so got rather hot I slept the sound and peaceful sleep of the just been fucked. It wasn't till I perched briefly on a kitchen chair while drinking my morning coffee and eating my Corn Flakes that I had any inkling of discomfort in the vicinity of my arse and began to think through the implications of that for the day that lay ahead, sitting for six hours in the far from luxurious confines of a Bristol Superfreighter's co-pilot seat.

'Ants in your pants?' queried Captain Evans shortly after take-off on our first flight out.

'A bit of Dhobi's itch, I think, sir,' I improvised.

'Bath or shower often,' grunted Evans. 'Talcum powder. Regular changes of pants. No doubt they told you all that in the RAF.'

'They did, sir,' I said. 'I'll have it in check by tomorrow. Never fear.'

'Keep your eye on the Decca,' Evans said.

I might have felt offended by Evans's interference in what I'd let him believe was a matter of groin hygiene but actually I didn't. I had learnt less than an hour earlier that I would be flying with Captain Evans and only Captain Evans for the whole of my first fortnight. I guessed that he saw himself as responsible for me and not just in the cockpit. His fatherly concern for my health and welfare might prove awkward over the coming two weeks but I wasn't going to resent it.

'We follow the direct route as closely as possibly,' Evans now rammed home the point. 'Forty-three miles means forty-three, not fifty-three. So no going round by Boulogne because it looks interesting. It's a business we're running, not the armed forces, paid for out of the public purse. Petrol is expensive and margins are tight. That's not something they teach you in the RAF.'

'No sir,' I said.

Today we were flying G-AMWE, the City of York. Though we didn't refer to it by its given name: that was something dreamt up to charm the passengers, it was not for the likes of us. We called our planes by the last two letters of their reg. sign. So G-AMWE became Whiskey Echo. Though that, I thought, had a pleasingly whimsical sound to it: every bit as good as City of York.

Ours was the third flight out of Lydd that morning on the Le Touquet route. By chance, Mike would be following us, in ten minutes' time, aboard the fourth. As first officer still, sitting like me in the right-hand seat. As we crossed the French sand dunes looking towards Étaples, Mike would be coasting out over the shingle wastes of Dungeness beach. We two would be flying along the same radio beam though twenty-plus miles apart. Then I would see his plane (Whiskey Foxtrot, often shortened to Whiskey Fox) roll onto the apron at Le Touquet a few minutes before mine started its engines again, ready to head back to Lydd.

I found these curious circumstances strangely moving and the emotions they aroused in me came from somewhere very deep inside myself. They chimed with my growing feeling that Mike and I were very close. And yet, after last night... I had to shuffle in my seat again as my thoughts returned to that. The physicality of what had happened between Will and me had drawn us two even closer than we'd been before. Alone in the bathroom this morning I'd been aware of the lingering, pleasant, smell of Will's cock. It was as though he'd marked me – as if I was his territory – for life. It hadn't been an intentional thing, it was a sort of by-product of our shared experience. But it had affected Will too. Had he too been brought up short by the sudden smell of *me* about *him* while he was doing his morning ablutions? I tried not to think too hard about that. I knew, though, that he'd been as deeply affected by the experience as I had. I could tell by the eloquent look on his face when he confronted me at breakfast.

'Keep a lookout,' Evans interrupted my reverie sternly. 'Near the coast. Light aircraft following it up and down... Summer morning like this.'

'Don't Le Tooks tower warn us about cross-traffic as a matter of course?' I asked.

'Indeed they do,' the Captain said. 'But they're only human, like the rest of us. Admittedly, if they slipped up and failed to warn us they'd go to prison for it. Though we wouldn't live to enjoy the satisfaction of knowing that.'

'I see, sir,' I said, feeling very sobered as well as taken down several pegs. 'I'll keep a lookout to starboard, sir.' Starboard – right – was the side on which I sat. I peered out into the morning sun's brilliance. Below us stretched the long sweep of Le Touquet's sandy beach.

I didn't know whether I was coming or going. That was an old-fashioned expression I'd heard my mother use. But that day it applied to me quite literally. Six crossings each way – twelve separate trips – in seven hours, with a forty-minute lunch stop and two tea or coffee breaks while they refuelled the aircraft. Lunch was in the canteen at Le Touquet, by the way. It was my first experience of French grub and I made the most of it. Surreally, Mike walked into the canteen just as Evans and I were finishing our lunch. With his Captain of the day. Coming to have their lunch. And munching on my first ever *croque-monsieur*, a delicious, fussed-over, ham and cheese toasted sandwich, I did know I was in France, at Le Touquet, during that lunch stop.

The same was not true, though, of every moment of the afternoon that followed. Several times I had to look carefully at the Decca, or to note the sun's position in the sky, to check whether I was heading towards England or to France. And when, as Evans taxied the plane slowly onto the apron and I popped down the ladder to undo the clamshell doors I'd find I'd lost track of where I was. When the doors opened would they give me a sight of the terminal building at Le Touquet or the one at Lydd? This despite the fact that I'd been peering towards the building in question from the window of the cockpit just seconds earlier. Twice I was happily surprised by the sudden appearance, as I opened the doors, of Will at the front end of the ramp. His surprise would be equally happy. It showed in the form of a smile blossoming quickly on his face. When this happened, at least, there was no doubt that I was at Lydd.

I couldn't guess whether the coming-or-going confusion would put itself right as I did more and more Le Touquet trips or whether it would get even worse. It was something I could ask Mike about. But there was something else: something that I wouldn't have to ask Mike about. As the day wore on, so the soreness around my arse wore off.

Mike was very sweet and gentlemanly when we got undressed that night. He said to me as the three of us stood around the bed, peeling our clothes off, 'Would it be OK with you if I fucked Will tonight?'

I said, 'That's fine with me. But you might have to ask Will what he thinks.'

All three of us laughed and Will said, 'He already has.' I decided there was no point being jealous about this. We would inevitably have to take turns with one another's arseholes and pricks. We weren't going to work out a list of whose turn it was to do what to who –

sorry, to whom – like the batting order in a cricket match. And part of me was a bit relieved that I wasn't going to get fucked again that night. No need to specify which part of me that was.

Will seemed to become a little nervous as Mike laid him on his back and arranged his legs around his neck. Not only was it his first time, but Mike had the biggest dick among the three of us. Mine was the middle-sized one, while Will's own (the one that Mike had considerately arranged for me to be initiated with last night) was by a small margin the smallest. As Mike made his preparations with a moistened finger I hovered, kneeling beside them on the bed, stroking various parts of Will in an attempt to relax him further. Those parts included, of course, his springy cock.

But Mike, though big, was gentle. His slow plunge into Will ('Imagine you're swallowing it, like a boa constrictor,' Mike told him) caused Will to moan a bit but not to shout. And once the two of them got into their stride together Will was calm and comfortable enough to tell me to lie beside him on my back. And so, while Mike pounded away between Will's beautiful round buttocks, Will and I gave each other an energetic hand job.

I came first. It went everywhere, as it usually did. The sight of that liquid firework display immediately caused Mike to lose his load inside Will, and that in turn set Will off. He exploded with a shower of sperm that easily equalled mine in quantity, energy and scope. Not until a couple of minutes later did he allow Mike to remove his emptied cock from his arse.

The arrangements of this three-way event might seem a tad mechanical, set down in print. But in reality they were nothing of the sort. The whole thing was as big a bonding moment as the previous night's adventure. Not only volumes of spunk but also an abundance of affection and positive feelings were released amongst us. I'm being circumspect about naming those feelings. When two people have sex together and it's more than just sex then we call that making love. But when three people are in on the act...? My mind didn't want to go too near that dangerous thought.

Over breakfast the next morning – I mean, during that brief five minutes of sitting around the kitchen table together with coffee and Corn Flakes – I noticed a new fondness in the looks, and occasional half-accidental touches, that Mike and Will exchanged. The previous day I'd noticed, enjoyed, and basked in, a new closeness between Will and me, following our first fuck. Yet now, had I lost out to Mike? Would this new bond be swapped back and forth between us, depending on what we did and who we did it with? (With whom we did it?) I remembered the 'token' – that tennis-racquet-sized object that was handed to each train driver at Appledore signal box as he entered the single track, then handed back. Always the same token. Unchanging. Would the new closeness that had arisen, first between Will and me, then between Mike and Will, work like that? Handed first to one pair within our threesome, then passed on to the next? And so on... Or would the bonds, the ties of affection, grow stronger and bigger among the three of us as we continued to experiment?

On the other hand, I wondered less optimistically, would we eventually just grow tired of our unusual arrangement? Only time knew that answer to that.

As the days passed Captain Evans grew more confident in my abilities as a pilot. He let me speak to the Lydd and Le Touquet controllers on the radio and occasionally 'gave me control' so that I became the person who was actually flying the aircraft. Sometimes he was relaxed enough with me to talk about things other than the altitude, the wind or the compass heading. I can't go as far as to say we chatted, but he occasionally gave me the benefit of his opinions on general matters, or asked me questions about myself which I would answer as best I could.

One day he said, 'You three sharing a house together – Mike and you and that car-driver chap – how do you get along, all of you? Cooking and suchlike. Cleaning. Washing up. I hope at least one of you's got a girlfriend to pitch in with some of that.'

'None of us has a girlfriend *right at the moment,'* I said, and I heard with dismay the dishonesty of my answer in that emphasis. 'But we manage all right. Take things in turn.' (I meant him to understand, the cooking and the washing up.) 'And luckily all three of us are able to cook.' He seemed satisfied with my response. But his question had come like a warning shot from society at large. The people we worked with, our parents, other friends... None of those people would be able to contemplate the fact of three men co-habiting indefinitely, with no girlfriends in sight, without eventually questioning it.

On another occasion Evans, who sometimes talked to me about the RAF, telling me of his experiences and asking me (though this less often) about mine, came out with this. 'Trouble with national service is, you get a lot of homos in the armed forces. When you have a professional fighting force it's different.'

'Um, why?' I asked. This was about as far as I dared go, I thought, without revealing myself.

'Poofs won't fight unless they have to. In the War, perhaps some did. But in the main they haven't the stomach for it. They get out of it. Join some reserved occupation instead.'

'Are you saying that all homos are cowards, sir?' I queried. I owed it to myself to challenge him as far as that.

'In the main, yes. Why? Do you know some that aren't?'

'I don't think I know any homos at all, sir. Not to my knowledge at any rate.' Thank God we had no poultry among the cargo. The cock that I heard crowing at that moment was only in my head.

And thank God that it was the precise moment in the flight for the change of radio frequency from Le Touquet tower to Lydd. 'Get onto Lydd tower,' Evans abruptly changed the conversation. 'Position report.'

'Yes, sir,' I said.

A homo. A queer. Neither of those labels was one I wanted. Yet no others existed yet. I was simply a young chap who liked having sex with other young chaps. Before this spring it hadn't happened often, but now, after my wonderful chance encounters with Will and Mike and moving in with them, it could and did.

I didn't want to go too deeply into it. Didn't want to analyse too much. It was one of those subjects it was better not to think about. Like the question of whether you believed in God or not.

Being homosexual in England in 1963 meant being an outcast. If you were caught having sex with another of your kind you would go to prison for it. In most parts of the world it was worse than that. (It still is.) So I lied to Captain Evans. I lied – by omission, I think the expression is – to my parents and to everybody else. In a way I was lying to Will and Mike and they were lying to each other and to me. None of us came out and said to each other, 'Right. We're queer. Let's admit the fact and then confront the world with it. Teach them to face it.' We didn't think of ourselves as cowards. We'd been in the military. We were brave enough to fly planes; we would readily have flown into war zones and into combat. Evans had been wrong about homos in that respect... But we weren't brave enough to tell the world the truth about us.

Most people had never knowingly met a homosexual. Though an idea of what to look out for was prevalent enough. A homo, queer or poof was an effeminate creature, lisping and high-voiced. He couldn't be trusted, as he had no investment in the systems – family and so on – that depended on trust. He wouldn't be any good in a fight and (Captain Evans had actually voiced the popular belief) would do anything rather than defend his country if it came to it. More than that – and this was deeply unfortunate for the homosexual community's social standing in general – he seemed to be readier than most to betray his country to the most unattractive takers. Burgess, Maclean...

On the other hand, paradoxically yet obviously, many people had first-hand experience of homosexual women and men. They found them among their sons and daughters, among their siblings, and among their nephews and nieces. Even, occasionally, among their parents. But they then stoically buried their knowledge and denied the fact to themselves and to everybody else. So the likes of Will and Mike and me went undetected in society at large for years and years. Decades. Centuries. Until some catastrophe caught us out.

TWELVE

In the days, or rather the nights, that followed we ran the gamut of possible pairings. I got to fuck Will – on the giving end for the first time in my life. It was a lovely experience. It was also a rite of passage (excuse the pun) and had, for me at any rate, something about it of a religious experience. Then Will fucked Mike. Then Mike fucked me... I was a little apprehensive about taking the thrusts of his rather bigger dick but in the event it didn't hurt too much; Will had prepared me, so to speak, with his smaller cock. At last I got to fuck the bigger, senior, Mike. And then the circuit, for want of a better word, was complete.

There was no question, for me, of preferring one or the other of my two partners when it came to sex, or of preferring the active or the passive role when it came to anal intercourse. Both my lovers, and all the possible permutations that we'd tried and would go on repeating indefinitely, seemed to be parts of a single wonderful sexual and emotional experience. And I know, because eventually we talked about it, that exactly the same went for the two others. Even to think about the possibility of a preference on my part between them, or of preferences on their parts among us, would have seemed wrong – in almost a moral sense.

The bonds between the three of us seemed to strengthen as the days passed and we explored the permutations of what we could do all together in bed. It was a real chicken and egg situation. The more we fucked and sucked and wanked one another the more we bonded. The more we bonded the more we sucked and fucked and wanked. It wasn't possible to say, and we didn't waste time thinking about this, which was cause and which was effect.

But would we eventually get tired of our three-way arrangement? If I had any anxiety at all about the situation, then that was it. That we might divide up into one pair and one isolated person whom the pair shut out? That was a horrible thing to contemplate, but as that beautiful warm May gave way to a sparkling June I was determined not to contemplate it. Nothing had gone wrong yet at least; the only thing to do was to enjoy the present and make the most of it.

My probationary fortnight, flying to Le Touquet and back under the authoritarian supervision of Captain Evans, seemed to be going on for ever. But eventually it came to an end. I had a weekend off. By chance, so did both Will and Mike. We all went off separately to visit our respective parents at home in their different parts of the south-east.

I didn't know about the other two, but for my part I found myself edgy and nervous. I could only talk about my work life, my flights, Captain Evans, my first visits to France, my first mouth-watering encounters with *croque-monsieurs* and the superior, French version of hot-dogs *(hot-dogs)*. My heart was bursting to release the wonderful news that I had found two lovely like-minded lads who I slept with and had sex with, and that they felt the same thrill and delight at the arrangement as I did. But of course that was out of the question. My imagination couldn't even envisage the ensuing scene, even as the wildest fantasy.

I felt uncomfortable and out of place at my parents' home. For the first time in my life I had that growing-up feeling: the knowledge that my home was no longer here but somewhere else. I didn't know if Will and Mike, at home with their parents in London and Hampshire respectively, were having the same feelings, thoughts and experience... But I could make a pretty shrewd guess. It was a relief to return by train to Lydd on Sunday night.

That following Monday I found myself on the later shift, flying afternoon and evening flights to Le Touquet with a Captain who was about the same age as Mike and as pleasantly relaxed with me in the cockpit as Evans had been formal and stiff. His name was David Cook. So, yes, Captain Cook. Though when I met him at the beginning of our first shift together and addressed him very properly as Captain he laughed and said, 'No, please don't. I'm David to you. And if I may I'll call you Jack.'

'Yes please,' I said. And when, at an early stage of our work together in the cockpit, I called him sir almost automatically he said,

'No sirring me, please. We can still be perfectly professional without being reminded of the Air Force all the time,' it was my turn to chuckle and say, 'OK David.' Then I went on with calling out the items on the pre-take-off check-list.

Working with David that first day was a lovely, happy experience. Quite apart from the relaxed atmosphere that quickly established itself between us, I found David to be a delightful chap, entertaining and interesting. He was also very handsome, in a way that managed to be quite masculine yet also almost pretty. He was very blond, very blue-eyed, and had the kind of delicate fair skin that never tans but is ivory smooth and golden-white. I quite often found myself fancying chaps who were a few years older than me – as Mike was, and now David. But I wasn't going to allow myself to fall for him. Partly because I was involved in a set-up that was complex and unusual enough already. Partly because David was married and his wife was at that time expecting their first child.

Doing the later, overlapping shift meant returning late from Le Touquet on the final evening flight. Neither Le Touquet nor Lydd was fully equipped for night landings. But Silver City had become a major player in civil aviation precisely by pushing boundaries of all types. So our last crossing of the Channel, at nearly nine o'clock on these June evenings, coincided with the sunset, which at the beginning of the month occurred at about ten past nine and ended up, by the longest day, at twenty past. We would take off from the French airfield facing directly into the sun's blazing ball of crimson and climb up among the long red streaks of the sky as if mounting the branches of a burning tree. The sprawl of the Romney Marsh would soon appear across the luminous water, a black flatness ahead of us, and we would line up for Ferryfield's runway in the speckling dusk, only just able to make out its grey shape against the grey of its surroundings in the oncoming gloom. Cars that travelled the nearby roads already had their headlights on. As we taxied back towards the apron we used our own headlights to show the way, and the cars would be unloaded by the light of overhead arc-lamps.

I had started my new job working the same early shift as both Mike and Will. This was wonderfully convenient but of course it was a matter of pure coincidence. It wasn't going to last, and it did not. It wouldn't be every week that I could expect a lift to and from work in either Will's Mini or Mike's Ford Anglia. I bought a very second-hand bicycle from one of the car drivers who worked alongside Will, for the princely sum of two quid. It was all I needed. The journey between the airport and the place I now thought of as home was little more than two miles and, except for the hump of the railway bridge beside the station, as flat as a billiard table. And with a forethoughtful view to those late evening returns home

I'd made sure that my new transport had lights that worked.

A few days after I started working with (Captain) David, my bed-mate Mike became a Captain himself. Will and I wished him well for his first day – he had the early shift – and we agreed we'd have a small drink together in the pub in the evening, after we'd all finished. I asked Mike who his co-pilot would be on his first flight out. He pulled a face and said, 'Captain Evans.'

'Oh no,' I said. 'How come?'

'It's fairly standard,' Mike said. 'It's the company's way of checking up that they haven't made a mistake in promoting you. Anyway, it's just for one day. After that I'm with Paul for the rest of the week.'

Will and I had to say we were glad about that, though I wasn't entirely sure we were. Paul was a very junior First Officer, barely a fortnight longer in the job than I was. He was also very cute and personable, with very expressive dark brown eyes. And he didn't have a girlfriend. Anyway, one day at a time, I thought. Mike had to survive his day with Evans first. I wondered if he would say sir to his temporary co-pilot.

It was ten o'clock when I cycled up to the door of the pub near the station, the Railway Hotel of happy memory, my front light bravely announcing my arrival to the other two who were already inside. They had eaten together at home; I'd had supper in Le Touquet. And now we celebrated Mike's promotion with a half pint of Tankard bitter. It sounds a bit tame as celebrations go and it was. But Mike would be airborne again soon after nine the next morning. By drinking even that small glass of beer at ten the night before he was technically in breach of the twelve-hour rule. However, a half pint wasn't going to harm him. None of our colleagues or superiors was in the pub at the time; no-one was going to know. The drink was only a symbolic one anyway.

When we got home – Will and Mike in Mike's car, me arriving five minutes later on my bicycle – Will said something that none of us had said in all the nearly twenty evenings we'd spent together. 'I'm a bit whacked. Are you two OK if I leave you to it tonight and get my head down on my own?' He looked at Mike and me anxiously to see how this would go down.

It was actually a relief. Since we'd started fucking one another we'd felt rather obliged to go on doing it night after night. Not exactly in strict rotation, but not a single night passed without one of us getting fucked by one of the other two. And all of us always ejaculated at some point; sometimes twice. I think that all of us felt it would have been somehow disloyal to the trio, disloyal to the idea of 'us' to want to call a halt to the merry-go-round and ask for a night off. But now Will had been brave enough to do just that.

Will was rewarded by smiles from Mike and myself. 'That's fine by me,' Mike said. 'We don't need to fuck each other every night if we don't want to. There's no rule that says we have to do that. Actually I'm quite tired myself...' Mike looked at me. I felt dismay at that moment. If Mike decided that he too wanted to sleep alone in his bed there would be no place for me except the living-room sofa. But Mike seemed to read my thought. 'It's OK, mate,' he said. 'We can sleep together. But you might end up just getting a cuddle rather than a fuck.'

'That's fine,' I said; my relief must have been plain to see on my face as well as evident from my voice. 'Cuddle'll do nicely. I'm also a bit bush-whacked.'

Mike and I said goodnight to Will in the hallway with hugs and a kiss each. Will then disappeared into his own bedroom and Mike and I went into Mike's. Will left his door ajar, we both noticed, and Mike and I didn't shut ours completely either. I had a moment's fantasy in which the three of us moved into a bigger house, in which there would be one huge bedroom with three big beds in it. I quickly dismissed the fantasy as ridiculous and shut it out.

Mike and I got undressed and took it in turn to go to the bathroom. There I found myself coinciding with a naked Will and we took the opportunity for a further brief goodnight hug and kiss – after we'd shared the toilet bowl for a pre-bedtime piss. Then I was in bed with Mike. We did cuddle briefly before turning away from each other to sleep. 'Night, Jack,' Mike said quietly.

'Goodnight Captain,' I said back to him, and we both giggled at that.

I woke up in the middle of the night. Something was happening on the other side of the bed. It had woken Mike too. It turned out to be Will, climbing in next to Mike. 'Sorry,' I heard Will say. 'It felt odd being on my own. I suppose I was lonely…'

'Come here,' Mike told him, and wrapped him in a warm embrace.

From behind Mike's back I found myself also welcoming Will. 'We missed you too,' I said. I reached an arm around, across Mike's naked torso and Will, sensing my movement in the dark, reached for my hand, found it, and for a moment held it tight.

I've written 'in the middle of the night' but actually it was what people called the small hours; and because we were in June the tight embrace of the darkness was already beginning to loosen with pre-dawn light. Mike and I wriggled sideways a little to allow Will a ledge of space and then Mike, in the middle between Will and me, said, 'Perhaps let's all just lie back and get a bit more sleep.' Will and I murmured sleepy agreements to that.

But not many minutes passed, not enough for me to fall asleep in the growing light at least, before I heard Will's voice say quietly and diffidently, 'Would anybody mind if I gave myself a bit of a wank?'

There was a moment's pause before Mike said, 'No problem. You go ahead, mate.'

Another moment passed and then I heard the rustle of the top sheet as Will got quietly to work. I know my own cock had started to stiffen soon after Will joined Mike and me in the bed. Now as I heard him begin I became fully erect. I said, 'If no-one minds I might join in myself.' I reached down to my cock and found it as big and hard as I'd ever known it. I started to stroke it.

Immediately I heard Mike heave a rather theatrical sigh and say, with a very transparent pretence of reluctance, 'Oh well, might as well join you both.' And I felt the movement as his own hand dipped down below his waistline beneath the covers and heard the rub and rustle as he began slowly to touch himself.

At first we only heard each other. But the dawn was approaching rapidly, and it was growing lighter not simply by the minute now but by the second. So that very soon we could all see clearly the movements of one another's hands beneath the sheet and blanket. It was like watching three piston engines working away slowly, but at different speeds and never quite in synch. It was a very sexy sight.

Suddenly I felt Mike's strong fingers in my groin. They gently explored the landscape there, then wrapped themselves around my balls. 'That's nice,' I said.

'Only fair,' said Mike sleepily. 'Will's doing the same to me.'

I heard Will say, 'Mm,' to that. Silently I crept my free hand towards Mike and caressed his chest with it. The action was a bit awkward and probably not very arousing for him, but it was the thought that counted.

I could sense that we were all climbing towards our climaxes. Like three of the planes we flew gathering speed on the runway. I felt my semen rise behind my balls and at the same time Mike and Will simultaneously threw back the bedcovers exposing us all to the dawn. Three very stiff dicks, three pumping hands, three firm young bodies whitely high-lit by the gleam of morning, and linked lightly by exploring hands.

'I'm coming,' I heard Will say.

Mike grunted, 'Me too.'

As for me, I didn't get time to say it. It just suddenly poured out of me and went everywhere. The other two grunted again as they saw my dick disgorge its load into the grey dawn, and then they very quickly followed suit. Mike a half second later, Will – for all that he'd been the first to feel his orgasm stealing up on him – a half second behind him.

In the moments that followed, as we shuddered and convulsed together, side by side and at moments in one another's arms, I realised there was something I wanted to say. I wanted to say it so urgently that it was almost bursting out of me. But I couldn't say it. I didn't know how to say it. Not in the circumstances I found myself in. It was just three words. Three words that had been used, at some point in their lives, by almost every human being since the dawn of speech. But had anyone in human history ever used them … and if so, how had they managed to say them … when there were two other people involved in the experience?

THIRTEEN

We had been blessed with gentle south-westerly breezes for the whole three weeks since I'd had my interview and done my flying test. High pressure had brought with it the settled conditions, warmth and blue skies that are its summer hallmarks. The hump had usually become visible within moments of our left-hand turnout towards France shortly after take-off, and the estuary of the Canache would come into view, ten miles south of it, a moment after that. But one morning towards the middle of June that all changed – as inevitably it would at some point – when the wind swung round to the north.

Our take-offs and landings went the other way round. We took off into the wind as always but now starting from the other end of the runway, (zero three) heading north. Heavy windscreen wipers swept the driving rain out of our view for half a second at a time, then the next half second brought it hammering back. As we rode up through the wind the plane would shake as though someone was trying to get salt or sugar out of it. It was a tense enough experience for us in the cockpit, working together at our dual control yokes to keep the plane as steady as we could. God knew how the passengers below us, behind the vehicle hold, felt. During these days of north wind and rainfall I worked with several Captains, but mainly with David.

We would turn out to sea over New Romney and Greatstone and double back along the coast till we met our familiar radio beam: the one that stretched like an invisible tightrope between the beacon at Le Touquet and the one at Lydd. Then we turned left and followed that. Thank God for Decca. We could only glimpse the sea occasionally, a thousand feet beneath us through the murk. There was no view of any coastline ahead.

But when things were this way round the landing in Le Touquet was straightforward. We flew all the way to the beacon, which was located just behind the beach. The runway lay directly ahead of us, its threshold just a mile away, and we were perfectly in line with it. It would come into view within seconds of our flying overhead the beacon, by which time we were well into our descent. This was called, by aircraftmen everywhere, the 'straight-in' approach.

On the way back, of course, we did the thing in reverse. We took off from Le Touquet heading inland and had to double back over Étaples, picking up our radio beam a mile or two off the coast. With any luck the Dungeness lighthouse would come into view just before we crossed the English coast, and we would turn as we crossed it, and find ourselves (we hoped) lined up for the north-easterly (03)runway at Lydd: the one from which, just over an hour ago, we had taken off.

Will was to be seen from time to time, driving cars, manoeuvring ramps on the apron, now clad in sou'wester and oilskin cape. Because of the high winds the aircraft were shackled down by their wheels to rings embedded in the tarmac every night. At home the wind rattled the windows while we lay in bed. What would this place be like in wintertime? I wondered. I was like the grasshopper in the fable, I realised. I hadn't given the winter very much thought.

I didn't want to find myself feeling sorry for Will. That he didn't have as exciting a job as Mike and I did. As Captain David and Mike's co-pilot Paul did. That while we were aloft, jousting with the clouds, Will was earthbound, driving cars across the tarmac and manoeuvring them into place in the freighters' holds. He too was a pilot. It seemed a cruel piece of fate that he simply hadn't completed as many hours of flying as Mike and I had done while in the RAF.

But Will didn't want to be pitied for his humbler role at the airfield. He had a smaller salary than Mike and I did, but he almost made up for that with the (admittedly modest) rent that Mike and I paid him for sharing a room in his house. 'I'll get there one day,' he told us one night. 'I mean, be a pilot.'

'Of course you will,' said Mike comfortingly, and tweaked his knee beneath the supper table to show him that he believed that.

In the meantime, Will had told us the details of his job. The arriving cars were driven by their owners through passport control and customs, then their drivers and passengers got out and walked into the terminal to join the few foot passengers who might also be on their flight. They handed over their keys to Will's immediate boss, who distributed them among the drivers. Will and his fellow drivers then took the vehicles from the airside car park towards the apron via a tunnel through the terminal and control block. Here they halted briefly. Inside the tunnel were marks on the ground and a height gauge that exactly duplicated the dimensions of the freighter's hold. It was here that any discrepancies or problems could be dealt with before loading the aircraft. Then the ramp was driven up to the aircraft's nose, and the cars brought out of the tunnel and carefully driven up it and into the plane's gaping mouth.

'The only person except for us who's allowed to drive a car on board,' Will said, 'is the Queen's chauffeur. He's considered to be good enough for the job.'

'Not bad,' I said.

'Mind you,' Mike put in, 'When the Queen and the Duke of Edinburgh flew with us the Duke insisted on flying the plane across.'

'Really?' I hadn't heard about that.

'Though he did let the Captain have control on landing,' Will said. He looked at Mike. 'Isn't that right?'

'There was a strong crosswind at Le Tooks,' Mike said. 'Apparently the Captain on that occasion did the last bit.'

'What takes the time,' said Will, 'is the business of chaining them up.'

'What?' I said. I was still thinking about the royal family, and Will's comment seemed a bit bizarre in the context.

'Chaining the cars up. Four shackles per car. One for each wheel. It takes an age and a half.'

'It's true,' said Mike. 'We're usually all done and ready to go about five minutes before you lot can give us the all clear from down below. If you could find a quicker way to do your bondage stuff on the cars we'd get away a bit quicker.'

'Quicker turnarounds, more flights,' I said. 'More income for the company.' I had no head at all for business but even I could work that out.

'Well,' Mike said to Will, 'maybe you should get to work on it. You spend half your day knotting chains and un-knotting them. I'm sure that with a little thought you could sort something out.'

'Hmm.' Will gave a little snort. He might have been a bit displeased by Mike's suggestion. No-one likes to be told of an obvious way to improve his working practices that he hasn't come up with himself.

Two things happened a day or two after that conversation. The wind went back to south-westerly. That meant a rise in pressure, and the return of blue skies, sunshine and warmth. Will dispensed with his oilskin cape and sou'wester and could now be seen striding about the apron with his muscular legs attractively clad in shorts. The other thing that happened was Mike's saying to me, 'Guess what. You're flying with me tomorrow. And to make a real change for you we're flying to Ostend and back.'

'Wow,' I said. For a second I couldn't think of a more intelligent comment. I was excited by the prospect of flying side by side with the man whose bed I shared almost every night. I was also happy at the thought of going to Ostend. In Belgium. It would be the second foreign country I'd have visited. It lay ninety-six miles away from Lydd; the flight time was thirty-five minutes. It was still a very short flight but after a month of plying to and fro between Ferryfield and Le Tooks – less than half the distance – it seemed like an adventurously big trip.

In the crew room I went through the library of charts with Mike. We would have copies of them in the cockpit too, but this was my preparatory homework. Not that I would be flying the plane this first time. But there was always the remote possibility that Mike, a fit man of thirty-one, might drop dead or become incapacitated in some way en route, and you always had to think of that.

In bed that night I kept squeezing Mike in excited anticipation of the next day. Mike noticed, of course, and so did Will. 'All excited about tomorrow?' Will asked with a laugh in his voice, and Mike snickered.

'Yes,' I said. 'I know. Silly, isn't it.'

'No, it isn't silly,' Will said sturdily and gave my stiff cock a squeeze as he spoke. 'I'd be excited if it was me. Sharing a cockpit with Mike…'

'As opposed to just a cock,' Mike said.

'I'm serious,' said Will.

'You're not jealous, I hope,' I said cautiously. I had become aware that we were all three of us treading on eggshells these days, talking to one another very sweetly and politely so as not to give offence. Like characters in an Enid Blyton children's book. I knew that all couples, married or otherwise, had to be careful of each other's feelings. Otherwise the relationship would not last. But I was finding that when there were three people involved the diplomacy and tact required to make sure than no-one felt left out of anything needed to be dredged up in quantities that were greater by an exponential, not simply arithmetical, amount.

'Jealous, no,' said Will after a moment's thought. 'Envious, though... Perhaps a little bit. But there's nothing unhealthy about that.'

'No,' I agreed.

'I just need to get on and find a way to become a pilot,' Will came back unexpectedly. There was an unusual edge of determination to his voice.

'That and find a way to shackle the cars more quickly,' Mike said teasingly. 'That lot'll give you plenty to think about while we're away in Belgium tomorrow.' Will pounded lightly on his Mike's chest with his fists. They both laughed, then I laughed. And then Mike licked Will's shoulder affectionately like a cat.

'You don't want me to call you sir, I hope,' I joked to Mike as we walked out to the plane in our uniforms – Mike proud of his new jacket with its four gold stripes.

'I certainly hope you won't,' he answered. 'Mind you,' he added more quietly, 'it was nice when you called me Captain in bed last week.'

'Then maybe I shall call you Captain sometimes,' I said as we climbed the ramp into the car hold.

'That is allowed,' said Mike solemnly. 'Provided it's as a joke.'

'You notice the plane they've given us?' I said.

'Couldn't help but notice,' Mike said deadpan. It was Le Quatorze Juillet, July the Fourteenth. Otherwise known as Whiskey Kilo. Or in full, G-ANWK.

But what we did next was anything but a joke. Mike had to walk round the outside of the plane, checking carefully that everything that was supposed to be attached to it really was attached, and correctly positioned and fixed. I mounted the ladder to the cockpit meanwhile and did the initial inside checks, reporting these to Mike when he emerged through the hole in the floor behind me a minute later. Now we were deadly serious: a professional team of pilot and co-pilot, Captain and First Officer, responsible between the pair of us for the lives of twenty other people as well as twenty-eight tons of expensive equipment in the form of their transported cars and our company's aircraft.

We took off towards the south west, into the wind, though very much in the opposite direction from our destination. This meant a turn of nearly a hundred and eighty degrees around Dungeness Point before we could intercept our radio heading – that invisible tightrope whose other end this time was the beacon at Ostend on the Belgian coast.

It was a brilliant morning and we were soon in sight of the coast of France, but heading this time to the north of the hump, towards the point where Cap Gris Nez drove itself into the middle of the Channel like a spike. On the English side we were soon passing Romney, Hythe and Folkestone, then Folkestone Warren, where the railway line runs dramatically beneath the towering white cliffs. We could even see trains, minute worms at this distance, running along the beachside track. Our heading took us straight past Gris Nez and then Cap Blanc Nez a few miles further east. The white cliffs of Dover glistened in the morning sun just fifteen miles to our left. The white cliffs of Blanc Nez did the same five miles off to our right. Both sides of the Strait seemed so close in the clear morning that you could imagine that had we dipped our port wing its lowered tip would have made contact with Dover Heights and if we'd dipped the starboard one it would have brushed the French white cape. Beyond the twin pillars of high cliff – like Scylla and Charybdis – the whole northern end of the Channel opened out ahead of us like a funnel of blue water whose open end disappeared in a misty sparkle that was North Sea and Dutch coast. I couldn't help it: 'This is beautiful,' I said to Mike.

'I know,' he said. 'Grab the binos. Take a proper look.'

I did. And there was all the beauty writ large. 'Twas Nature still, but Nature magnified. After half a minute I put the binoculars back in their compartment.

When we were in Mike's car and he was driving I would often lay my hand on his nearer thigh, or, if no gear change seemed imminent, wedge my hand between his legs towards his crotch. The present situation seemed no different. We were travelling in a dead straight line, we had long ago reached our cruising altitude of a thousand feet and there wasn't a cloud, let alone another aircraft, in sight. The only difference was the rather larger gap between our two seats. The cockpit was as wide as the cab of a lorry, even though I've previously compared its lack of comfort to a Jeep's. In order to carry out the manoeuvre I was used to performing when in Mike's car's passenger seat I had to lean sideways and stretch across. Nevertheless I did it. Then I slipped my hand between my Captain's legs.

I wondered for half a second how he would react. Then I knew. He didn't move a muscle. But he sighed quietly. Then he said, not turning his head but still gazing steadfastly through the windscreen, 'Oh Jack. My little sweetheart.'

To say that that astonished me would be an understatement. I was astounded, thrilled and aroused by the endearment, coming at such a moment, in such a place. Though I was almost equally astonished by the reply that came unbidden to my lips. It took me by surprise, yet it sounded almost as though I'd been practising it, so smoothly did it slip out. 'You're my sweetheart too,' I said. I added, for the sake of precision, 'My big sweetheart.' Before this moment I think I'd never used the word sweetheart in my life.

Mike said, to my further astonishment, still keeping his eyes fixed on the way ahead, 'I've always imagined how wonderful it would be if a pilot I was flying alongside did that.'

'Me too.' It was true. It was one of the things that, over the years, I'd fantasised about in bed. I partly undid my safety harness and leant even further over to wards Mike, planting a kiss on his nearer cheek. I didn't expect him to return the compliment and he did not. I re-engaged my safety harness and re-inserted my hand between his legs and kept it there for a full minute. He made no objection to that.

Our route remained dead straight. But the coast of France had turned a corner at Gris Nez; it now lay approximately west to east, and our route ran right alongside it, a few miles offshore at first but steadily, mile by mile, closing on it. We passed the docks of Calais, flying right overhead a Dover ferry that was pulling out of the port, and then the industrial sprawl of Gravelines and the harbour of Dunkirk. Mike pointed that out to me. *We will fight them on the beaches.* I couldn't prevent the words coming into my head.

By now we could see the runway at Ostend ahead of us, just behind the beach. Helpfully, as if deliberately, it lay directly in line with our approach. 'Can we go straight in, do you think?' I asked Mike. Strictly speaking that would have been a downwind landing, something frowned on, but this morning's westerly breeze was extremely light. And the airport was bigger than Lydd and Le Touquet, the runway longer. That made it a safer place to land with a tailwind anyway... Mike checked with the Ostend tower and they granted our request for a simple straight-in approach.

Our course met and then crossed the line of the beach like scissor blades gently closing and a moment later we were on the tarmac. 'Welcome to Belgium,' Mike said.

We made three return trips to Ostend that day. It was more relaxing, in the end, than the usual six frenetic round-trips to Le Tooks. The only disappointment for me was that our lunch break coincided with a stop at Lydd. I'd heard tales of a wonderful Belgian favourite dish: *moules et frites*.

On each of our crossings that day I leaned across and placed my hand between Mike's legs for a minute or two, and twice he did the same to me. It seemed to have become a ritual between us. Our special bond. It was *the thing we did* when flying together. We didn't speak about it again, though, until we were coming to the end of our last homebound flight in the afternoon run around three o'clock. Mike suddenly said, 'Do we tell Will about this?'

'What? This little thing...' I wasn't sure how to express it. 'Or what we said this morning?'

'Either,' said Mike. 'Or both.'

'Well,' I said, 'we do the same thing in the car, don't we? And Will and I do it – put our hands between each other's legs when we're driving together...'

'Do you?' asked Mike.

'Well, yes. I assumed you'd assume that. I didn't think of it as something one ought to confess.'

'No,' said Mike. 'I suppose it's not.' There was silence for a moment while beneath the port wing the town of Calais came and went. Then Mike said, 'Do the two of you call each other sweetheart?'

'No. Do you and he…?'

'No,' said Mike very quickly. 'I mean we haven't done up to now.'

'No,' I said, equally quickly. 'We've never done that yet.'

'No, right.' Mike nodded his head a couple of times slowly, in a way that was very Captain-like. The engines just outside the windows seemed noisier than ever just then. Five minutes later the church tower of New Romney came into sight across the water in the distance ahead.

FOURTEEN

There was a social club for staff at Lydd airport. It was called the Wingspan Club. Unlike English public houses at the time it was open for most of the day. For the use of off-duty staff. Will and Mike and I used it occasionally. The day of my first flights to Ostend with Mike was one of those occasions. We'd finished early – it was little past mid-afternoon – and knew we could treat ourselves to a drink or two without falling foul of the twelve-hour rule. Will would also be finishing early. I tracked him down in the car park; he said he would join us in half an hour.

A few of the other younger pilots also came into the bar. David (Captain Cook) was one of them. Another was the young First Officer Paul.

David came up to Mike and me. He looked at Mike, but jerked his head towards me. 'How did he get on?' David asked Mike.

'Absolutely fine,' said Mike. As far as the others were concerned our relationship was a purely professional one, even if we did share the same address. 'You trained him very well.'

'You're making me jealous now,' said young Paul. 'I thought I was the up and coming flying ace round here.'

'And so you are,' Mike reassured him. He gave his shoulder blade a light but masculine slap.

David added, 'Of course you are. It's just that now it looks as though there's two of you.'

'I take it the two of you were teamed up today,' I said, meaning David and Paul.

'Indeed,' said David. 'Six trips to Le Tooks.'

It was only yesterday that I'd done exactly that with another, older Captain, Captain Wimbush. (He was famous for smoking small cigars, Tom Thumb or Panatellas, in the cockpit.) Now, after my three trips to

Ostend with Mike, it seemed a long time ago and a very humdrum thing to do.

Paul turned half away from our group. 'Hi there. Come and join us.' He was greeting Will. I thought that nice of him.

'Careful on the bridge corner,' Will and I both warned Mike as we drove off, the three of us in Mike's car, two hours later. It had been a jolly couple of hours, meaning – among other things – that we'd had three beers each. The road home was easy and short. The only problem that staff and crew tended to encounter when leaving the airport after such a session lay just a hundred yards along the access road from the car park. The little road made an unexpected dog's-leg twist where it crossed a stream. The stream, more properly a drainage dyke, was big enough to swallow the front end of a car. It had done so on more than one occasion after someone's pleasant session in the Wingspan Club.

'Cheers, I will,' said Mike, slowing down. Then he navigated the dog's leg carefully and successfully.

We hadn't shopped for supper. Instead we drove on towards the beach next to the Pilot Inn. We walked, a carefree trio, along the shingle, while the later planes clattered overhead on their way to Le Touquet. Then we got fish and chips from a shack near the inn and took them home.

Neither Mike nor I came out and told Will how we'd touched each other intimately while we flew that day. I realised that we didn't need to. He sort of automatically knew. We also somehow knew, all three of us, that we would in some way make up for this.

We did, as soon as it was bedtime. We went to Will's room: it was an unspoken agreement that for tonight Will was in charge. Once we were naked we all piled on top of Will's bed and there Will fucked first Mike and then me straight afterwards. He came both times, inside each of us, while Mike and I stroked each other to orgasm – orgasms which were spectacular in their energy, and more visibly so than Will's two out-of-sight explosions inside the two of us. Mike and I took turns with the toilet bowl afterwards.

Nothing had been said. I had come to think of our three-way relationship as being like a flying aeroplane. You kept it aloft by careful adjustment of the flying surfaces – ailerons, rudder, elevators and flaps. What had happened between Mike and me that day on the way to Ostend had unbalanced things a bit. By fucking the pair of us in a single session Will had efficiently re-trimmed the craft.

It was back to the Ostend run for Mike and me next day. Shortly after we reached cruising height (our majestic one thousand feet) and were headed along the radio beam that led to the Belgian airfield, Mike casually leaned over, laid one hand on my thigh and stroked it lightly. I would have been more cautious and waited another minute or two before doing that to him. However, he was flying the plane; I was happy for him to be in charge, to have control of things.

'You never do this with young Paul, do you?' I asked jokingly.

Mike laughed. 'Of course not.' He paused for a second. 'I'd quite like to, mind. He's very attractive, isn't he.'

'Yes,' I agreed.

'Will seems to think so too. They were very matey yesterday in the club.'

'I did notice. Though I wasn't going to say anything. But I couldn't help thinking the attraction might have been mutual.'

'Yes,' said Mike, applying a little more pressure to my thigh. 'I thought that too.'

We were silent for a little while. We were coming up to the Scylla Charybdis moment – the point at which the white cliffs on either side of us stood sentinel, guarding the gateway to the North Sea. It was a beautiful thing to see and feel, a spot on the globe that was heavy with history and resonant with symbolic import.

Mike broke our thoughtful silence eventually. 'Do you think Paul is one of us then?'

'It's a possibility,' I said neutrally. I thought for a moment. 'It'd be nice if he was, actually.'

'Maybe,' said Mike in an open-minded sounding way. 'Are you thinking he might come and join us at the bungalow and we'd have two beds between four?'

I laughed. 'I wasn't thinking quite that far. Anyway – what about Captain David? He's another handsome chap, don't you think?'

'We'd need an extra bed,' Mike said.

'I certainly wasn't thinking *that* far. He's married, with a pregnant wife.'

'Exactly the point in their lives when married men go off the rails. No sex at home…'

'Come off it.' Naughtily I crossed my arm over Mike's and tweaked his knee.

'I was joking,' Mike said. 'About David anyway. Though yes, I had noticed his looks. I'm surprised you thought about him, though. He's ten years older than you.'

'Hmm,' I said. 'But then so is someone else I know.' I removed my hand from Mike's knee and he wormed his hand between my legs and pressed it up against my packet. We were passing by Cap Blanc Nez. The white wall of chalk towered alongside us; at five hundred feet – half as high as we were – it seemed to reach out to us in the sky alongside it.

A few days later Mike and I parted company – though only during working hours. I was back in harness with David, Captain Cook. For the whole of that next week I studied him carefully. Yes, I fancied him. But in all the hours we spent sitting side by side in the intimate confines of a Superfreighter's cockpit, I could see not the smallest sign that he fancied me. I certainly wasn't going to touch his thigh as we flew to and from Le Touquet, although it was a very nice thigh, and it grew more and more tempting day by day, laid out for my inspection just two throttle levers away. I had to conclude that he was a normal heterosexual man. And if by any chance he wasn't. well, I was pretty sure he wasn't going to be leaving his wife for me.

On the other hand he did tell me some interesting news. 'The company's opening up the Geneva service in a month's time,' he said. 'They've ordered three new planes. Carvairs.'

I thought I knew what a Carvair was. But I checked to be sure. 'That's – er – a converted DC-4.'

'That's right,' said David. 'They carry five cars not just three. Freddie Laker's started using them on his routes from Southend to Calais and Geneva.'

The DC-4 was the next size up from the famous 'Dakota' DC-3. Nearly twice the size of the Dakota it had four rather than two piston-prop engines and had 'tricycle' undercarriage (that is, it had a nose wheel, like most newer aircraft, rather than a tail wheel to sit back on like the older types). With the coming of the jet age the pre-War DC4 was pretty well obsolete, but the entrepreneurial Freddie Laker had seen an opportunity. He'd bought a number of them up cheaply and modified their front ends to carry cars, with the cockpit raised above the hold in a hump, along the lines of the Superfreighters we flew.

'What about loading?' I asked. 'They'll be too high for our ramps surely.' The Carvair's fuselage sat above its wings, eight or more feet above the ground; it wasn't slung beneath them like our freighters were.

'Yep,' David agreed. 'We're getting a scissor-lift for Lydd. Hopefully Freddie will let us share the ones at Geneva that are already there. The board are negotiating it, as they say.'

'And who'll fly the Carvairs?' I asked.

'New pilots coming in,' David said. 'Though if all goes well and the service expands some of us may get trained up on them during the winter months.'

During the winter months. I was still deliberately shying away from thinking about the lean winter ahead, when car-ferry traffic would drop dramatically away and most of the summer pilots would be laid off. That was the pattern every year, and I hadn't been led to expect anything else. But now, because hope springs eternal in the breasts of twenty-one-year-olds, I found myself wondering optimistically if I would be spending my winter learning to fly Carvairs.

David said, 'Did you try mussels and chips when you were on the Ostend run with Mike?'

'*Moules et frites?* No. I wanted to, but our lunch stops coincided with a return to Lydd every day. So it was mostly hamburgers.'

'Well, don't worry. They do them at Le Touquet too. If they come to more than the company voucher I'll treat you.'

'Wow, thanks, David,' I said, surprised. Then, 'Cross traffic at two o'clock high.' I was still a novice First Officer, but I seemed to have made the grade with David, socially at least.

I hadn't had much to do with Wing Commander Davies since he'd interviewed and tested me. If we coincided in the crew room he always greeted me by name and asked me how I was getting on but, though his manner was marginally less gruff than Captain Evans's there was never more to it than that. But a few days after my first taste of *moules et frites* in Le Touquet, generously sponsored by David, the Wing Commander came up to me in the crew room and told me this.

'Special assignment in a couple of days. We're putting you on the cheese run. You'll be going with young Captain Purcell.' (That was Mike. My 'sweetheart'.) 'I understand you live in the same house as him, so I presume you won't mind sharing a hotel. Separate rooms of course.'

'No, of course not,' I stammered. 'I mean … wow… Thank you very much sir.'

'Don't thank me,' said Davies as he strode away. 'Thank Michelle.'

'I will, sir,' I told his departing back view. Michelle was Davies's personal assistant and secretary. It was still a bit of a mystery the way the pilots' roster was handed down from On High. But I suspected that Davies had more of a hand in it than he pretended.

The cheese run was considered a bit of a perk. Almost a reward for good behaviour and uncomplaining toil in cramped cockpits. Every few days a Superfreighter left Le Touquet early in the morning loaded, not with cars, but with French cheese. The cheeses were unloaded onto a lorry at Lydd and then taken by road to one of the big markets in London. The pilots who brought the cheese back from Le Touquet flew out the night before and were put up, and given an expense-account dinner, in a smart hotel. This little adventure had now been offered to me. A night with Mike in a French hotel. It would be the Hotel Bristol, I knew, because it always was. It was one of the top hotels in Le Touquet. The words kept repeating themselves in my head. A night in a French hotel with Mike.

I waited before announcing this to Mike until the two of us were sitting down to supper at home with Will. I didn't want to have to tell Will later on that Mike and I had known about this for some time before he got to hear of it himself.

'Ah, so you know too,' Mike said when I made the dinner-table announcement. He gave me a look that made it clear that he too had been wondering how to break this bit of news to our bed-mate.

'You're not taking me then,' said Will. He made a pantomime of pretending to feel hurt and left out. But it was a double bluff, which both Mike and I easily saw through.

'Take you next time,' Mike said consolingly. Then he got out of his chair, went round behind Will's and cuddled him from behind, very strongly, very ... affectionately. And that was the real consolation, as we all well knew.

When the day came we were given a late-starting shift. We didn't have to turn up for work till four. We did two round-trips to Le Touquet, then after our third outbound flight we left the plane parked up for the evening and night on French soil. A taxi took us from the airport to the Hotel Bristol. I looked out of the window as we made our way. 'This isn't typical of French towns,' Mike told me. I took his word for it. But I'd never seen a place like Le Touquet.

The airport had been carved out of a forest next to the river estuary. The town had been carved out of the same forest, fitting snugly into the angle between the airport runway and the sea. The quiet little roads ran through deep tunnels of overhanging trees: limes, oaks and pines. Smart modern houses lay back from the roads, their gardens too were full of forest trees which half hid the coy houses. Our way emerged from the forest just before we reached the sea. There was room for only a small grid of streets, lined with smart shops, casinos and hotels, in the little strip between the trees and the beach.

Then there we were, stepping out of a taxi together, Mike and I, still in uniform and carrying our flight bags, and being ushered along a colonnade through a cloister-like garden, into the foyer of the grandest hotel I'd ever seen the inside of.

As the Wing Commander had promised we had a room each. We inspected them both. One was a single, the other a double. I said, 'We only need the one.'

'Of course,' said Mike. 'And we'll only use the one. But we won't be telling them that. I've heard it's common for men in France to share hotel rooms with a double bed. It's done to save costs and nobody thinks anything of it. And nobody at the hotel here would turn a hair if we told them they could free up the single room and sell it to someone else. But when the bill went back to Silver City and Michelle or someone saw that we'd used only one room, not two...'

'I see. Of course. It's obvious. I hadn't thought it through.'

'What usually happens,' said Mike, my mentor and guide in this new experience, 'is that we dine early. That means we can have some wine with our meal.'

'Good thinking,' I said. 'I'd better ...'

'Freshen up?' Mike took the words out of my mouth. 'But we'll go down to dinner in our uniforms, I suggest. We get more attentive service that way.'

'I see.' I thought for a second, then added, 'I wonder why?' Though I thought perhaps I knew.

I ate oysters for the first time in my life, in that grand dining room. Mike gently advised me against that choice. 'If by any chance you got a bad one the flight back would be a nightmare…'

'It's only twenty minutes,' I said carelessly.

'Twenty minutes is a very long time in a nightmare,' Mike cautioned.

'Well, so long as you don't have them too,' I said cheekily. 'Anyway, I'm sure I'll be OK.'

'All right, you win,' said Mike. 'But if it all goes pear-shaped in the night don't blame me.'

'I promise.' I was drinking something called a *kir royale* while we perused the menu. It was sparkling, alcoholic and blackcurrant flavoured. Just the first sip of it had sent my mood sky high. I felt as bubbly and effervescent as the champagne in the aperitif. I tweaked Mike's knee-cap under the table. You could do that in France, I'd heard. Homosexuality wasn't illegal here. Anyway, there was a long white cloth on the table and nobody could see what I was doing. In the unlikely event that anyone would have cared about it.

FIFTEEN

There was steak and chips on the *carte*. I looked at the words *steack-frites* longingly. I'd never eaten steak. It was not the sort of luxury we had at home. And it hadn't been a menu item in the RAF canteens either.

I wasn't sure whether to admit this lack of sophistication (lack of family money?) to Mike. But I quickly decided that if you'd openly called someone your sweetheart you owed it to them to be frank about yourself, warts and all. So I told him. He said, 'Then you shall have it tonight,' like a fairy godmother. Though he added, 'On Silver City.' And then, 'I'm going to have it too.' He suggested we asked for the steaks to be cooked 'medium'. For a starter he ordered pâté and toast for himself – I had my oysters – and it turned out he even knew how to ask for a medium steak in French. *À point.*

The oysters were exotic and magical. So was the steak. Even the chips were better than any I'd had in England. We shared a bottle of Beaujolais with our meal, which we capped off with chocolate mousse. When we left the dining room I felt I was walking among the clouds. And I knew what I meant. I brushed their cotton-wool shapes every day of my life these days. It was an integral part of my working week.

'It's still light outside,' Mike said as we sauntered towards the door that led out of the dining room. We could see the cloister garden beyond it: green trees and blue sky.

'We could go for a walk along the beach,' I said.

'My sentiments exactly,' Mike said. Still in our uniforms we strode purposefully out into the street.

The beach was just a block away. Even at this hour there were couples walking along it and people riding horses, some at a gallop, on the edge of the surf. The pounding hooves sent up fountains of spray that shone in the low sun like showers of sparks. The beach faced due west. It was a suntrap in the afternoon and even now the sun, an hour away from setting, still blazed in the sky in front of us. There was no sign of England on the horizon. Because the Dungeness shingle spit rose only a few feet above the waves there was no chance of seeing it from down here, forty miles away on the opposite beach.

Some instinct made us turn north together; neither of us said, 'Left or right?' We didn't need to discuss it. As if with one mind we made our way in the direction of the piece of coast we knew – the bit we flew over every day, beside the estuary.

The seafront promenade gave up before that point. We left its over-civilised parade of hotels behind us and now the beach was backed by scrub-grown dunes. We were in a little forest again. A forest of broom bushes and low, wind-sculpted pine trees. A network of footpaths and bridleways wove its way among the trees. Suddenly I knew what I wanted to do next.

I swung round towards Mike and kissed him on the mouth. He kissed me back and wrapped his arms around me. I dropped down in front of him. It was the same movement I might have made if I'd been going to ask him to marry me, but that wasn't my intention. I unzipped his fly instead.

'Not here,' Mike said quickly. But he didn't mean zip him up again. He went on, 'Get among the trees.' So we shuffled a little way into a recess between the clumps of broom. And there I pulled his trousers down to his knees, knelt in front of him and took his long hard prick in my mouth. I stroked the backs of his thighs and buttocks urgently. He rumpled my hair and fondled my ears as my head drove back and forth; his breath came in loud heaves and he occasionally thrust his hips towards me while I sucked him till he came in my mouth.

My first oysters. And now, as the sky turned red and gold behind Mike's thighs, my first mouthful of another man's salty spunk. It was turning into quite an evening.

Mike didn't return my compliment there and then. He kissed me fondly and deeply and pulled his trousers up and said, 'You'll get your go at bedtime.' Then he rumpled my hair again and we walked on.

We came to a place where there was a fenced-off clearing among the trees. A notice warned of high voltage and mortal danger to anyone who climbed the fence. In the centre of the enclosure was a small brick-built structure with an aerial mast rising from its flat roof. 'It's our beacon, isn't it?' Mike asked me.

'I think it must be,' I said. This was the anchor point of that invisible tightrope in the sky that we crossed almost every day as we flew here from Ferryfield. This insignificant hut, the size of a public toilet, among the trees. It was an oddly anticlimactic moment. Like Dorothy's meeting with the Wizard of Oz.

We turned round and walked back towards the town in the dusk, re-entering its lit-up streets just in time. Just before the darkness became total and disorienting among the trees and sand dunes.

'You know what?' Mike said.

'What?'

'We could be naughty and have a nightcap before bed. Just one.'

'You're the boss,' I said.

We went to the Bar des Sports, next to the casino. It was homely and cosy inside, almost like an English pub, with a long wooden counter and a ceiling full of beams. And, like an English pub in a rather classy seaside town it was rather full of English men and English couples, who looked as though they'd come to Le Touquet for the golf.

We stood at the bar and ordered glasses of blond beer. Dressed as we were in our uniforms we were a bit of a magnet for the golfing British folk, all of whom had either flown here by Silver City or knew someone who had. It was my first taste of celebrity. I enjoyed the moment and yet felt uncomfortable with it at the same time. In the years since, I've heard the same mixed feelings expressed by real celebrities.

Back in the hotel I made a bit of a charade of opening the door to my single room noisily and going into it. Then, when I was sure there was no-one in the corridor, I slipped out noiselessly and entered Mike's larger one like someone playing a part in a film or a farce.

We undressed each other silently. While we still stood beside the double bed Mike ran his hands over me in a reverent way, like someone handling a priceless piece of porcelain that had come into his hands by a stroke of luck. His hands seemed to be expressing wonder at the situation in which they found themselves. I felt – and I was sure from the way he was touching me that Mike felt it too – a profound sense of the mystery of *now*. The uniqueness of the moment.

'Let's get you to bed,' Mike said eventually. 'Don't want you to get cold.'

Once we were between the sheets Mike held me tightly. Then I heard him whisper, 'Darling,' and my heart nearly stood still.

I didn't say anything in reply and Mike said no more. Instead he wriggled round on top of me and took my ready-to-burst cock into his mouth. In a way he seemed to be taking my ready-to-burst heart into himself as well.

I came inside his warm mouth only too readily. I warned him when I was just about to but he didn't release my cock. He went on sucking to the end and swallowed all of me.

When he was sure I'd drained myself into him and would squeeze out no more Mike disengaged and we wriggled around until we were the same way up, heads together on the pillows the way couples usually position themselves in bed. We kissed, and I found myself tasting and smelling the exotic scent that was a blend of Mike's familiar breath and sweat and my own spunk.

And then Mike said it. He whispered it so quietly that I had to think it over for a second afterwards. Had he really said that? But yes he had. I whispered it back to him, awed by the solemnity of the utterance, the importance of the moment. 'I love you too.'

We said it a couple more times, but we didn't say anything else. We didn't elaborate, or try to pick apart the meaning, let alone the implications, of what we'd said. We started to masturbate each other gently, but it was only going to be a loving fondle; we both knew we weren't going to come again tonight. After a while Mike fell asleep, and I knew it would only be a minute before I went to sleep myself. I just had time during that minute to worry about the oysters I'd eaten. I ran through the worst eventuality I could imagine. That I would wake up and be sick in the small hours. Stomach pain and stomach cramp. I would be too ill to fly alongside Mike in the morning. The flight would be cancelled. The cargo of cheese would rot and go to waste. A major financial loss would accrue to the company. I would be summarily dismissed and so would Mike. A small sigh escaped my lips. It was an oddly contented sigh though. I discovered that if all those disasters came to pass I wouldn't mind a bit.

I wasn't ill in the night. On the other hand, Mike's wake-up knock at the door came far sooner than I could have predicted. There was no way I could get back to my own room in time to respond to my own wake-up knock. I jumped into my clothes as quickly as anyone on a military exercise, ran back to my own room and threw back the pristine sheets. It was the best I could do. The hotel would bill Silver City for the two rooms. They weren't going to add a note to say that one of the rooms looked as though it hadn't been used much. I didn't know much about the big wide world but I was fairly sure of that.

I rejoined Mike in the dining room for breakfast. A quick coffee and a croissant. But I managed to say brightly to Mike, 'See. No ill-effects from oysters.'

He looked across the table at me with a very serious face. 'Good. But this morning I find I still love you. Can't guess the consequences of that.'

My sang-froid crumbled. 'I still love you too,' I said hoarsely. In the voice of a frightened kid.

Work is the salvation of the frightened. We had work to do and we threw ourselves into it. The taxi picked us up as arranged, to the minute. We were wafted surreally through the woodland glades of Le Touquet's mini-suburb; the morning sun glimmered through the leaves at us, making jewelled canopies of our tree tunnels. When we emerged from this fairyland we were already at the airport. The contrast with arrival at Lydd's stern terminal on the bleak and treeless flatlands could hardly have been more stark.

The cheese was loaded, pallet after pallet, by forklift truck and pallet wheels beneath our windscreen as we did our checks. Mike went down with the dispatcher and checked the cargo, pallet by pallet, against the manifest. Then, doing what was normally my co-pilot job, he closed the clamshell nose doors before clambering back up the ladder to rejoin me in the cockpit. 'Want to drive on the way back?' he asked casually.

'Why not?' I answered. It seemed a fitting thing to do after you'd proclaimed your love for your commanding officer – and had eaten oysters and managed not to be sick in the night.

Though I kept my right-hand First Officer's seat, it was I who had control as we started the engines, taxied to the foot of runway 32 and opened the throttles up. It was I who slipped the footbrakes as the engines spooled up. It was I who chose the moment to push forward on the yoke to raise the tail-wheel, though Mike joined me in the push. And as we climbed over the radio beacon we had stood and looked at last night at sunset it was I who had the view, not only of the Channel sparkling into life ahead of us but of the broad placid estuary of the Canache to the right. But it was Mike who looked out and down, left-side, trying to see the exact spot where I had sucked him off last night. I know that, because I saw him doing it.

I had control of the plane. I was, for the moment, in charge of the situation. I took advantage of the moment. I inserted my hand between my Captain's legs and boldly squeezed his half-stiff cock.

I flew the rest of the way home. I did the landing, without any interference, but only support, from Mike. After the cheese had been unloaded we took off again, this time for Ostend. I flew us all the way there and Mike flew us all the way back.

Our day was finished at lunchtime. We waved to Will across the car park, said 'See you at four,' to him and then took ourselves off to the beach beside the Pilot Inn. We had fish and chips and a pint of bitter each in the pub. We were boisterous, and careless of what anyone else inside the Inn might have surmised from our behaviour. We behaved, in other words, like any two young people in love.

129

A miniature railway ran, and still does run, a few yards inland from the beach. It ran from Dungeness Point, through New Romney and Dymchurch, all the way to Hythe, where the flatlands of the Marsh came abruptly up against the cliff wall of the North Downs below Lympne Heights. The line ran directly behind the Pilot Inn. A strip of concrete raised an inch above the surrounding shingle had been constructed alongside the track. And a wooden board behind this rudimentary platform announced PILOT HALT.

'I haven't been on the Romney, Hythe and Dymchurch since I was a kid,' I said to Mike.

'I've never been on it,' Mike said. And I heard the voice of his childhood self, disappointed by some minor setback, returned to him in that moment.

'Then let's go on it,' I said.

'What? Two grown men, just the two of us, without any kids?'

'Oh don't be so conventional,' I said.

At least we were no longer in pilots' uniforms. We'd changed into shorts and Aertex tops on a brief stop at the bungalow on the way from airport to beach. There was something indefinably different about the bungalow, I'd thought, but I couldn't have put my finger on it. I hadn't mentioned it to Mike.

We waited for the next train to pull in. It was southbound: its destination, just a mile away, was the terminus at Dungeness. That was just as well perhaps. We could wait with the train while it turned around and then come back on it. Had we gone the other way, got carried away in our enthusiasm and ridden all the way to Hythe, we'd have been half the evening getting back to where the car was and Will, arriving home at teatime, would have wondered what had happened to us.

Two sets of parents with their children waited on the platform with us. I was glad of that: it made us less conspicuous. A few minutes later the train's smoke appeared between the nearby houses and we could hear its businesslike chuff-chuff-chuff. Then it came shimmering and shimmying into view a little way up the single track, wagging from side to side a little with each alternate piston stroke.

The gauge of the railway was a mere fifteen inches. But trains are about twice as wide as the tracks they run on and twice that again in height. The locomotive that pulled the train towards us, belching steam and smoke from every orifice, came almost up to our shoulders, and it was magnificent. Modelled on the Gresley Pacific engines (think Flying Scotsman) this specimen was dark green painted, with highly polished copper and brass pipes. Its name was Green Goddess I saw as it hissed to a stop beside us. 'It's the same one I travelled behind when I was a kid,' I told Mike.

The conductor got off and sold us tickets, we squeezed into one of the open wooden coaches and the driver, seated like an ogre over-filling the cab he worked in, eased the engine once again into forward movement.

The ride itself was faintly anticlimactic. At ten miles an hour across featureless shingle... But the kids we shared the carriage with were excited enough by the experience and some of that excitement rubbed off on us. We got out of the train when it stopped at Dungeness and along with other passengers clustered round the engine while it took on water. Then we got back inside again when it was ready to set off.

There was no need for the engine to be turned on a turntable in order to make the return trip. The Dungeness end of the line was furnished with a loop. So we simply continued in the direction we were going and circuited the loop. Ten minutes later we were back at the Pilot Halt.

'That was good,' I said, when we had extricated ourselves from the cramped compartment (it was more like a small church pew than any other train compartment I'd had experience of.) 'Beautiful little loco.'

'Beautiful little you,' Mike said.

I could see that he wanted to kiss me then. I knew that was what I wanted to do to him. But on the platform of a kids' holiday attraction... There was no possibility of that.

We spent the next hour lying on the shingle, talking about ourselves, and then it was four o'clock and time to go back. We arrived at the bungalow at the same time as Will did. He was getting out of his Mini when we drew up. We all walked into the house together. As we entered the hall I realised what it was that had made the place seem different when Mike and I had gone in to change a few hours earlier. The place smelt of cigarette smoke. And although most men smoked in those days it so happened that Will, Mike and I did not.

I didn't say anything about it. It was Will's house, not mine or Mike's. He could smoke in it if he wanted to, or invite other friends who did.

But for once Mike and I were not on the same wavelength. Mike said to Will immediately, 'Had visitors round?' He said it in a perfectly friendly way, though. And when Will looked surprised at his comment he explained it. 'Slight smell of cigarettes.'

'Oh right,' said Will, giving a little start. 'Yes. Actually Paul came round for supper last night.'

'Good,' I said cheerfully. 'I'm glad you had some company. I felt a bit guilty, leaving you alone while I was gallivanting with Mike in Le Tooks.'

'Actually we had a bit of a session,' Will said a little sheepishly. 'As neither of us had an early start. I mean

132

we drank a bit. I thought he probably shouldn't drive himself home...'

'So...?' Mike said, now sounding a bit discomfited.

Will drew himself up to his full height and looked at us both. There was a challenging look in his eyes that I'd never seen in them before. I found that I didn't feel very comfortable with it. 'So he stayed the night.'

SIXTEEN

I was afraid that Mike might say something like, 'I suppose he slept in my bed then,' and that Will would then be obliged to say, 'No, he slept in mine,' but this didn't happen. Perhaps that was just as well but what actually did happen wasn't very much easier to deal with. What happened was that we all stood in the hall, rooted to our separate spots, staring at one another in silence. That is to say that Will stood glaring at Mike and me. And – though I can only guess what we may have looked like – I suppose that Mike and I glared back.

After half a minute of this I looked at Mike. By now I was hoping that after all he would say something. He was the leader of our little pack. I, ten years younger than him and a year younger than Will, could think of nothing to say at all. But the mere sight of Mike, looking lost and rudderless, told me that he hadn't a clue how to react either.

Eventually Will broke the silence. 'Well? Why are you both looking at me like that?' (So we were looking at him like that.) 'We don't have rules, do we? Do you two own me? Nobody's said anything about that. What am I expected to do? You two go gallivanting off to France...' Yes, he did use the word gallivant. 'Don't tell me you didn't have sex together. Without me...' He tailed off.

We didn't need to tell him we'd had sex together. It must have been written on our faces. And though we certainly weren't going to tell him we'd said we loved each other, I thought there was a good chance that fact was equally easy to spot. We might as well have had the words tattooed on our forearms or even foreheads. I love Jack. I love Mike.

Then at last Mike did speak. 'Jack, why don't you go and put the kettle on? I think I owe Will a hug.' He stepped towards Will and took him in his arms. Will didn't shake him off but neither did he throw himself wholeheartedly into the embrace. He did put his arms around Mike's shoulders, but they hung there limply. He was accepting of Mike's gesture, his half-hearted response seemed to be saying. Perhaps he was even appreciative of it. But it clearly had done nothing to put things right. I decided to follow Mike's very sensible suggestion. I went into the kitchen to put the kettle on and left them to it.

'Tea's in the garden,' I called to them a few minutes later. I thought that was a sensible idea. To be in a less confined and intimate space than the living room or the kitchen. I'd already taken a tray of mugs out.

To my relief they came out meekly together and we all picked up our mugs, then went and sat down on separate rustic seats, making only occasional eye contact like three cats. It struck me as an essentially British way of handling the situation. To sit down over a cup of tea in silence. Yet no-one had hit anyone else, no-one had even shouted at anyone else. The cup of tea solution, absurd though it was, was at least preferable to those alternatives.

Eventually we started talking. About the cheese cargo. About the magnificence of the Hotel Bristol. Our moment of celebrity in the Bar des Sports. The fact that I'd eaten my first oysters and not been sick in the night.

But that we'd taken a walk at sunset in the beachside woods and that I'd pulled Mike's Captain's trousers down and given him a blow job... Well, we prudently left that bit out.

Equally prudently Will didn't choose to enlighten us as to what he and Paul had done together in bed.

It wasn't an easy evening. We cooked supper together and were polite to one another, but none of us could eat very much. It was quite a relief when bedtime came and Will went off to his bedroom while Mike and I went to bed in Mike's. Unlike the last time this had happened, just a week or so ago, we didn't leave the doors open.

Even when we were in bed together Mike and I didn't talk about what had happened. Neither of us knew what to say about it. The situation in which a husband or wife goes away on business, sleeps with someone else and returns to find that their spouse has done the same thing in their absence is common enough, and the various possible consequences have been explored by humankind since – we could reasonably assume – the beginning of marriage and monogamous relationships. But our situation was quite different from that. We weren't married to one another; we'd made no commitments to one another; we weren't monogamous. We didn't know what the rules were, or how this sort of thing was supposed to work.

Mike and I lay unhappily side by side together. We made no attempt at any kind of sexual contact. Occasionally we clasped hands for mutual comfort but that was as far as it went. Eventually I went to sleep and so, I assume, did Mike.

In the morning Mike and Will both had early starts. Mike would be flying to Le Touquet and back till mid-afternoon… 'Not with Paul, I hope,' I'd been unable to stop myself saying when he'd told me that. 'No,' he'd answered. That was a small mercy for all of us. Including, presumably, for Paul himself.

Mike and Will drove off in their separate cars. They did that sometimes, even if they were on similar shifts, but this morning it seemed a more noticeable thing, a more significant fact. I was working the later, overlapping shift, starting at two o'clock. I was off on another slightly unusual assignment and had been looking forward to it. I had told the others about it and they'd wished me well with it. But this morning the thought of any treat in store – even one so small as a slight change of routine at work – was like tasting ashes in the mouth. That's the conventional phrase. But it really did feel like that. I spent the morning pottering around the house – moping, I suppose was the real word for it – and trying half-heartedly to tidy the place up a bit. My mother used to say that if you were in a bad mood or feeling low there was no better cure for it than to get the Hoover out. I did get the Hoover out, and even used it, but it didn't really cheer me up.

I cycled to work and walked into the crew room. I had to brace myself for that moment, thinking that Paul might be in there and wondering what I'd say to him. But he wasn't there. Neither was Mike. They were both out somewhere in mid-Channel, in separate aircraft – mercifully for them both. Through the window I caught sight of Will, busy manoeuvring a ramp into place.

My Captain for the day was David. Captain Cook. I was glad of that. When you're feeling bruised by life there are some people you wouldn't choose to be with because they are rough-edged... I can't find a more precise phrase than that. But I found the company of David a rounder, smoother experience. Am I making sense? Anyway, I was going to spend the day with David. And it would be a short and easy one, as well as, for me, a new and different experience.

We weren't going to cross the Channel today but would head inland instead. To an airfield called Blackbushe, which was near Camberley on the border of Hampshire and Surrey. That was where Silver City Airways had its headquarters and carried out major maintenance. Our job was to take one aircraft in for servicing (Whiskey Bravo, alias the City of Salisbury) and bring another one back (Whiskey Echo, City of York). The direct-line distance from Lydd to Blackbushe was eighty miles but, despite the company's policy of always taking the shortest possible route, flying the direct course was not an option: the route went directly over the runway of London's second airport, Gatwick, and because of its extreme busy-ness the airport was protected by a zone from which all aircraft except Gatwick arrivals and departures were excluded. We could not go bumbling through Gatwick's terminal manoeuvring area at two thousand feet.

So our route diverted slightly to the south. There were two beacons to pass en route: Mayfield and Dunsfold, both of which served principally as guide-posts for arriving and departing Gatwick traffic. As usual, David took me through the route on the charts in the crew room before we boarded the aircraft. 'Hey,' I said. 'We fly right over the village I was born in.'

That was hardly an earth-shattering discovery as the village lay less than fifteen miles inland from Lydd. But David was kind enough to show an interest in what I'd said. 'Which one's that?' he asked.

I pointed it out. 'Wittersham.' Actually we would pass about three miles to the south of it.

'Have you ever seen it from the air?' David asked.

'No.'

'Then perhaps we can let you have a look at it.' I wasn't quite sure what he meant by that but I chuckled anyway by way of acknowledgement. We checked the weather reports. Clear skies all the way to Blackbushe, and a light summer breeze from the west.

Take-off was sudden and quick. It took me by surprise though it shouldn't have done. I was well aware that there were no cars in the hold – and no cheese or passengers or anything else for that matter – but my brain hadn't properly processed the fact. We were about four tons below our usual take-off weight.

We looped round to pick up the beam that we would follow to Mayfield. That took us across the Romney Marsh. Within a couple of minutes the town of Rye, where I'd gone to Grammar School, came into sight on the left. And a minute later, there was Wittersham, a little way off to the right. I pointed it out.

'Aha,' David said. We clattered on till we had were exactly abeam of it, then David said, 'Let's take a closer look,' and to my astonishment he calmly banked and turned to the right.

We made a leisurely orbit of the village, all the time banked to the right. Seated as I was in the right-hand, co-pilot's seat, and what with the sky being cloudless, I had a perfect view of it. There was the square-towered medieval village church. Next to it the village school where I had gone as a small child. A field I'd played in, with a pond in the middle of it where I had caught tiddlers. And there was the house that I'd been born in. The house that had once been my parents' and now belonged to someone else. I could see the garden, the plum tree and the apple...

I started crying suddenly. I tried to be quiet about it but I didn't manage to be that quiet. And I had to reach my handkerchief from my pocket and blow my nose into it. There was no way that David could fail to notice that.

But his reaction surprised me almost as much as the flow of tears itself. He took one hand off the yoke and, as we still continued our orbit, leaned over towards me and laid his palm gently on my leg. 'Don't worry,' he said. 'I'm not surprised. Seeing your home from the air can be quite an emotional experience.'

My defences down, I blurted out, like a kid, 'It's not just that.'

David didn't say anything to that. Instead he gave the top of my thigh a quick little rub, then returned his hand to the yoke.

I wasn't sure what had tipped me over the edge. Whether it was indeed the sight of the scenery of my childhood viewed unexpectedly from two thousand feet. Or whether it was David's gentle kindness in giving me the aerial tour in the first place.

We completed our circuit, intercepted the radio beam to Mayfield and re-engaged with it. After a further minute back on our straight track, during which we continued to cross roads and fields and villages that were familiar to me, David spoke. 'What's up, amigo?' He went on, 'You didn't seem quite your usual perky self when we met in the crew room. You needn't tell me if you don't want to but you can if you like.'

I wanted to hug David at that moment. It was probably fortunate that I was strapped tightly into my safety harness. I said, 'Nothing really. Bit of a problem at home, perhaps.'

There was a second's pause. Then David asked, 'Do you mean home-home, or home with Will and Mike?'

'Home with Will and Mike.'

As I heard myself say the words I felt that I'd admitted something huge; and not only to David but to myself.

'I saw Mike in the crew room earlier,' David said matter-of-factly. 'He wasn't looking his usual self either. Very down in the mouth, I thought.'

You can't have silence in a plane whose two engines are firing on all their twenty-eight huge cylinders like machine-guns, but the pause in the conversation that followed David's last observation was the nearest thing to it. Eventually David broke it himself.

'I may be a married man,' he said. 'But I saw the world a bit first.' Another pause. 'I'm pretty broad minded. I mean, about the different ways that different people live their lives. I mean … I'm trying to say that though it's up to you whether you want to talk about things or not … if you do … well, I'm not going to be shocked.' Pause. 'In case you were worried about that.'

I said, 'Thank you. Yes, I was worried about that.' There was another little silence, if you could call it that. Then I said, 'You know that some people get into partnerships with people of their own sex…'

I saw the corners of David's mouth twitch slightly upwards. 'Yes,' he said. 'I did know that. I went to boarding school. I've been in the RAF.'

'The thing is…' I said, beginning to feel safer, and finding I really did want to get this off my chest, 'the thing is that it's like that with me and Mike. As I realise you've guessed. But it's also like that with me and Will. And with Will and Mike.' It was easier, I found, because David and I weren't facing each other, but looking forward together through the windscreen. We could see each other's profiles, but only if we turned our heads a fraction in order to do it.

'That is interesting,' David said. 'And yes, I had wondered if that was the case. But I told myself I was being too imaginative, if that's the right way to put it.'

'You weren't being too imaginative,' I said.

'Do you want to tell me about it?' David asked.

'Are you sure you want to hear it?' I checked.

'I certainly am,' David said.

SEVENTEEN

The whole story came tumbling out. About our chance first meetings (David laughed aloud at the story of me going to sleep in Mike's bed and having to announce myself when he returned in the night) and about everything that had happened since.

We passed the beacon at Mayfield, and adjusted our course northward by about two degrees. A few minutes later we saw planes coming in to land at Gatwick, then others taking off, a few miles away to our right. After a few more minutes we reached Dunsfold and made a bigger turn right, and I was still telling David about the events of the cheese run (or some of them) and its aftermath. 'Please keep this to yourself,' I said when I'd eventually finished. 'Especially about Paul. I wouldn't want everybody knowing…'

'I'm not sure that I was surprised even by that,' David said. 'Not that Paul's in any way obvious about it. But in a way I'd sort of … well, wondered about him. Not to put it any more strongly than that. But yes, of course, this stays between us. I'm not the sort of person to betray a confidence.'

'I didn't think you were,' I said.

And then we were rattling our way over the town of Aldershot and talking to the tower at Blackbushe to prepare our landing approach.

David made an impeccable touchdown. The whole flight had lasted barely forty minutes, but for me it had seemed like a major event in my life. Though in exactly what way I couldn't have said just yet.

We had tea and, believe it or not, toasted muffins, despite its being the middle of summer, while we waited in the canteen at Blackbushe for them to get our return aircraft, Whiskey Echo, and the relevant paperwork sorted out. David and I sat opposite each other at the canteen table. This gave us quite a different perspective on each other from the profile views we'd had in the cockpit. I found myself wondering if this made any difference to anything. Certainly David's face appeared even more attractive today than it ever had done in the past... Not that there was much of a past. I'd only known him for a few weeks. But I fancied him no end now, I discovered. I knew this had something to do with his wonderful kindness, first in breaking the rules so that I could see the village I'd been born in, and then for patiently listening to the story of my current troubles. However I also fancied young Paul – as well as Mike and Will of course. Perhaps it was just a facet of being twenty-one. That I would fancy almost every attractive looking male I met.

David cut in on my rambling thoughts. 'I'm sorry I haven't been much help.'

'Oh but you have.'

'OK. If listening to you get it off your chest was any help...'

'It really was.'

'But I haven't offered you any practical advice. It's a situation that's ... well, it's outside my own experience. And I can't even say I have other friends who've been through anything ... anything very much like it.'

Other friends. The words sent a small private thrill through me. Did the choice of them mean that he classed me as a friend now? Among the others. As from today he was certainly one of my friends. One of the best.

'But I'm sure you'll sort something out,' he went on. 'Three handsome chaps like you are. Four handsome chaps, I should say. Paul's got it in the looks department too.'

'So have you.' The words were out before I'd had a chance to weight them up.

Was it my imagination or did David faintly blush? He said, 'Oh,' in surprise, then smiled at me – perhaps trying to cover either the surprise or the blush. Then he said, to my own surprise, 'But I'm a married man these days.' Did I also imagine a wistful nuance to his voice? Though even the words themselves would give me a lot to think about in the hours and days ahead. Now I discovered that he hadn't finished yet. 'Not that that's something I can take full advantage of just at the moment. It's hand jobs only for the foreseeable future.'

'With your wife being pregnant,' I said. Somehow, amazingly, I managed to say this in a level, easy tone of voice and to nod sagely as I spoke. Meanwhile my thoughts had turned into a kind of mush, like scrambled egg.

David shrugged his shoulders. Then he stood up. 'Come on. Let's see if this aeroplane's ready for us.' But he gave me a very penetrating look as he said it. A look whose meaning I was unable to work out.

We went back the way we had come. At least, that was how it started out. Heading south east to Dunsfold. By the time we'd done that twenty-mile leg the Channel was visible ahead of us, even from our modest altitude of a thousand feet, flashing silver at us, winking enticingly from between low hills. 'Passing Dunsfold at a thousand,' David told the tower at Blackbushe. 'Mayfield next. Now changing frequency to Lydd. Good-bye. Thank you.' Then he reached out to the radio tuner and changed the frequency. To something. With hindsight I think it probably wasn't Lydd.

'Fancy a run back along the coast?' David said. That startled me quite a bit.

'Are we allowed to?' I asked like a stupid kid.

David turned towards me with the naughtiest grin I'd ever seen on his face. I hadn't thought till now that his face was even capable of such a look. 'No,' he said.

'Will we be in trouble?' I had turned into the timid little brother who is being coaxed by his elder sibling into mischief.

And David had slotted into his role too. Wonderfully easily. 'Only if we get caught,' he said. 'And we won't get caught.'

So instead of turning east we turned south, straight towards the sea at its nearest point, about fifteen miles ahead of us. 'This is fun,' I said.

'I thought you could do with a bit of cheering up,' David said. 'Give you a bit of a treat. Take you out of yourself.'

I thought that was wonderfully sweet. But then I also thought about his extraordinary reference, in the canteen, to hand jobs. Had he been obliquely hinting that he would be happy for me to give him one of those? That he too needed cheering up a bit and taking out of himself?

I didn't really want to believe that might be the case. A whole can of worms would open up if it was. But if it was… If it was… I didn't know where such a thing could possibly take place between us. Except in the cockpit of a plane while we were at the controls of it. My imagination now went off on a wild and crazy journey. Was it conceivable that airline or military pilots occasionally pleasured each other in that way across the throttles? There had been plenty of smutty talk in the mess rooms of the RAF but I had never heard stories of anything like that. Although it would have been physically possible I could barely manage to visualise it taking place. Instead I found myself imagining the wording of the official report that would follow the almost inevitable accident. *The uniform trousers of both pilots were found to be lowered to the knees, along with their underwear. Their safety harnesses were unfastened. It is not within the remit of this report to speculate about the possible reasons for this. But there is no doubt that the failure of the crew to monitor the instruments and to keep a lookout played a major part in...*

'And here we are,' David said. The silver sea was opening out in front of us, filling our forward view as if poured into it. Arundel castle floated beneath us. A minute later we had crossed the coast. 'Littlehampton, I think,' David said, nodding towards the town that lay underneath.

'Yep,' I said. 'There's the river mouth.'

David turned the plane left, towards the east, and we followed the wavy line of the shore. We paid no heed to Decca or the compass. You couldn't get lost when walking in clear weather along a beach.

There was Worthing. There was the river Adur looping into the sea at Shoreham beside the power station, then there was Brighton with its two piers. 'One of them's the Palace Pier,' I said. 'I never know which is which.'

'The other one's called the West Pier,' said David archly. 'Maybe now even you can work it out.' It was fun to be teased by him like that. I reached across and gave his thigh a playful slap, then thought that perhaps I shouldn't have done that. Not only was he ten years older than me (to say nothing of being married) but he was my Captain and I was his First Officer; we were on duty and in uniform... Of course the same conditions applied when Mike and I touched each other in the cockpit, but we were lovers, were in love with each other, which made it different...

David slapped my thigh playfully back. My imagination returned to its earlier fanciful flight. With difficulty I throttled it back.

We cruised past Newhaven harbour. The long nose of Beachy Head jutted into the sea directly ahead of us. 'The Seven Sisters,' I said. The sun was lighting up those seven side-by-side cliffs of chalk. David banked the plane, we eased to the right and we followed the Sisters down to the tip of the Head, where the lighthouse was. Then it was turn left, and up the other side of the Head. Eastbourne underneath.

David got onto the radio and made contact with Lydd tower at last. 'Passing Mayfield by the south,' he told them. That was true. He didn't spell out the fact that we were at least twenty miles south of Mayfield, off the coast east of Beachy Head.

'We won't be on Lydd radar yet,' David told me. 'At least I think we won't. All the same it might be prudent to head back towards our official course.'

We followed the coast as far as Hastings, then turned inland. A few minutes later we intercepted our official radio beam just north of Rye. As we turned onto the track I saw my home village of Wittersham for a moment, first dead ahead of us then swinging astern by the left, but I decided not to mention that.

'Fingers crossed,' David said. He clicked on the radio and spoke again to Lydd. He told them we had ten miles to run and re-confirmed our landing approach. He turned to me. 'I think we've got away with it,' he said.

I had an urge to rub his thigh again at that point. Out of gratitude. From happiness. But I resisted it. I think perhaps he felt a similar urge but he too resisted it. We might not have got away with that.

We flew on across the Romney Marsh towards Ferryfield in what writers like to call companionable silence. (Always excepting the din of the engines of course.) I wondered, was some nosey member of the public going to phone Silver City and tell them they'd seen one of their Superfreighters joy-riding along the coast off Brighton or Eastbourne? I doubted it. At least I hoped not.

We landed, then taxied, not to the apron in front of the terminal where the cars and passengers were loaded, but round to the side by the hangar. We parked at the spot we'd been told to by the control tower, then David switched the engines off. I started on the routine tasks that made up my part of the job of shutting the plane down until it was needed next. David turned to me. He said, 'I've been thinking about what you told me. You say that Mike and you have told each other that you…' He faltered.

'That we love each other,' I helped him out.

'And that you're in love with each other.'

'Yes.'

'But you're also both in love with Will, aren't you?'

'Yes.'

'Well, I understand that,' David said. 'Because life is complicated and it doesn't always go the way that people think it's supposed to…'

'Like our flight this afternoon,' I said.

'Exactly. So, if you and Mike both love Will, maybe you should tell him that. You've said it to Mike and Mike's said it to you. Now perhaps let Will in on the secret. Tell him you both love him and see what he says to that.' He thought for a brief second. 'Of course it may not do any good. And what do I know about anything anyway? But I can't see how it would make your present situation worse.'

'God, David, you're wonderful,' I said. I felt tears prick at my eyes again. Mercifully none came out. I felt like throwing my arms round David and telling him I loved him too. But fortunately someone came banging on the nose doors just then, setting the whole plane clanging, wanting us to open up and hand over the paperwork.

I cycled home. Mike had got in a few minutes before me. I guessed that Will would be arriving just a few minutes after us. Mike came to the door to greet me. As soon as I was inside we gave each other a kiss. It was like being newly-weds.

'I've had an amazing day,' I said.

'Mine was fairly ordinary,' Mike said. 'Six trips to Le Tooks and back. With a fairly ordinary co-pilot. Tom Parkes. I didn't cross paths with Will all day. Or Paul. Perhaps that was just as well for all of us.'

I remembered what David had said about Mike being down in the mouth when he'd met him in the morning. And that I too had looked down in the mouth. Mike still had that aura about him now. Whereas I had lost it. I was radiant. I wondered if Mike had realised that yet. 'So tell me about your amazing day,' Mike said.

I told him it all. In the kind of detail a lover has a right to expect. Though I left out the more alarming bits. I didn't mention that David had talked about his sexual frustration and about hand jobs. Or our minor hand to thigh contacts. But Mike still found it amazing enough.

He blew air into his cheeks and then blew it out. He said, 'I can't tie this up with the David I thought I knew. That I've known for the last three months. We've flown together often enough. He never ... I never knew him do anything as irregular as that.'

'It wasn't as irregular as *all* that,' I said. Back-tracking a bit.

'All the same,' said Mike. 'Taking you on a scenic tour of the village you were born in... And then all along the coast on the way back. I really take my hat off to him. And to you both for managing not to get caught. But ... I just find it difficult to imagine our Captain Cook doing all that.'

It went through my mind that perhaps Captain David had been showing off to me because he was more attracted to me than I'd previously thought, and wanted to impress. I dismissed the idea. I certainly wasn't going to – it wasn't the moment to – share it with Mike. Instead I said, 'I think he was just trying to cheer me up. After... Well, after last night.' I'd already admitted to Mike that, encouraged by David and his assurances that he was an open-minded person, I'd blurted the whole story out.

'Anyway,' I went on, wanting to get to the crux of the thing before Will came back. 'Anyway, David gave me what might be sound advice. Though we won't know till we try it. And I need to discus it with you first.'

Mike gave me a puzzled look. 'Discuss what? David's advice? What advice? Has he suddenly turned into an agony aunt?'

I'd used the time it took me to cycle the two miles home to think about how I would get David's message over to Mike without putting Mike's back up. I thought I had found a good way to put it. But it turned out that I wasn't going to get the chance. We heard the sound of Will's Mini drawing up outside. The sound of its door opening then closing as he got out of it. And I saw Mike's face fall again as he braced himself for our imminent encounter with our landlord and ex-bed-mate.

Mike and I had been sitting in the kitchen. Mike had put the kettle on when he saw me getting off my bike but we hadn't got round to making the tea yet. 'Better put the kettle back on,' Mike said grimly, and I was getting up to do just that when the back door opened and Will came through it, grinning almost insanely, I thought, with childish delight.

My first thought was that he'd managed to have sex with Paul after finishing work. But I checked the time mentally. He wouldn't have had time to do that. Less than ten minutes had elapsed since Will knocked off at four o'clock. They'd barely have had time for a conversation or a quick kiss. And even if they had done something – a thirty-second wank in the crew toilet? – I knew Will well enough to know that he'd have had the politeness to hide the fact, or at least not to be so brazen about it as to come home with a triumphant grin on his face.

'Oh hallo there,' said Mike, brightening up. No doubt relieved at not having to confront a surly truculent housemate. 'You look a bit…'

'I've cracked it,' said Will jubilantly. 'I really have.'

I said, 'Cracked what?'

'The turnaround time,' Will said. 'I think I can get it down to eleven minutes.'

'Come again?' said Mike uncertainly. Neither of us had managed to home in on what he was talking about.

'We talked about it the other day,' Will said. His eyes wandered around the kitchen and he was finding it difficult to stand in the same place.

'I'll make tea,' I said. I was already standing. Now I took the three paces to where the kettle was

'We keep you waiting for five minutes on each turnaround,' said Will. He sat down opposite Mike at the table at that point, while I listened to what he had to say from the vicinity of the sink. 'Because of the time it takes us to chain the cars' wheels up. But … as I've just said … I've cracked it.'

Mike looked at him narrowly across the table. 'How?' he asked.

'I've invented something,' Will said. I'd never heard anyone come out with that particular announcement in my life before. And neither have I since.

'Invented something?' Mike said, and I added, 'What?'

'I'll get a pen and paper and I'll show you,' Will said.

I'd made the tea by the time Will had got a biro and a blank shopping list from the window sill. The full mugs sat untouched on the table in front of us all as he drew his diagram.

I have to say that it didn't look all that simple. But I wasn't an engineer or a mechanic, even if I'd always been fairly quick at maths. Both Will and Mike were ahead of me when it came to the mechanical engineering stuff. I watched as Will drew an arrangement of chains and anchor points. A major piece of the contraption was a thing shaped like a massive pen-knife with a ratchet running down the core of it, a pump-handle attachment, and a big hook on each end of it, one attached to the chain, the other to the floor-ring set in the deck.

Mike was enormously impressed. 'I think that's brilliant, mate,' he said. 'But listen. Have you told anyone else about it?'

'No.' Will's tone of voice made it clear that he understood the significance both of Mike's question and of his answer to it.

Mike didn't let this go just yet. 'Not any of the chaps you work with? Not Paul perhaps? Just letting it fall by accident…?'

'I've told you No,' Will said very firmly. 'You're the only people who…' He didn't try to finish the sentence.

'Well,' said Mike, 'I think you've done brilliantly. I take my hat off. I could never have thought up anything like that.'

'And I certainly couldn't,' I added for good measure. Neither Will nor Mike took any notice of that. They probably already knew that I couldn't.

'The next question,' Mike said slowly, 'is whether you've made any headway with the matter of how to become a pilot.'

Will grimaced. 'Sadly, no.'

'Don't worry,' said Mike. 'Because I think I have.'

EIGHTEEN

All three of us started doing mental arithmetic. Multiplying the number of minutes saved per turnaround by the number of flights per hour and then by the number of hours that the freighters flew in summertime. We reckoned that if Will's calculations were right the company could squeeze in either four or five more round trips to Le Touquet each day.

'What you should do,' Mike told Will, 'is let the Wing Commander know you've got something that could boost the company's revenue and say that you'll give it to them in return for training you up as a commercial pilot.'

'It sounds a bit cheeky,' I said.

Mike looked at me a bit heavily. If a look could be classed as heavy. 'Well, what else is he going to do? Sit quietly on the idea till he's an old man and then inform the National Office of Useless Inventions? It's not going to be useful to very many companies, I'd have thought. Who else chains cars to floors against the clock? Only air ferries, I'd have thought.'

I saw Mike's point. I also suspected he was getting his own back on me for listening to advice from David and singing his praises. Though perhaps I was being oversensitive.

Will said, 'Cheers Mike. And you're right. But it's a bit scary. I don't think Davies even knows my name. I can't just knock on his office door or buttonhole him in the canteen.'

I said, 'Talk to Michelle.'

It was still early. We went to the beach, the three of us. We took towels and wore swimming trunks under our shorts. You could swim quite safely near the Pilot Inn. A few weeks ago Will and I had done it. The beach sloped gently away below the sea. The situation was different just a mile away at Dungeness Point. The 'Ness' jutted into the sea like an underwater cliff and dangerous currents swept round the corner of it.

I'd been flying in sight of Dungeness Point and Cap Gris Nez almost every day for a month. And, though a bit less often, also Cap Blanc Nez. I'd been using the words together, almost in the same sentence, without the obvious striking me. Till now. As I swam a not very stylish breast-stroke around and among the other two. Mike was also doing breast-stroke, I noticed. That was reassuring somehow. Only Will had learnt to do the crawl. And very impressive he looked doing it.

The obvious thing that had struck me was that Ness, Nez and Nose were all the same word. Just with different accents. They went back to a time when both sides of the Channel belonged to the same cultural bloc. Perhaps to the days of the Normans, perhaps the Romans too. What was the Latin word for nose? I wondered. Nasa? Nasum? As in Nasal? I remembered what Will had told me about the medieval fishermen of Dungeness sailing across to Boulogne when they wanted a woman, rather than flail across the shingle and marshes to Rye. I felt a satisfying sense of the seemingly random but truly wonderful interconnectedness of everything.

But we were only just into July and the water was cold. We abandoned our attempts to swim after a minute or two. We stood together, waist-deep in the water, jostled by unthreatening little waves, touching each other's chests and arms, and chuckling a little when we met one another's eyes.

'I need to piss,' Mike said.

'Then do it,' said Will. All three of us giggled.

'That's better,' said Mike. Then, 'Ooh.' I gathered that Will had grabbed his cock beneath the water while he was in the middle of doing it.

'It's gone all small,' announced Will.

'So's yours,' I told Will. I had just grabbed his dick playfully too.

'Don't squeeze too hard,' Will told me. 'I'm trying to pee too.'

I laughed and decided to add my own drop to the ocean. I didn't really need to. I was just being companionable. Showing solidarity with the others. With my two... My two whatever they were. 'Hoy,' I called out. One of them had grabbed my dick through my trunks too.

'It's tiny too,' said Mike, laughing into my face. So now I knew who was holding me. I wrapped my spare arm round Mike's wet shoulder. He copied the gesture, placing an arm round Will, and Will completed the chain by wrapping his free arm round me.

I realised that I had something to say and that I must say it now. I hadn't had a chance to consult Mike and had no idea how it would go down. 'Will, 'I said, 'I told Mike in Le Touquet the other night that I loved him. I need to tell you that I love you too.' I waited for the sky to fall.

I waited for perhaps two seconds in which nobody spoke and nobody moved. Perhaps we all simply continued to pee beneath the waves. Then Mike said, 'That goes for me too, Will. I love you. I love Jack too, and I told him that in Le Touquet. You should have been there with us. We'd both have told you that we loved you too.'

Will's reaction was bigger than I'd expected. He started to cry. In a small voice he said, 'I love you both. I love you both "like crazy" as the Yanks say. But I was afraid...' His voice became a whisper. 'I was afraid that you didn't love me.'

Of course that set Mike and me off too. We both welled up and the tears spilled over. I don't think either of us had heard anyone say they were afraid we didn't love them – before today.

We left one another's dicks to do whatever they wanted to and hugged each other wetly, the three of us together, with all our arms. Just a little way out in the surf, where other people could see us. But we didn't care.

How odd this moment was. I'd dreamed up all kinds of stagey ways in which Mike and I might tell Will we loved him, as per David's advice. I hadn't remotely envisaged it happening in circumstances like these. And yet, as so often, as I was discovering, it was the physicality of the moment, the sexy touching, that had pulled the trigger and set the declaration off. The untangling of our knot of experience and feelings had come about because of a gentle physical contact. I found myself thinking the words – excruciating pun, this, and even at the time I felt ashamed of it – *at a stroke.*

What with crying, and the knocking waves and the fact that we'd all just emptied our bladders into the sea, it was about the wateriest experience you could imagine without being drowned. Talk about watersports. I wondered if a three-way declaration of love had ever been made in such unusual circumstances. And I still do wonder that.

'You're very much loved, my darling,' I heard Mike say to Will, as he nuzzled his cheek with his own. 'Never fear otherwise.'

I said, 'Seconded.' And I wormed a hand down the back of Will's swimming trunks to show that I meant it. 'Now let's get out of this bloody water and get warm again.' The others clearly thought that last idea of mine a brilliant one. At once we were trampling the waves in an energetic scramble towards dry land.

Holding up towels for each other, we took off our swim trunks and dried ourselves. We walked to the Pilot

Inn and went in for a celebration pint of beer. We realised that we'd overlooked one thing. We'd had the foresight to put our trunks on under our shorts before coming out but hadn't brought underwear to put on when we changed back into them on the beach. As we entered the pub I wondered how see-through our three pairs of white shorts might be. But it couldn't be helped. We were here now. 'Three pints of Best,' I heard Mike say. In a very manly and Captain-like voice.

'I don't know Michelle very well,' Will said unconfidently. 'Mike, would you come with me? Introduce us properly. I won't know what to say.' He lifted a forkful of scampi to his mouth and posted it inside. We'd moved on from The Pilot to The George in Lydd High Street. We were treating ourselves to a rare restaurant meal. Celebrating Will's invention. Celebrating our declarations of mutual love. Celebrating one another. Celebrating ourselves.

Mike said, 'Jack'll go with you.'

'Oh come on, Mike,' I said. 'You know Michelle better than I do. You've been here weeks longer than me.'

'She likes you better than she does me,' Mike said. 'I've seen the way she smiles when she talks to you. You're younger than me. And prettier. She fancies the pants off you.'

'She doesn't!' I said, laughing. 'And I may be younger but I'm certainly not prettier.'

'Who are you trying to kid?' said Mike.

Will said plaintively, 'I don't care which of you it is. I just want one of you to come with me. I don't mind if you draw straws. Or toss a coin.'

'Toss something else,' said Mike sniggering.

'There's always someone who lowers the tone,' I said. Mike responded by topping up our glasses of Mateus

Rosé. 'All right, Will,' I said. 'I'll come with you. First thing tomorrow.' I thought it rather funny the hoops one had to go through. That Will had to persuade one of his two lovers (both equally reluctant to shoulder the responsibility) to represent him before Michelle, so that she could make the case for his idea to her boss, the managing director, so that he could present it to the board. And then I thought that it was also rather sad that life had to be this way. So difficult. Everything always uphill.

And yet there was scampi and chips and Mateus Rosé. And wall-mounted lights in the cosy beamed dining room of a Georgian coaching inn. In Lydd High Street. Oh. And ah. The *now*ness of that moment.

It hardly needs to be said that the three of us slept all together in the same bed that night. That we had joyous sex together. That we *made love*. As we wound down afterwards, preparing for sleep, Will said, 'I wonder if three young chaps have ever told each other they all love each other in quite the circumstances we did.'

Mike said, 'One another.'

'One another?' queried Will.

'It's each other when there's two of you,' Mike explained sleepily. 'One another when it's three.'

'Are you sure?' I asked.

I felt Mike's shrug all the way through Will's shoulders, which lay wedged between him and me. He said, 'All I'm saying is that that's what we were taught at school.'

'I bow to the wisdom of your teachers,' murmured Will.

I said nothing. I was nearly asleep, and very contentedly so. But I've tried to be mindful of Mike's teacher's rule when setting down my account of things in this narrative.

Will stood beside me as I knocked at the door of Michelle's office the next morning just before nine. I was relieved, when she opened the door to us, to find that Davies wasn't in there with her. One step at a time, I thought. We weren't ready yet for step two.

'Hallo Michelle,' I said. 'I've brought someone to see you. I'm not sure if you know Will…'

'Of course I know Will.' Michelle smiled warmly at both of us. She was a dumpy little brunette lady with very shiny bobbed hair. 'I know him very well.'

I thought this was as good a start as could be. 'The thing is, Michelle, we want to enlist your help,' I said.

Michelle sat back down behind her typewriter. 'I'm all ears,' she said, even more encouragingly. There was a tinge of French accent in the way she pronounced the words. She had an English father and a French mother. She was a treasured linguistic asset to a company that traded across the border between their two countries.

I swallowed my nervousness and announced, 'Will has a proposal to put to the Wing Commander. It's an idea that could substantially increase the company's revenue. We wondered what would be the best way to approach him.'

Michelle laughed but then re-composed her features. 'What sort of an idea?'

Will spoke for the first time. 'It's an invention. I've invented a system for shackling the cars down in the holds much more efficiently and quickly. It's a special kind of chain mechanism. I'm certain it could shave five minutes off each turnaround.'

I added, 'We think Silver City could put on five extra flights a day if we used it.'

Michelle looked from me to Will and back again. 'This isn't a leg-pull, I don't suppose?'

'No,' said Will. 'I can draw you a diagram…'

'It's all right,' said Michelle, perhaps wanting to spare herself a lesson in mechanical engineering. 'If you're serious and would like to talk to the Wing Commander about it, then I'll tell him what you've just told me and see if he's prepared to listen to you.'

'Hey, thanks, Michelle,' I said. It seemed as though we were two schoolboys again, asking Matron if she'd put in a kind word for us with the headmaster. Will echoed my thanks a little more formally.

I remembered something. If I didn't say it, then maybe Will wouldn't. 'There's another thing, Michelle. Our friend Mike had a further idea about this…'

'Mmm?' Michelle said.

'Will's hoping to get his commercial pilot's licence but he doesn't have the money for it. Mike was thinking that if the board liked Will's idea and wanted to reward him for it…'

Michelle's eyebrows went up. She made a guess as to how I might have wanted to end the sentence. 'They might do so by paying for his training to get the licence?'

'That's about it,' I said. Will only managed to nod his agreement.

'I'll try to remember to mention that too,' Michelle said. The nod of her head indicated that the audience was at an end. A little smile played around her lips.

We were on the way to the door when Michelle spoke again from behind her Remington. 'I can't promise anything, boys, but I'll do the best I can. And, Will, I suggest that if the Wing Commander does agree to see you, you bring along a copy of your diagram already drawn. Preparation is – what? Nine tenths of something, I think.' She smiled at us again and this time her eyes twinkled along with it.

We had to stop ourselves from running away down the corridor whooping in exultation. And we were both basking delightedly in the warmth of that word *boys*.

I was on the Le Touquet run that day. Flying alongside one of the older pilots, Captain Wimbush who, like Davies and Evans, had flown in combat during the War. Captain Wimbush the smoker of Panatellas and Tom Thumbs. We had our lunch in the Le Touquet canteen. We shared a table with another pair of pilots. By chance they were Captain Evans and Paul. (Who is this *Chance*? And where did he get his sick sense of humour from?) It was the first time I'd clapped eyes on Paul since he'd slept with Will. And now I found myself staring into his soulful brown eyes – they looked troubled now – across the intimate small space of a canteen table while we ate lunch together. In the company of two medal-bristling Captains of the old school, who were rampantly heterosexual and thirty years older than we were.

I had to say something to Paul. I needed him to know there was no bad feeling from Mike and me. At least, not any more. I had to say it now. But I would have to say it in code. 'Good to see you, Paul,' I said.

Paul said flatly, 'Good to see you, Jack.' Then, 'Things OK at home?' Even more flatly.

'Things are fine.' I smiled at him. 'Are things OK with you?'

'Yes, fine,' he said. The troubled look deserted his eyes and he returned my smile cautiously.

Paul was sitting next to Evans. Captain Wimbush was next to me. Evans could have seen my smile; Wimbush could have seen Paul's; neither of them could see the two.

'What is it with the young these days?' Evans said to Wimbush. 'They have a language of their own. Impenetrable.'

'Like a code,' Wimbush agreed with him. 'Worse than Enigma. Can't understand a word they say.' Then the four of us laughed together in quite a friendly way. Laughter is the most international language of all. The most inter-generational. And more healing than any words.

During the afternoon, as we flew back and forth three more times, I found myself imagining a wonderfully Polyanna-ish scenario in which Paul got off with David, and left Mike and Will and me alone together. Just the three of us. And neither Paul nor David would end up as losers: they'd have each other. I realised quite early on that there was a flaw in this scheme. There would be a couple of losers. Paul's wife and their unborn child. I realised that I was still a novice in the business of unsnarling life's tangles.

'You'll never believe it!' Will called excitedly to us when he arrived home an hour later than usual. 'Davies came looking for me in the car tunnel during the afternoon. He checked that he'd found the right person, then asked me to go and see him in his office when I finished.'

Mike and I were in the living room listening to the new Beatles single, From Me to You, which had just arrived. Will's voice carried through to us from the kitchen. We left the Beatles to play among themselves and went through to join him. 'And so...?' Mike asked.

'I'd taken Michelle's advice. I had a very clear diagram prepared. I did it in my lunch break. Anyway, Davies sat me down and made me take him through it. He's asked me to present it to the board at the next meeting.'

'Hey,' I said. I moved towards Will and hugged him. 'That's brilliant news.' Then I had to step away from

Will and let Mike have his turn. You have to remember little details like that when there are three of you.

Will said, when Mike had released him, 'He wants me to produce a demonstration model. Just a single example. He said I can use equipment and materials in the maintenance hangar and do it there in my spare time.' Then his face fell slightly. 'I'm not much good at metalwork. I'd have to ask one of the blokes in the hangar to do it for me. They'd want money... I mean, they're nice chaps but I don't know them very well. They'd see at once what it was for and know it was worth something. They might try and pinch the idea and flog it to another company.'

'I've got a better idea,' Mike said. 'You know the motor-bike repair place down towards the army camp?'

'I know where it is,' Will said. 'I don't know anyone there.'

'The guy who runs it is a friend of David's. David just happened to mention that one day.'

I jumped in with the obvious. 'You're thinking Will could get it done there.' But I was thinking, Mike knew things about David that I didn't. I was pathetically jealous.

Mike said, 'The point being that they wouldn't need to know Will works at the airport. They wouldn't necessarily guess what it was for. Safe from industrial espionage.' He laughed at his own use of the grandiose phrase. But he'd made a good point, as Will and I both knew.

'First one of us to run into David,' Mike said, getting into team leader mode, 'get the name and phone number of the chap from him and we'll give him a call.'

'Aye-aye, Captain,' I said.

'Where does David live?' Will asked. It sounded as thought he'd never thought about this before.

Mike and I both knew. 'They have one of those new bungalows on the edge of town. Army camp side. Towards the motor-bike place.'

'We're practically neighbours,' said Will. 'We must have him round some time.'

'Have *them* round some time,' I corrected. 'Have *them* round.'

Mike said, 'What about the pilot training idea? Did you say anything about that?'

Will smiled very serenely. 'I didn't have to. Davies brought the subject up. If the board are at all interested in my idea he's going to propose that to the board himself. So...' he turned to Mike and bowed slightly, '...So thank you for that idea, Mike.' Then he turned to me and again bowed slightly. 'And thank you, Jack, for broaching it with Michelle. I wouldn't have had the guts to.'

I nodded a little bow back to Will. 'Of course you would have. If I hadn't been there you'd have done it. Anyway, don't thank me; thank Michelle.' The words sounded oddly familiar, I thought.

NINETEEN

Most of us wore dark glasses when we were out flying, at least for some of the time. But we didn't wear them around the terminal or in the crew room. That would have been considered rather bad form: affected and pretentious. So it was a bit of a surprise when I ran into David in the crew room the next morning to find him wearing his sunglasses. I didn't comment.

Instead I came straight to the matter I wanted to talk to him about. 'Have Will or Mike spoken to you this morning?' I asked.

'No,' he said. He addressed me without taking off the sunglasses.

'We wanted to get hold of a contact of yours. The chap at the motor-bike repair place.' I explained what it was about.

'I'll phone him tonight,' David said. 'I'll tell him to expect a visit from Will. Or...'

'From Will. But please don't forget. Time is of the essence. There could be a lot riding on it. For Will. Financially.'

'I'm intrigued,' David said. 'You said he's invented something and needs a demo model? What sort of invention?' He sounded very intrigued indeed but he still didn't take his glasses off.

I felt myself wriggling a bit. 'It's still under wraps at the moment. I hope you don't mind me saying that. But Davies has asked him to present it at the next board meeting. Which is in two weeks. That's why I said time is of the essence.'

'Of course,' said David. 'I understand. And no offence taken about the secrecy thing. Careless talk costs wives and all that.'

Had he meant that as a deliberate joke or was it a Freudian slip? I didn't acknowledge it. Just in case. I said, 'Are your eyes all right?'

For answer he lowered the dark glasses down his nose and I saw at once what the trouble was. His right eye was narrowed to a slit, the lids puffed up and red. So was the whole area of skin around it. Another twelve hours and he'd have the most amazing shiner. I felt a sudden anger. David was my newest friend. He had a beautiful right eye. Now someone had gone and blacked it.

'Oh my God!' I said. Without thinking I clasped his nearest hand. 'How did you get that?' Amazingly I managed to stop myself asking, 'Who did it?'

'I walked into the door of an open kitchen cupboard,' David said. Well, that's what everyone always says. And of course no-one believes them. I certainly didn't believe David.

'Oh God, I'm sorry.' I found to my surprise that I was still clasping his hand. He hadn't freed himself from my grasp. He was actually clasping my hand back. Quite tightly. He didn't pull the glasses back up immediately. He gave me a look... I couldn't interpret it. An old-fashioned look? Though that expression meant something else, I thought. Yet those were the words that came to my mind. Perhaps there were different types of old-fashioned look. Then David returned the sunglasses to the 'on' position and we disentangled our fingers – though without undue haste, I noticed.

'It's a bit embarrassing, all the same,' David said.

'Yes, it must be.'

'Hence the dark glasses.'

'Makes sense,' I said. Then, 'When are we next flying together?'

'Tomorrow as it happens,' David said. 'We're on Calais. *Moules et frites* at lunchtime. I'm buying.'

I giggled at that, but very happily. Someone else came into the room then. 'I'll look forward to it,' I said. And we walked off in different directions.

David was as good as his word. Actually even better. Apparently he phoned his wife at lunchtime, got the phone number of his friend at the motor-cycle repair shop and then rang him, told him to expect a visit from Will and roughly what Will wanted. David managed to pass the news of this progress to Will when their paths crossed during the afternoon out on the apron. By the time I next saw Will, in the evening, he'd been to the repair shop, had told David's friend what he wanted doing and they'd agreed a price for it.

'We'll all chip in,' Mike said generously when Will told us what the price was. 'After all, we put you up to it.' Mike was, of course, being generous with my money as well as his own but I found I didn't mind that. In fact I liked it. It was a sign of the easy intimacy between us. Mike would have shared his last crust with me. And I would have done the same for him. The same went for Will... I won't go through all the six permutations.

'Thank you,' Will said. 'That might be helpful. Though just as a loan, obviously. By the way, I saw David all day long in dark glasses. He didn't even take them off when he came and spoke to me. Has somebody biffed him?'

'He walked into the door of an open kitchen cupboard.' I said it as convincingly as I could but I could see that neither Will nor Mike believed me.

I'd had time to think by then about that old-fashioned look of David's. I'd tried to translate it into words. The words too came out as old-fashioned. *It is thou hast done this to me.*

Me? How could I have done it? But my imagination came up with a fanciful, rather awful hypothesis.

167

Supposing David really had been signalling to me, even perhaps unconsciously, that he wanted me to give him the companionable relief of a hand job. Maybe the story of the goings-on between Mike and Will and me – not to mention Paul – had turned him on a bit or even made him envious. Suppose then that in his frustration he had approached someone else in the hope of a bit of male bonding. That he'd chosen the wrong person and had got thumped for his miscalculation. But who had he approached and where had he approached them? I hadn't seen anyone at the airport going round nursing a bruised hand or with bandaged knuckles. So where then? In a pub? In a public toilet? That thought, I'm ashamed to say, excited me as much as it appalled me.

But it truly was an awful thought. And I wondered how he had managed to explain to his wife how it had happened. I knew that over the years and decades many married men had found themselves in the same excruciating situation. For a stupid moment – *It is thou hast done this to me* – I felt as though I *had* been responsible for what had happened to David. But only for a moment. I wasn't responsible for interpreting his unspoken desires. I certainly didn't owe it to David to be unfaithful to Mike and Will for his sake. But the trouble was, I'd got too fond of David.

I didn't share these thoughts with the others. Not even when I was snuggled up in bed with them that night. The David thing had been going on too long now – for several days at least – and had gone too deep. It would have been difficult to explain it and for David and me to appear innocent in the eyes of the others, despite the fact that nothing beyond a bit of hand holding and thigh rubbing had happened between us. I didn't want there to be another awkwardness for us all to go through, as there had been when Will had slept with Paul a couple of days earlier. Only a couple of days? I could hardly believe that.

But that reminded me, I hadn't thanked David for the part he'd played in sorting that little difficulty out. I would do it in the morning.

The route to Calais was the same as the route to Ostend, except that you only went halfway to Ostend before you landed. The distance, at just under forty miles, was even less than the distance to Le Touquet and the flying time much the same: between fifteen and twenty minutes. The small airport lay about five miles east of Calais town centre and two miles in from the coast. Getting there was easy enough from Ferryfield.

Once David had got us onto the Decca course a few minutes after leaving Lydd I told him. 'I'm very grateful for your advice the other day.'

'What advice was that?' he asked.

'You know perfectly well what advice.' This wasn't the correct way to speak to one's Captain while in the cockpit. But I felt that David and I were on pretty intimate terms these days. 'About me and Mike and Will. Telling Will that we both... You know.'

'You did that?' David said.

'Yes.'

'And it worked?'

'It certainly did. You've seen the three of us together lately?'

'Yes, I have,' said David. 'And yes, I did think, something's happened to ease that little difficulty. Well I'm glad. Though I'm sure I had very little to do with it.'

'Don't underestimate yourself,' I said. And without conscious thought I reached across, put my hand on David's thigh and briefly rubbed it.

David didn't respond to that, either in speech or in movement. But a moment later he said, 'It's good to tell people that you love them. Most of us do it too seldom. And to too few people.' There was a second's silence. Then he added, 'Well, that's today's sermon.'

'It's a very good one,' I said, trying to sound nonchalant. Trying to feel nonchalant. I still had my hand on my Captain's leg. I thought it would offend him if I took it away smartly at that point. Besides, I didn't really want to. But I wasn't sure what either of us was going to say next. I was flying an aeroplane with my hand on my Captain's thigh, exactly the way I would do when I was flying with Mike. And this Captain who wasn't Mike, with my hand trespassing in his lap, was talking about love.

At that moment the starboard engine gave a polite cough. It happened sometimes. One of the cylinders (there were fourteen per engine) would miss a beat. It was known as the 'Bristol cough' and was considered quite a normal occurrence, though the first time it happened to any pilot it frightened the life out of them. (Not for nothing had the aircraft been dubbed the Bristol Frightener.) The Bristol cough had frightened the life out of me the first time I'd experienced it. That had been during my first fortnight, flying with Captain Evans. But his calm and casual, 'Don't worry: they do that,' had set my mind immediately at rest. When it had happened in the intervening weeks, which it had done three or four times, I had thought nothing of it. But this time I took it as a sign that I should leave David's right thigh in peace. I moved my hand back to the no-man's-land between us.

By now we were approaching Dover Strait. Dover Castle up on its Height above the white chalk-face, Cap Blanc Nez on the right: Scylla and Charybdis. Up to now this had always been a special moment in the flight; because I'd always been flying with Mike when we passed this point. It was one of our private places – if the airspace above the Mythic Strait could ever be said to be private. Now here I was sharing it with David. I decided not to comment on it.

But David said suddenly, 'Isn't this just gorgeous? This sight. This spot.' His right palm landed on my thigh as he said it. Rather high up. Almost as if that had been the spot he was talking about.

'Yes it is.' I didn't move a muscle. But I was thrilled to my core. I didn't want to be but I was. It was a physical thing. I couldn't help it.

David's hand moved a couple of inches, as if it had accidentally slid. It just brushed the shaft of my penis through my trousers. 'Oops,' said David, and removed his hand as though it really had been an accident. But he had felt my cock all right. He'd felt it just long enough to have realised I was stiff.

'Right,' David said, now all professional and businesslike. 'Better get ready to land this bus. I'll call tower. You start descent and landing checks.'

'Yes, David,' I said with alacrity. I almost called him sir by accident.

That summer nearly a dozen of our planes were buzzing back and forth every day between Ferryfield and Le Tooks. One flight each way every ten minutes. But the demand for car-plus-passenger air transport to Calais and Ostend was very much smaller. Not least because our main competitor, Freddie Laker's Channel Air Bridge, was already in the market, flying to both destinations from Southend with his Bristol Freighters and, this year, his Carvairs. Silver City's share of the Calais and Ostend market could be delivered by just two of our planes on the route from Lydd each day, one serving each airport. There were three daily flights to Ostend and back, and six to Calais.

Today Mike and Paul were doing all the Ostend flights. (I'd have loved to be a fly on the wall of that cockpit: it was the first time they'd flown together since … well, you know what.) While David and I would take all six flights to Calais.

We got through the morning without touching each other again in the cockpit, and without any further mention of the word love. I think we both had a feeling that we needed to rein back a bit. But David did buy me mussels and chips at Calais, in the terminal building, as he'd promised, and they were very tasty.

The plane we were flying was Le Quatorze Juillet – Whiskey Kilo – the one whose registration letters were G-ANWK. I hadn't drawn David's attention to this during the morning. I was being careful of all sorts of things for all sorts of reasons. But on the way back across the baking tarmac to our warhorse after lunch I did rather gleefully, and perhaps ill-advisedly, point it out.

'I used to see this plane when I was a twelve-year-old,' I said. 'Even then I thought its reg. amusing. Being the anagram it is.'

David laughed. 'You know, you're the first person I've met who's dared to say it. Though everyone must have spotted it. I know I saw it at once. It's the mind I've got.'

'The mind we've all got,' I said. 'Will and Mike and I often joke about it.'

'Ah,' said David with quite a lot of feeling in his voice. 'You're lucky people, you three.'

I thought there was rather too much cargo in that observation for me to risk replying to it, so I didn't. Anyway we parted at that moment. David to do his exterior walk-round check, me to climb the ladder to the cockpit to start the other checks. Up and down that ladder forty-eight times a day most days of the week. No wonder we all stayed svelte and fit.

The afternoon was uneventful. Until the last outbound flight a little before four o'clock. Whiskey Kilo's starboard engine gave another discreet cough shortly after we passed Cap Gris Nez. It didn't faze us. It was also completely unnecessary. Neither of us was fondling the other, nor were we talking about anything remotely suggestive or dangerous. The engine coughed again as we passed Cap Blanc Nez three minutes later. A minute after that, as we flew abeam Calais docks it had a positive fit of coughing. Only then did David and I feel remotely perturbed by it. But we didn't spend long being remotely perturbed. After another prolonged seizure it stopped completely. 'Crikey,' said David, peering past my head at the wind-milling prop outside my right-hand window. 'Your bloody engine's out.'

'Shit,' I said, while an awful gaping hole opened up in the pit of my soul and the pit of my stomach.

'I'll fly the plane,' said my Captain calmly. 'You try and re-start it.'

It could have been worse. The Bristol Superfreighter was designed to be able to limp along on one engine for quite a distance. And we were only three minutes from touchdown. Through the windscreen I could already see the runway waiting for us like a welcome mat. All the same it was a frightening experience. I quickly found the engine re-start drill among the library of papers and charts on the clipboard attached to my yoke. I went through the steps, while David throttled up the one remaining engine and worked the rudder bar with his feet, pulling the rudder hard over to the left to counteract the plane's new tendency to wander to starboard.

It was lucky that our approach to Calais that day involved a 180-degree right turn onto finals after we'd flown past the airport on our downwind leg. Even so, David would need all his skill to judge the turn exactly when the time came in a minute.

'I can't start it,' I told David. Superfluously. He was well aware that I couldn't.

'Don't worry,' he said. 'We'll land perfectly safely. But you can go on trying if you like. Just for the fun of it.' Then he turned to me and gave me a confident grin. He took one hand off the yoke just long enough to give me a thumbs-up.

At the same moment I heard a sound below the ladder. Then a woman's voice called up. 'Is everything all right?' It was our stewardess who had left the passenger cabin via the connecting door, had crept sideways along the car deck, and was now shouting to make herself heard above the din of the remaining engine.

'Tell her we're fine,' David instructed me. I sat nearer to the hole in the floor than he did.

I shouted down the hole, relaying David's message. 'All under control. Seat-belts on. Landing in two minutes.'

I was overwhelmed by David's sang-froid. By his bravery and coolness. I hoped fervently that my real Captain, my own Captain, my lover Captain Mike, would have been as … soldierly. I don't know a grander word for it.

David called the tower. He said we were just starting our turn onto finals. He added, as though it was an afterthought, that one of our engines had stopped working, and could they have the emergency services on stand-by just in case? Then, as though adding PPS to a postscript, he very calmly said, 'Pan, pan, pan.' That was just one level below a Mayday.

The plane turned towards the runway only too easily. The difficulty would lie in stopping it from going on turning and taking us back out to sea. That was if we didn't roll completely over first. But David managed it. We wavered and wobbled our way down from our thousand feet in a wany sort of straight line. I could see two fire engines making for the runway threshold as we approached it. As we crossed the threshold at fifty feet they turned towards the runway, one either side of it, ready to dash towards us, or race after us, depending on what happened in the next three seconds.

They raced after us. We'd landed impeccably. At least David had. I'd given up trying to start the right engine a few seconds before touchdown. All David's seat-of-pants calculations would have been thrown into confusion if it had roared back into life at the last second.

A couple of minutes later we had rolled to a stop outside the terminal building. A minute after that the two fire engines drew up one on either side of us. They kept their engines running until we'd shut ours down.

Only then did I remember I was supposed to have gone down and unlatched the nose-doors. I did so then, and two firemen rushed in as soon as they were open. I didn't think anyone was particularly worried by my lateness.

TWENTY

I spent the next hour in a daze. Perhaps I was in shock. I sat in the Calais crew room with David, drinking coffee after coffee. Through a haze of unreality such as surrounds you when you are admitted to hospital I heard news coming and going. The airport manager coming and going. Our handling agent coming and going. David being called again and again to the phone. Little by little things fell into place, like the white flakes in a snowstorm paperweight.

The plane would not be returning to Lydd today. The engine needed stripping down. It couldn't simply be restarted and flown out across the Channel again, hoping for the best. Aero-engines don't stop for no reason. The reason needed to be found and the fault fixed.

Three car-loads of passengers who had booked on our return flight had to be dealt with. For once, luckily, there were no foot-passengers, no travellers unconnected with any of the three vehicles. And happily we were at Calais, just a few miles from the sea-ferry port. The handling agent made the arrangements. Our three cars and their occupants would be taken to Dover on the next ship out. Financial adjustments to be dealt with in due course.

That left us – David and me and the stewardess Marianne – twiddling our thumbs at Calais airport. The handling agent pulled a face. 'The hotels round here aren't exactly the best…'

'What about central Calais?' David asked quickly. 'What about the Georges Cinq?'

The handling agent looked taken aback. I said, 'Oh come on. You're talking to a hero. He's saved fourteen lives as well as an expensive bit of machinery…'

The agent stopped me, nodding vigorously. 'Of course,' she said. 'You're quite right. The Georges Cinq it is. I'll phone them now to make the arrangement. And I'll organise a taxi.'

'Well done, boys,' said Marianne quietly as soon as the agent had gone away to her office.

'How do you say in English?' the agent said when she came back. 'Good new, bad new? Yes, you can stay at the Georges Cinq. But they have only two rooms, not three. One room is a double.'

'That wouldn't be a problem for me,' I heard David say evenly. 'I don't mind sharing with Jack. Unless...' He turned and looked at me through the dark glasses which he hadn't taken off all day. I couldn't see the expression on his face.

'It's not a problem for me,' I said, trying to sound as though it was a matter of no interest whether I shared a room with David or whether I didn't. Actually my thoughts were in turmoil. Of course they were. I was full of excitement. And guilt. Guilt? I hadn't done anything! Yet.

David said to the agent, 'Might I use your phone for a minute? I need to speak to my wife.'

'Of course.' said the agent. She looked expectantly at me and Marianne.

Marianne said, 'If I may...'

And I said, 'There's someone I'd like to phone too, if...'

'Of course,' said the agent.

We formed an orderly queue. When it was my turn I phoned the number of the bungalow, unsure whether there would be anyone there or not. I was disoriented by events, unsure of the time, of what shifts Mike and Will were on. But the phone was answered almost at once. By Mike.

I told him exactly what had happened as briefly as I could. He was at first horrified, then over the moon to know that I was all right. I told him about the hotel arrangement, though I left the most alarming detail out.

'Are you really sure you're fine, darling?' Mike asked. 'Not in shock? You sound a bit…'

'It's been an odd experience. But, yes, I'm fine. And anyway there are three of us. We'll look after one another.' (I'd even got the grammar right.) 'I'll be home tomorrow by hook or by crook. Whether Whiskey Kilo's fixed or not.'

'Well, take good care of yourself,' Mike said. 'And I love you.'

'I love you too.' It was a bit of a whisper actually, though the others had made a point of talking among themselves in the corridor outside the office so as not to appear to eavesdrop. 'Give my love to Will.'

'Bye darling.'

'Bye darling.' I hung up.

As the taxi drove us through the bright warm streets of Calais I found myself surprised to see the sun still high in the sky. It was the same feeling I'd get when coming out of a cinema after a matinee and the daylight took my breath away.

The Georges Cinq, I eventually realised, was named after the British King George the Fifth. A solid modern building in the town's main shopping street, the Rue Royale. We checked in and nobody at the hotel seemed remotely surprised that David and I were going to share a room with a double bed in it. If Marianne was surprised she had the good grace not to show it. Not that she actually saw the double bed.

We arranged, the three of us, to meet downstairs in half an hour and take a walk around the town to while away the time before dinner. Then David and I were alone together in a room with a double bed in it.

Immediately David threw himself down on it. Rather inconsiderately, I thought, he chose the side nearest to where I was standing, so that if I wanted to throw myself down on the bed next to him I would have to walk round him to the other side of it. But I did want to throw myself down on the bed. I needed to. So I did.

David exhaled long and loudly. So did I. We both still had our shoes on, even our uniform jackets. But at that point David took his sunglasses off. 'Now you're on that side of me,' he said. 'You won't have to look at this.' He jabbed a finger towards the eye that he'd taken care and forethought to keep out of my line of vision. I felt ashamed of myself for thinking him inconsiderate.

We lay side by side, looking up at the ceiling, like a stone monument to two dead pilots. Neither of us attempted to touch the other. 'Wow, what a day,' I said.

'Thank God for you,' David said.

'Not me. I didn't do anything. Except fail to re-start the engine.'

'That's not what I meant. It was your being there. You kept me calm and gave me strength.'

'You kept me calm,' I mumbled. 'You gave me strength.'

'I nearly went to pieces,' David said quietly. 'I didn't think I was going to be able to handle it. But you...'

I couldn't speak. I found David's hand. It was protruding from a hefty sleeve with four braid stripes and brass buttons on it. I clasped it.

When we came down to the foyer Marianne was waiting for us. We walked out into the sunshine, the three of us.

British people tut-tutted about Calais. A charmless town of charmless buildings and streets. Hastily re-built after the War... But people forgot why it had to be re-built. We, the Allies, destroyed the old town in the last days of the War, in the effort to get the Nazis out. What should its population, homeless and jobless, have done in the circumstances? Waited a generation for the continent's best architects to restore it to its ancient Bruges-like beauty? Calais is Calais. Take it or leave it. And neither its Nazi occupiers nor its destructive liberators had managed to destroy the town's spirit, its essential vibrancy as a lively commercial and fishing port that gave an open-hearted welcome to its visitors.

We dawdled by shop windows, admired the trunk of a Roman lighthouse (War had destroyed everyone's homes and businesses but had spared a Roman lighthouse – oh, the sick humour of Chance) and eventually found ourselves by the harbourside. Here some two dozen fish stalls were lined up along the edge of the quay at which small fishing boats were tied up. The stall holders called to us, and called to everyone, with a cheerfulness I'd seldom met in English market traders. Around a corner, from where we could see the open sea between the distant arms of the harbour breakwaters, we could also look across the haven to the two car ferry berths. Beyond them the harbour railway station.

'Have you ever come here on a ferry?' David asked me. His tone was stiff and formal and Marianne must have picked it up.

'No, never.' I heard myself sounding equally stiff and starchy. 'I never came to France before I started work at Silver City.'

'I have,' said Marianne, who hadn't been asked. But now David encouraged her to talk about her visits to France as a teenager, and I was glad of that. She couldn't have failed to realise that something had changed between David and me since we'd gone to our hotel room.

A train pulled into the harbour station behind the ferries. A steam engine pulled it, a big tender-engine belching grey smoke. It was the same size, shape and sooty colour as an English one, but its details were noticeably different. It was somehow unmistakeably French.

We turned back towards our hotel and an early dinner. Whatever tomorrow might bring or not bring it would certainly involve an early start. We had shrimps for a first course, then a Dieppe-style fish stew that had wine and cream and mussels in it. And, rather inevitably, because we all knew it would be wonderful, chocolate mousse. Then there arose the delicate question of how the three of us would spend the interval before bed. David dealt with it with grace. He and I, he told Marianne, would probably go out to a bar for a drink. He hadn't asked me about this but had probably realised he didn't need to. Marianne answered with equal tact that she would probably go straight up to her room. She had brought a book. And it had been a long day.

'And eventful,' I said.

'Indeed,' she replied, and gave me a rather thoughtful look.

After dinner David had another phone call to make. To the maintenance hangar at Calais. In a mixture of English and French they told him that the engine had been stripped and the problem diagnosed. A build-up of dirt in the fuel intake ports. The mechanics were going to stay late and clean the engine out. It would be put back together and ready for us in the morning. David told them we would be at the airport for eight o'clock.

The plan, arranged over the phone with Ferryfield, had been that if the plane was airworthy by the morning we would fly her back to Lydd empty first thing, ready for her first scheduled flight back to Calais at nine-thirty. It seemed now that we were on track to carry the plan out.

We discussed it with Marianne and then arranged our early morning wake-up calls and taxi with the clerk at the reception desk. Then David and I bade Marianne goodnight.

David and I walked a hundred yards up the Rue Royale to the Café de Paris. We sat out on the pavement and watched the evening strollers walking past. David had his dark glasses on, of course. At least it was still light. 'Every French town has a Café de Paris,' David informed me. 'It's worth seeking out. It usually tends to be the best one in the street.' David, ten years older than me, as Mike was, seemed to know infinitely more about France than I did. Between them he and Mike seemed to know infinitely more about everything in life. I wondered if I would ever catch them up.

As we sipped our small blond beers we talked of ordinary things. We didn't touch on what had happened while we'd lain together on our hotel room bed. In one way nothing had happened, yet in another way everything had. After David had confessed to nearly losing his nerve in the cockpit and I'd taken his hand, we had rolled towards each other and into a tight embrace. A full hug, if you're both lying down, requires a bit of conscious effort. Both of you have to lift your torsos up for a moment, just long enough for the other to get his other arm round underneath. You can't just slip into the intimacy the way you can when standing up. David and I had quite deliberately carried the exacting manoeuvre out.

Because we were both in full uniform, including braided jackets (though mercifully not the peaked caps) it had felt a bit odd. But it had still been very tight and muscular and intense. Because of the uniforms we had almost managed to convince ourselves that it was a friendly rather than a sexual embrace.

Almost. But then I had gone on and given David's cheek a soft and gentle kiss. Then he had given my cheek a soft and gentle kiss. After that we'd simply held each other tightly, not speaking but rocking each other occasionally. And then it had been time to go and meet Marianne and go out for our walk…

David and I finished our beer at the Café de Paris. We walked back to the harbourside. By now it was quite dark. Arc-lights from the docks across the water, and light from the port-holes of the ferry that was tied up there for the night, shone back at us from the rippled surface of the water in a constant movement: a movement that was like quiet and soothing music. Above our heads the stars were out.

I felt David's fingers tunnel in amongst mine and we stood, clasping hands and looking at the silvered water for some time in silence. Then David spoke. 'Come on. Let's go to bed.' He turned towards me and kissed me on the lips.

We watched each other as we got undressed. David was obliged to look me full in the face with his sunglasses off. 'I must look an awful sight,' he said.

'Your right eye does,' I said truthfully. 'But the other one looks splendid. So does the rest of you.'

David was slightly smaller than Will or myself, and a good deal smaller than Mike. But he had a similarly good physique. He might have been a civil airline pilot for a few years longer than us but, like us other three, he still had an ex-serviceman's fitness and body shape. 'You look gorgeous,' he said. Simultaneously we dropped our underwear and showed each other our erect pricks. The moment was as if choreographed.

David's was the same size as Will's was. That is, a fraction smaller than mine. But unlike ours it was circumcised, which made it look different. As soon as we were naked we were all over each other on the bed. But we hadn't romped for long together before David turned me over on my tummy and fucked me from behind. He explained his choice of position. 'You don't want to be looking at my right eye while we do this.'

He came very quickly inside me, then rolled us round onto our sides and brought me off while his cock was still inside me, very expertly catching my ejaculate in his fingers before it went all over the hotel's bedspread. I helped him out by fishing from under the pillow my handkerchief, which I'd put there when we were getting undressed. 'Thank you,' David said as he wiped his fingers and my dick on it. 'Be prepared. Were you in the Scouts?'

Then we got into bed properly and turned the lights out. We lay side by side, sometimes caressing each other a bit anxiously, each busy with our own thoughts. After a while David sighed and said, 'Oh dear. I have a feeling I'm going to feel bad about this in the morning.'

'Spoken for both of us,' I said.

'I don't know. You're not the one who's married, with a pregnant wife.'

I was stunned. I felt myself turn both hot and cold and my body started to shake. I wasn't sure what emotion was causing this until I heard myself speak. 'How fucking dare you,' I said. The emotion was anger of course.

'What do you mean?' asked David, startled.

'You're saying that your heterosexual feelings for your wife, your bond with her, are more valuable than mine are. Of a different order of magnitude. Well, you're completely wrong. It's a fucking insult.' I found I had grabbed David's shoulders and was shaking them.

'It is different,' David argued. 'All right, I accept that you can't compare one person's feelings to another person's and say that one's deeper than the other. But

184

it's a different degree of commitment. Could you please stop shaking me like that?' I stopped shaking him. I hadn't realised that I was still doing that. 'Thank you,' he said. 'But it's a matter of vows made in church. I've done that. You haven't.'

I protested. 'That option isn't open to the likes of Will, Mike and me. Even if we wanted to, we couldn't. Anyway, talking of commitment, you've broken your vows tonight.'

'So have you,' retorted David. 'Even if you've only made them in your own head.'

'Only…?' I said, outraged. 'There happens to be no other place.'

'Even if you could do it in church they'd never accept a three-way agreement.'

I calmed down a bit. 'No. I suppose not. Though that's not really the point.'

There was silence between us for a moment. Then I broke that. 'But what you said at first really was a bit of an insult.' I heard an aggrieved, almost petulant tone come into my voice. I wasn't pleased with it.

'OK,' David said. A bit huffily. 'You're right. I was wrong. And you are right. It was an insult. But it wasn't intentional. I didn't mean it. I wasn't thinking straight. Anyway, I withdraw it.'

There was another second's silence. Gently I touched David's face. I ran my finger tenderly around the bruised rim of his right eye socket. 'The swelling's going down already. It'll be fine in the morning.'

'Oh my darling,' David said.

I had never used the D-word before this afternoon's phone call with Mike. I felt I wasn't old enough for it yet. I'd never said it to Will, nor had he to me. When Mike had first used it to address me that had been a major moment in my life. Now David had suddenly hit me with it.

'I'm sorry I lost my temper,' I said.

'Justifiably,' whispered David. He sounded very upset. Very choked.

'I'm sorry for shaking you just now.'

'I'm sorry for saying the things I said.'

'It's OK,' I said. We kissed each other's lips in the darkness.

There was another little silence. Then I said, 'I'm not the first man or boy you've had sex with, am I.' I was pretty certain of this. Especially since he'd given me such an expert fuck.

'You're right. I told you I'd been to boarding school. And then there was the Air Force. Of course we've all been in the Air Force...'

'Yes,' I said. A couple of very personal memories came blearily back.

'But never since I married Gillian.'

'No,' I said firmly, as if I naturally knew that.

'I thought that getting married might do the trick. Might cure me, if you like. But it seems it hasn't.'

'No,' I said. Then, 'I'm sorry I upset you. What you said was reasonable enough. After all, nobody in my immediate circle is pregnant.' I heard David giggle faintly at that. 'On the other hand,' I went on, 'you've only been unfaithful to one partner. Think of me. I've cheated on two of them at a stroke.'

We held each other again, this time more gently, and – we couldn't help it – both laughed. Then we snuggled together and nuzzled cheeks and noses. Without comment we felt the wetness of tears on each other's cheeks.

I'd been right about one thing. David's right eye was no longer swollen when I looked at it in the morning. The eerie-looking slit had been replaced by a sparkling blue brightness that matched its partner. On the other hand David had that delicate alabaster skin that either bruises easily or shows the bruises – I don't know which. This morning the affected area, which up to now had been merely crimson, had gone the colour of a shining blue-black damson.

TWENTY-ONE

The first of Freddie Laker's Channel Air Bridge ferries
was already landing when we arrived at the airport. The
first of the day, that was. Our aeroplane, Whiskey Kilo,
Le Quatorze Juillet, was waiting for us on the tarmac.
And in the office so was a certain amount of paperwork.

'I don't feel very happy about sitting in the passenger
cabin all on my own,' admitted Marianne. I too was
frightened by the prospect of flying the plane back. So,
I'm pretty sure, was David. It was just that he and I were
not admitting it.

'If you like,' said David, you can come up into the
cockpit. It's a bit cramped but there is a tiny third seat.
And it is only for a few minutes.'

'That's very nice,' said Marianne. 'I'd like that.'

Then the three of us walked out across the tarmac. I
felt I was marching out to face a firing squad.

It had originally been intended to include a radio
operator among the Superfreighter's crew and so the
cockpit was equipped with a small sideways-on seat
immediately behind the Captain's. The march of
progress had rendered the radio operator redundant, but
the third seat remained in the cockpit. Today it would
prove its continuing usefulness. Marianne climbed up
the cockpit ladder with us and strapped herself into it.

Both engines started perfectly. We taxied and took off.
Two minutes later we were passing Calais docks. No
doubt David could have seen the spot where he'd kissed
me last night near the fishing boats if he was looking out
for it. I was on the wrong side for that. I had the distant
view of Dover Castle instead.

Marianne twisted round in her seat so that she could
see out through the windscreen, peering between our two
heads. She laid an arm along the back of each of our two
seats. It was as though she was bridging the gap between

us. Giving us, as an intermediary, the comforting hug we would have liked to give each other but couldn't.

'Gosh,' shouted Marianne above the noise of the engines. 'It looks so wonderful from up here at the front. You see everything all at once.'

'Not when it's cloudy,' I shouted back.

'Then aren't I lucky with the weather,' came Marianne's return shout.

'Listen to that beautiful engine note,' said David. 'Nothing wrong with that.' He was saying it to reassure Marianne, of course. Though maybe also to reassure himself. Or even me. Like whistling in the dark. But I was also glad to hear that staccato machine-gun roar just outside the window on my right. I hadn't enjoyed the scary half silence of the end of the last flight.

This was an extraordinary moment. I was flying alongside the man I'd slept with last night. The feelings we now had for each other were complex and difficult. We couldn't discuss them even if we wanted to, because of Marianne's presence right behind us. Nor could we give each other the comforting thigh pats that might have expressed those complex feelings more easily than words. But right now it was difficult to make sense of what had happened between David and me in any case. I was too preoccupied with, and too fearful about, the engine. Listening to it intently, waiting with nerves near breaking point for it to cut out or give a cough. In a way that engine was saving David and me from having to think too hard about each other. But it was the engine that, by its failure yesterday, had caused the mischief in the first place – by throwing David and me together in the same bed overnight. Oh the fiendish practical jokes of Chance!

Romney Bay grew wide ahead of us. We came in over Greatstone, turned and made a perfect landing at Lydd. The starboard engine was as steady as the port. As steady as a rock. I didn't need to go down and open the nose doors while we taxied onto the apron: we had no cars to let off. Instead I went down and through the door to the passenger cabin, taking Marianne with me. When the engines stopped I opened the passenger door and escorted her off the flight.

We hadn't got as far as the door to the terminal before Wing Commander Davies emerged from it. He greeted Marianne with a smile but then let her get on her way indoors. He turned his attention to me. 'You and Captain Cook are relieved from flying duty for the rest of the morning. Please tell Cook I want to see you both in my office as soon as you've handed the plane over. Say, in about five minutes.' Then he turned smartly about and followed Marianne into the terminal building.

I turned back towards the plane to pass on Davies's instructions to David. A figure came hurrying, almost running, towards me from the car tunnel. It was Will naturally.

'God, I'm glad to see you,' he said. 'I was worried about you. After Mike told me...'

'I'm OK.' I found myself suddenly nearly crying with emotion. I wanted to kiss him. Yet I found I felt ashamed and guilty. Undeserving of his concern. Of his love. His friendship.

'There've been some developments this end,' Will went on a bit breathlessly. 'Mike had a bit of a ... He left Paul behind yesterday. By mistake.'

'Left him behind in Ostend?' I was incredulous. 'He didn't say anything on the telephone.'

'He was only concerned for you when you spoke to him. No, not in Ostend. At the end of the runway.'

'What?!'

'I'll explain later. Got to dash now. Turnaround. There's another thing. Your mother phoned last night. She wants to come down on your next day off. Take you out to lunch. See the bungalow… Look, must dash. Talk later.' Will hurried off back towards the tunnel at a jog trot. I resumed my walk towards the aeroplane. But now I seemed to be walking on legs made out of jelly.

The Wing Commander was not alone in his office. On either side of his desk sat the two senior Captains, Evans and Wimbush. Though Wimbush was only dimly discernible through a fog of cigar smoke. David and I were motioned to sit in two chairs facing them. I'd seen scenes in films of Courts-Martial. With all five of us in uniform… I couldn't help feeling, with my heart in my boots, that this was very much like one of them.

The three senior pilots couldn't hide their surprise at the fact that David was still wearing dark glasses. David evidently felt he ought to say something about this before they did. 'Sorry about the glasses. I walked into a cupboard door at home and it doesn't look very nice. Would you like me to take them off?'

Davies tried not to smile but couldn't prevent the corners of his mouth from turning up just a little. 'No, it's fine. You can keep them on if you prefer.'

'Thank you, sir,' said David and we both took our seats.

'Right. Well, thank you for coming,' Davies said. 'And well done for yesterday at Calais.' He stopped. 'Oh dear, you do look rather alarmed, both of you. With or without dark glasses. This isn't an interrogation. But it is a de-briefing and we have to take it seriously. We need to know exactly what happened. In every detail.'

'So it doesn't happen again,' put in Captain Wimbush from behind his smokescreen.

'So,' resumed Davies, 'Let's start from the beginning.' Then he smiled. 'Captain Cook?'

At least, when they talked about needing to know every detail in order to prevent a recurrence of the incident, they weren't talking about what David and I had done in the hotel room bed.

When the half-hour de-briefing session was over it was a relief to find that David and I were still being praised for our handling of the crisis and had been freed from any suspicion of having done something to cause it. Nevertheless my thoughts were still in chaos. David and I would be flying to Calais and back three times this afternoon. (Two other pilots had been hauled in on their days off to provide emergency cover for the morning.) We would be alone together in the cockpit without the saving presence of Marianne. God knew what we were going to talk about. And then there was the astonishing thing about Mike leaving Paul behind on the runway. To say nothing of my mother's impending visit. I would need to get hold of Will when he had his lunch break and have a talk to him. Or rather, let him talk to me. There was rather a lot that I didn't want to tell him about.

David said in my ear as we walked down the corridor away from the office, 'I'm driving home for an hour. Just to clean my teeth and so on. Can I drop you off at your place, and bring you back on my return?'

I suppose I should have said no but I didn't. I said yes of course.

I gave David a quick tour of the bungalow. We kissed in the hallway. It was the most neutral part of the territory and neither of us was insensitive. We felt each other's dicks through our trousers. 'Now that's it,' I said. 'We must stop this.' I left him to decide whether I just meant the brief grope we were engaged in or the whole thing that we'd somehow started. I certainly didn't know which I meant.

We disengaged and David drove off. We'd agreed what time he would pick me up. I'd told David I needed to see Will at lunchtime. I'd told him what Will had told me about Mike abandoning Paul at the end of the runway, and David was almost as surprised by it as I was.

David returned very punctually and we returned to the airport without kissing. Though I did weaken and put my hand on his leg as we drove. Just for half a minute. In the canteen I found Will and we went and sat at a table. David tactfully didn't join us. But a moment later I saw him sitting and eating, sharing a table with Paul of all people. In a way I was glad Mike wasn't there just then. Much as I longed to see him, and for him to put his big arms comfortingly round me, there was a lot in my head that would need sorting out before that happened. I needed a little time to deal with it. First of all I needed to hear from Will about my mother's phone call.

Actually I wanted to throw myself into Will's arms too, but in the canteen that wouldn't be possible. For the moment I had to settle for gazing into his bright blue eyes across the table. The hugs would come later.

'I know you're worried about that,' Will said when I brought up the subject of my mother. 'Her seeing the bungalow and you don't have your own bedroom and so on. But Mike and I discussed it.' I found the thought of Mike and Will discussing my mother over a late night Horlicks or something. surprisingly touching.

Will went on, 'To make it less obvious... Mike's planning to go and see his parents at the weekend anyway. And you've got a day off on the Saturday. So if your mother came down that day she wouldn't run into Mike. His bedroom could become your bedroom. Not that it isn't already...' He stuffed a forkful of beans n toast into his mouth.

'I know what you mean,' I said. 'It might not entirely solve the problem but it'd be a step in the right direction. I can phone her this evening. Now tell me the other thing. About Mike and…' I glanced over towards where Paul was sitting, deep in conversation with David at their tubular-steel-framed table.

'Yes,' said Will. 'It was a bit embarrassing for him.' I wasn't sure whether he meant for Mike or Paul. No doubt that would become clear in the course of the story.

'You said he left him…' I jerked my head towards Paul again, '…at the end of the runway…'

'You know how the tail wheel sticks sometimes on some of them,' Will began. 'Well, you know that better than I do.'

'Yes, of course.' Our planes, dragging their tail wheels behind them, did not use them to steer with when taxiing, the way tricycle-type aircraft used their nose wheels. We turned instead by speeding up or slowing down one engine. The tail wheel simply followed the direction of the turn like a castor. A tail wheel that swung freely was perfect for taxiing and ground manoeuvring, but it was far from ideal during take-off and landing. So, when we were in position at the foot of the runway, ready for take-off we locked the tail wheel in forward-aft alignment. An electric switch on the control column shot a pin through the tail wheel's mounting that would keep it rigid. On arrival at the other end of the flight, when the landing roll was finished and we were ready to taxi to the terminal, we simply unlocked it. Just occasionally, though, the pin would be found to have jammed in the locked position.

The remedy was simple, though it might have looked alarming to the passengers. The pilot would halt the plane and put the brakes on. The co-pilot would pick up the crash-axe with which every aircraft cockpit is furnished and go down the ladder with it. He would emerge from the vehicle hold into the passenger cabin doing his best to look unthreatening, then exit the passenger door onto the tarmac. A hearty whack to the locking pin beneath the aircraft's tail would usually release it and the co-pilot would climb back on board the aircraft. A bang on the inside wall of the fuselage would announce to the pilot that the job had been successfully completed and he would start to taxi without needing to have sight of his co-pilot.

'Mike had done this before,' Will told me. 'But Paul hadn't. He released the jammed pin all right, but then he banged the axe on the outside of the aircraft to show that he'd finished...'

'Instead of waiting till he got back inside,' I said. I took a swig of tea from my mug.

'Exactly. Mike set off before Paul could run to the door, and left him stranded down at the turning point.' He gestured with an arm in the direction of the spot two thirds of a mile away from where we were sitting. 'When Paul didn't return to the cockpit Mike thought nothing of it. He assumed he'd stayed downstairs to be ready to open the nose doors. It wasn't till he'd parked up and the nose doors didn't open that he realised what had happened. That and the stewardess coming through and calling up the ladder to tell him.'

'Oh my God,' I said, though I couldn't help laughing a bit. 'And Paul had to walk all the way back?'

Will nodded. 'Mike's afraid that Paul might have taken it badly. That he thinks Mike did it on purpose.'

'Lord,' I said. 'Why does life always have to be so complicated?' A new thought struck me. 'They're not going to hold an enquiry into that, are they?'

'No,' said Will. 'Perhaps they would have done, but your engine failure yesterday's given them bigger things to think about. They're now going through the maintenance schedules and interviewing the mechanics.'

Will and I both looked towards the other table where David and Paul were still deep in conversation. I wondered if they were exchanging the same news that we were.

'Anyway,' Will said, 'that was a minor thing. It's you that's had the … what's the trendy expression? … the traumatic experience.' More traumatic than Will could guess. 'Tell me about that.'

'Oh gosh.' I sighed without meaning to. 'I don't know what to say.'

'It's not about the engine, is it.' Will's blue eyes pinned me. 'It's something else.'

I hesitated, looking indecisively into those eyes of his. 'I don't know…'

'Go on,' Will said.

Then I found that I couldn't not let Will in on it. However difficult it might be for both of us. 'There's something I need to tell you,' I said. 'Though I'm not sure you'll want to hear it.'

'We'll see,' Will looked at me very steadily as he said that.

'As you know, we had to stay in a hotel overnight.' I found I'd lowered my voice to little more than a whisper. 'It was very nice. David made sure they gave us the best. The Georges Cinq in the centre of Calais. But there were only two rooms. Marianne – do you know her? – yes – she had one, and David and I shared the other. We had a … a double bed.'

Will tried to smile reassuringly at me but it didn't really come off. 'You had sex.' I could see he was trying not to feel upset about this but I could also see that he was upset.

'I'm sorry, darling.' It was the first time I'd called Will that. 'Yes we did have sex. Actually he fucked me.' I saw the look on Will's face. I clarified quickly. 'He didn't force himself on me. It wasn't like that. I was more than willing, I have to admit…'

'He's married.' Will too was whispering now.

'We'd been flirting for days,' I said. 'I never thought it would lead to anything. I didn't see how it could.'

'Oh darling,' Will said, and even his whisper faltered. 'I love you. It was a mistake to sleep with Paul that night...' Our two pairs of eyes flicked nervously to the other table. But both Paul and David had left it and were not to be seen. 'But now you...'

'I'm so sorry, Will. So, so sorry. If I could un-happen it...' We were both on the brink of tears.

'It's OK,' Will said, though he didn't smile as he said it. 'We survived Paul, the three of us. We'll survive this.'

I said, 'I love you so much.'

'Have you said that to David?' Will asked.

'No, I haven't.' I didn't say that in a tone of outrage, blustering. There was no point. I wanted everything to be truthful between Will and me. I'd come very close to telling David I loved him. Will knew me very well. Almost as well as he knew himself. He would know how close I'd come to it.

There was a silence while we looked at each other, completely oblivious as to whether there was anyone else in the canteen or not. 'Thank you, Will,' I said. I didn't need to tell him that I was thanking him for my whole universe. Then, 'I now have to think about – and I'll need your advice on this – the question of what, or even whether, I'm going to tell Mike.'

Another big sigh was Will's answer to that. 'I don't know. I'll need to think about that.'

'Well, can you think about it quickly? We'll all be meeting up around five o'clock.'

'I'll do my best,' Will said. Then he flashed me a bleak little smile, the first he'd given me for several minutes. I was pathetically grateful for it.

I looked up at the wall clock. 'Now I've got to go and work,' I said. 'I'm on Calais with David. Three more trips.' I chased my last chip around my plate.

'I'm saying nothing,' Will said. 'Except good luck. Whatever I mean by that.'

'Thanks. I don't know how to say…'

'We'll say it all later,' Will said. 'Though perhaps not with words, I think.'

'You're wonderful…' Then a thought struck me that, oddly enough, I'd never had before. 'You say Mike's going away for the weekend. To his parents' place in Hampshire.'

'Odiham.'

'He told me they have a big house. What do his parents do? I mean, what are his parents?'

'It is a big house,' Will said. 'But they don't own it. It's the rectory or vicarage. His father's the rector there. Or vicar. Something like that.'

TWENTY-TWO

It might seem odd that Mike had been my lover for some six weeks and I hadn't asked him what his father did. But then I hadn't asked Will what his father did. And neither of them had asked me what my father did.

It was a generation thing. All our parents had been young adults during the War. Will and I had been born during it. Mike (and David) had been seven when it broke out; thirteen when it finished. Our parents had done amazing things in the War. Even my father, who hadn't flown in combat, had crossed the Atlantic several times between Britain and Canada in the most horrifyingly dangerous circumstances. Even laying aside the question of personal feats of courage it remained the case that they had all done an amazing thing simply by cheating death and coming through it. Millions hadn't. The War was the time through which their generation lived; in which it had been most thrillingly and terrifyingly alive. What they did in their civilian afterlives seemed somehow irrelevant. After what they'd experienced between 1939 and 1945 everything that followed was little more than an extended coda, a postscript, an afterthought.

'I'm really quite astonished by that,' I told Will when he announced that Mike was a son of the manse. 'It's not at all what I'd have expected.' I honestly couldn't have imagined anyone much less like a clergyman's son than Mike. A matter of having lazy preconceptions of course. 'What does your father do?' I asked Will. I braced myself. Perhaps Will would tell me his father was the Pope.

'He works in a shop. Quite a smart shop actually. A jeweller's in Bond Street. What about yours?'

'He's the bursar in a school near where we live,' I said. 'I mean, where they live.' We didn't ask each other what our mothers did. Most mothers of people our age had become housewives as well as mothers after putting their War work behind them with relief. There were exceptions of course. But most found this double role an honourable calling enough. And as few people had washing-machines, dishwashers or even fridges, it was quite a tough enough job.

'Will,' I said. 'I have to get back to the crew room. Re-join David. Get ready for take-off in forty minutes.'

'Back to Calais?' Will checked.

'Three more times before we finish.'

'Good luck with David,' Will said. 'Whatever I mean by that.'

'Will…' Daringly I reached across the table and touched the back of his hand fleetingly, the way he had done in the Railway Hotel the evening we'd first met. 'Thank you for being understanding. Thank you for being wonderful. Thank you for your love.'

'Thank you for yours.' Will stayed sitting for a second after I started to get up. His blue eyes looked up at me with an expression I would never forget. There was love and longing in it, but also anxiety and something like dread. Then he started to get to his feet and we turned away from each other to go our different ways to work. But I carried the memory of his blue eyes behind me as I walked towards the crew room, the way a peacock butterfly wears its eyes on its back.

Though David and I exchanged shy smiles as we prepared for the flight in the crew room and then the cockpit we didn't talk about anything except the tasks we were involved in until we had taken off and were in straight and level flight. Then, 'You had a long chat with Paul over lunch,' I said.

'You had a long talk with Will,' David batted back.

'He's my official boyfriend,' I said – to my own astonishment. I'd never even thought the word boyfriend in connection with either Will or Mike. I'd certainly never spoken it aloud to anyone. A boyfriend wasn't something a lad of my generation had.

'One of your official boyfriends,' corrected David. It was a reasonable retort.

'Did you tell Paul about us?' I asked.

David threw the question back. 'Did you tell Will?'

'Yes. It wasn't easy, but he was still my boyfriend afterwards, which is rather miraculous. I've asked him to advise me on whether or not to tell Mike.'

'And his advice was…?'

'I don't know. He says he needs some time to think about it.'

'Even so, it seems a hell of a lot easier among you three than it would be if I had to come clean with Jilly.'

'Can you imagine,' I said as a new idea struck me, 'if we were expected to come clean about any of this – about *any* of it – with our parents?'

David guffawed, which pleased me. The atmosphere needed lightening a bit. 'No,' he said. The idea was of course preposterous. Neither of us – none of us – had ever known or heard of any man who enjoyed sex with his fellow males who had voluntarily told his parents.

'What does your father do?' I asked.

'He's a barrister.' That explained David's having gone to boarding school. 'In London. Paul's father's a solicitor. Not so far from here. In Maidstone.'

'Birds of a feather,' I said without thought. Then, 'Yes, but did you tell Paul about you and me? About us?'

'No,' said David. 'Though I think he sort of guessed. He has antennae. They're pretty sensitive.'

So Paul wore antennae. And I wore a butterfly's eye markings on my back.

'He was curious about the dark glasses,' David went on. 'I told him I had a shiner. He asked me how I did it.'

'What did you tell him?'

David turned his head towards me and smiled beneath the glasses. 'The same as I told you.'

'It wasn't true, though, was it.'

'No. It was not.' He changed the subject slightly. 'He told me about Mike leaving him to walk home from the end of the runway. I suppose Will also told you that?'

'He did,' I said. 'He was afraid – he thought that Mike was afraid – Paul might have taken it badly.'

'Paul thought Mike might have done it on purpose. Though Mike did apologise to him profusely afterwards…'

'I'm sure he did. Mike would never do anything spiteful. It's not in his makeup. He just couldn't. If he wanted to criticise Paul over anything he'd come straight out and say it. And as far as I know he didn't even want to say anything to Paul about him and Will that night. It's water under the bridge for all of us.'

'Yes,' said David, sounding a bit reflective.

By now we were nearly across the Channel. There were a few cotton-wool clouds about. But not so many that we couldn't make out the white-cliff headlands of both sides coming and going between them. 'Here we are again,' said David rather gravely. 'Between Scylla and Charibdis.'

I couldn't think of anything to say that would be remotely intelligent or apposite. I leaned across and placed my hand like a wedge between his warm thighs and rested the blade of it against the trouser-clad form of his flaccid penis. It couldn't do any harm, I thought. There wasn't the remotest possibility that we'd end up in bed together again tonight. Unless an engine fell off.

There was no sign of Will at Ferryfield when I returned from the last of that afternoon's trips to Calais. Nor was his car in the car park. 'Can I give you a lift home?' David asked before walking across to his own car.

I was tempted but after a second's thought I said, 'Better not.' I hadn't seen Mike or his car either. If he had got home before me and saw me turning up in David's passenger seat… Well, if I was going to tell Mike the whole story – and I was still desperately looking forward to hearing Will's advice on this – I would want to do it at a time of my choosing, not of Mike's.

'Understood,' said David. 'Well, see you when I see you.' For the next couple of days I would be flying with Captain Wimbush.

'I'll look forward to it,' I said. I put the tips of my fingers to my lips and blew him a miniature, unreadable-at-a-distance, kiss. Still wearing his sunglasses he copied me minutely and blew me a tiny kiss. That created a tiny, delightful knot in my stomach for a second. I said, 'Sleep tight.'

'And you, my darling.' Then he turned and walked away quickly while I went off to pick up my bike.

When I got home neither of the others was there, though Mike's car was. I wondered if they'd gone to the beach in Will's Mini. But gone without me? Without leaving a note? I must admit that I spent a minute or two looking for a note. Under tables and chairs, below the windowsills. In case they'd written me one, left it on some flat surface or other and it had fallen off. But then I gave up and settled for making a cup of tea for myself.

I didn't have time to drink much of it, though, sitting in the shingly garden, before the Mini came into sight, drove up beside me, and Will and Mike got out of it. Will was brandishing something the size of a small hammer or crowbar and waving it excitedly about. 'We've got it,' he said exultantly. 'They've made it and it works.' Mike meanwhile was dragging a couple of lengths of metal chain from off the back seat.

The 'Shackle-it' as Will had decided to call it looked exactly like his original diagram of it. It was like an over-sized wire-tensioner with a big hook at each end but with a ratchet rather than a screw-thread running down the centre of it, and a pump-type lever attached halfway along it to lengthen and shorten it.

A few minutes later the three of us were excitedly practising using it. Mike drove two garden forks as far into the ground as they would go with a mallet, one on each side of the front wheel of Will's Mini. They would stand in for the rings embedded in the floor of the vehicle hold in every Superfreighter.

Will was the expert. He spent much of his working day chaining car axles to the deck, which Mike and I didn't. But he quickly taught us the method. One end of the chain was anchored to the tines of one of the embedded forks, the other was wrapped around the back of the Mini's front wheel, knotted around itself at the front, then attached to one of the Shackle-it's hooks. The other end of the Shackle-it was hooked to the half buried tines of the other fork. Then the lever was pulled once and the whole fastening immediately locked tight.

We took it in turns to carry out the operation, while the second member of our team counted off the seconds on his watch. The third person noted the timings on a piece of paper – and was occasionally obliged to lean heavily on one of the forks if someone else's enthusiasm with the pump-lever threatened to pull it right out of the ground.

As we practised with it we got better at it and the number of seconds required to effect the procedure grew fewer and fewer like the grains of sand in an hour-glass.

We had a second trial, using Mike's Ford Anglia as the guinea-pig, to see if this made any difference. After the first couple of tries it didn't.

'Right,' said Mike. 'Take those results with you to the meeting, Will. All of them. Not just the best. It'll show them how rigorously we've tested it.' The board meeting was less than ten days away now. Mike and I repeatedly wished Will good luck with it. We didn't talk about what might happen afterwards if the plan worked. If the company sent Will away to flying school … and he was lost to us for months. That was a future too uncomfortable to contemplate. But so was everything about the future. Once the summer was over and the pilots who'd been hired for the season, including Mike and me, discovered whether they'd be kept on through the winter or not.

Instead we went to the beach. We swam briefly and fooled around in the water. This time nobody felt the need to pee in it. Actually, although I've written nobody, I can only say for certain that I didn't. And that if anyone else did they didn't mention it.

By the time we'd dried off the Pilot Inn had opened its doors for the evening. 'Do you know something?' Mike said as we took our pints to an outdoor table that was effectively on the beach. 'That this place is called the Pilot, and we're all pilots, and I've never made the connection before. Never thought about it. I mean, the pub's so obviously named after a marine pilot. Either a person or a boat.'

I laughed. 'You're right. I hadn't thought about it either. For the same reason. There's the sea, the beach, the lifeboat station… You don't think of aircraft when you find the pub's called The Pilot.'

'We're not all pilots,' Will said. His tone of voice brought us down a bit.

'Yes we are,' said Mike. 'You were a pilot in the RAF. Once a pilot always a pilot.'

'I know what he means,' I told Mike. 'It's that he's still waiting for…'

'Yes, I understand that,' Mike said a bit curtly. 'But they'll pounce on the Shackle-it like hawks.' He turned to Will. 'You can be sure of that. You'll be a co-pilot here with us at Lydd in no time.'

'Well thanks,' said Will. He smiled graciously, though we all knew Mike had been whistling in the dark. Wanting to keep everyone cheerful and positive. That was Mike.

I knew at that moment that I did have to tell Mike about David. I'd wanted Will's opinion on whether it was a good idea or not. But I hadn't had a chance to find it out. Now I knew I just had to go ahead and do it anyway. 'Mike,' I began, 'there's something I need to own up to. It's something Will knows about but it's not fair if I don't…'

Mike cut me short. 'Is it about David?' he asked. There was a little smile on his face.

'Yes,' I said.

'It's all right. Will's already told me,' Mike said.

'And you're still talking to me?' I asked.

'Yes,' said Mike. 'That doesn't mean that Will and I wouldn't have preferred it if it hadn't happened. But it did, so…' He broke off and shrugged.

'I love you, Mike,' I said softly. Then, 'I love you, Will,' I added quickly so that there would be no danger of his feeling left out. Then, of course, we all had to repeat the mantra. It takes several times longer to go through the full set of permutations when there are three of you than when you are only two. As anyone who's ever tried it already knows.

I realised there was another matter that I wanted to broach with Mike. Although in the light of what I'd just learned about his conversation with Will I thought it was highly possible that this too had come up during their drive to the motor-bike workshop and back. 'I don't know if you've seen Paul today,' I said. 'David (if I'm allowed to mention him) thought that Paul might be a bit upset about what happened yesterday. Getting left behind out on the runway. That although he's accepted your apology he might be nursing the idea that you'd done it on purpose. I did tell David that you would never do a thing like that. That you were incapable of spite...'

'It's OK.' Again Mike cut me off. 'Will had the same thought. He told me in the car. But I've forestalled both of you. I met Paul in the canteen at Le Tooks this afternoon and had a chat with him. We've managed to put everything right. In fact I'm going to make it up to him properly. When I go back home at the weekend... Well, Paul's got the weekend off too. So I'm taking him to Odiham with me. To meet my parents.'

There's no describing the look that Will and I exchanged at that moment.

Anthony McDonald

TWENTY-THREE

There was nothing Will or I could do or say. Mike had displayed an almost superhuman degree of understanding, tolerance and forgiveness when Will had played away by bedding Paul and then again when I had done the same: by first flirting with David and then going to bed with him in Calais. If Mike now wanted to take Paul – Paul of all people! – home with him and introduce him to his parents and had had the civility and openness to announce his intention in advance… We weren't in a position even to query it. 'Are you sure that's a good idea?' 'We might find that a bit difficult to deal with.' Even gentle remonstrations such as those were not available to us. Will and I didn't just live in glass houses. We had already thrown stones and broken the windows. All we could do, and all we did do, was to smile nervously at Mike across the pub table and our half empty pint glasses and say with false brightness, 'Oh right. That'll be interesting. Hope you have a good weekend, then. Both of you. Say hallo to your parents.'

I had told David that spiteful or manipulative behaviour was absent from Mike's makeup. But several times during the course of that evening I found myself wondering, though feeling bad about doing so, whether I'd misjudged Mike, giving him credit for near saintly qualities that he didn't in fact possess – and that not many people in the world did. I wondered if in fact Mike, like the rest of us, was more than capable of behaving spitefully; I wondered if in fact he was an expert manipulator of other people and so practised at concealing that talent of his that those he manipulated remained blissfully unaware of it.

I managed to put both Mike's astonishing announcement and my suspicious feelings about it to the back of my mind as the evening progressed. We were celebrating after all. Celebrating the successful realisation of Will's brainwave in the demonstration model he'd shown us. Celebrating our success in proving that it worked: that by adding up seconds saved per each wheel shackled and multiplying up – four per car, three cars per flight, number of flights per day etc. – the time the invention would save the company would be very significant. Come to think of it we spent almost every day celebrating something, the three of us. Celebrating that very fact quite simply. The fact of being the three of us.

So we had a great evening. Beer in the pub. Wine with supper. Listening to music afterwards. Both Mike and I got our cheque-books out and gave a protesting Will our contributions to the bill he'd been given by the man in the motor-bike repair shop for making the Shackle-it. (I've written *a protesting Will*. Though he didn't protest so much as actually to refuse our cheques.) And then after that we went to bed; the three of us together; enjoying the healing, bonding balm of three-way sex. Of love. Having sex and making love. That was what happened that night. In a way that satisfying, satisfactory ending was unexpected. And yet it always turned out like that; so we should have expected it. But perhaps it was better that we didn't expect it; that we didn't take those happy endings, or one another, for granted. It meant that every time something went wrong among the three of us … and then we somehow put it right by having sex all together … that was a wonderful, magical kind of bonus.

'The Carvairs are coming in a fortnight,' Captain Wimbush told me the next morning as we coasted out near the Dungeness lighthouse en route for Le Touquet. He held out his pack of Tom Thumbs for me before taking one himself.

'No thanks,' I said. 'We're getting three of them, right?'

'Right indeed,' said Wimbush. 'But the first one's coming early. We're doing a proving flight next week. Invited customers, announcements in the press. Pity I won't be here to witness it. I'm on holiday all next week.' He struck a match and lit up.

'Lucky you,' I said. Not that I was envious. I was having a whale of a time. Living with Will and Mike. Doing a job I loved. And I hadn't been here quite two months. I wasn't ready for a holiday yet. And when I was ready for one … I wouldn't want it to be without my two mates. I asked, 'Carvair comes from…?'

'Southend,' said Wimbush. 'By way of Blackbushe.'

'What I meant,' I said, 'was the word Carvair. Who dreamed that up?'

'Car via Air,' said Wimbush, adjusting the trim-wheel with a confident hand, while balancing his little cigar between his lips. 'Freddie Laker's brainchild. We're behind the competition for once. He saw the old DC-4s were going cheap. Long haul's moved on. Jets. Pressurised cabins. Above the clouds at four hundred miles an hour and thirty thousand feet… The old piston engines pensioned off. Freddie made a cardboard model of a DC-4 converted for car transport. Five cars, thirty passengers. His board supported him and he had the conversions carried out.'

'New wine in old wineskins, though, isn't it?' I said. 'I mean the conversion's a good idea but the basic airframes are eighteen years old, aren't they? End of the War didn't they come out?'

'Yes,' said Wimbush. 'But have you never seen that old film The Gifthorse? You seize your chance, take what's on offer, and make the most of it. We won't be using them to cross the Atlantic anyway. Those days are past. We'll just be trotting them over to Geneva or

Rotterdam and back at three or four thousand feet.' He drew breath. 'A little more towards the Jura Mountains perhaps. But we won't be going right over the top of them. They're over five thousand feet.'

'They sound fun,' I said. 'I mean the Carvairs, not the mountains.'

'You'll clap your eyes on your first one next week. Now what's the Decca telling us?'

'Dead on course,' I said. 'And ... yes ... I can see the estuary through the haze ahead.'

The story of Freddie Laker convincing his board by making a cardboard model brought me back to Will and his forthcoming presentation of the Shackle-it. I wondered if Wimbush knew about that. I wondered whether, if he did know about it, he was wondering whether I also knew about it... Anyway, neither of us mentioned it.

But Will mentioned it when we met at home that evening. 'Fabulous news,' he said. 'I met Davies in the canteen. I mean, he was sitting there when I went in and he beckoned me over. He asked how the prototype was shaping up. I said it was made, and it worked, and that we'd done trials on it with timings... He said, "Good," and looked quite pleased, relieved almost. He told me that most things that got tabled at board meetings were in fact sounded out informally in advance. I mean the board members were sounded out and he's got the most important people's support already. Provided I can show the meeting that it works – which we know it does – they're really keen to have it and get it produced in quantity by a company that does that sort of thing. In which case...' Will paused and shook his head involuntarily. 'I can hardly believe this. He said they'd send me to flight school during the winter months. Keep me on the payroll at my present rate. And that if I passed my exams I'd be welcome to apply for a job here as a pilot. First Officer.' He stopped. He was looking at me with a wide-eyed, almost wild-eyed, look.

He'd said he could hardly believe it. I could hardly believe it either. I took him in my arms and said, 'That's wonderful. Well done, mate. You deserve it.' Then, 'Which flight school? Any idea yet?'

'Biggin Hill,' he said.

That made my heart do a little jump. 'It's only five miles from where I … from where my parents live. In summer you can see the planes landing and taking off.' I released him from my embrace and we looked into each other's eyes very intently, exploring each other's inner thoughts. 'It's wonderful news,' I repeated. I couldn't think of a more original way of saying it. 'You just have to get through the board meeting.' A thought struck me. 'Where do they hold that?'

'Usually in London. At the company offices in Brompton Road. But this one's going to be held at Lydd. So I can demonstrate the thing on a real car inside a real aircraft.'

'They're all traipsing down here just for you?' This was another thing I could barely believe.

'It looks like it.' Will modestly lowered his eyes a bit.

We chattered on for a bit until we'd exhausted the subject for the moment. Then I broached the other subject that was preoccupying us. I said, 'What do think about Mike's weekend plans? I mean going off with Paul? Have you seen Paul today? To speak to?'

Will exhaled audibly. 'Bit of a puzzle, that. I mean, when I spent a night with Paul all hell broke loose.'

I wasn't sure that three men glaring at each other for a few seconds, then making a pot of tea and sitting in the garden drinking it while carefully choosing other subjects to talk about constituted all hell breaking loose.

But perhaps Will was right. Hell was an internal thing, located in the head and heart.

'Do you think he's doing it to get his own back?' I asked. 'I mean, there was you and Paul, then me and David...'

'It's crossed my mind,' Will said. 'But I didn't want to think that. It doesn't seem like Mike.'

'My thoughts exactly.' It always made me happy when Will and I – or Mike and I – had exactly the same thoughts.

'But I haven't spoken to Paul,' Will went on. 'I think he may be slightly avoiding me at the moment.' I was amused by the idea of someone 'slightly avoiding' someone else, yet I knew exactly what Will meant.

I had another thought suddenly. 'You know Mike's father's a vicar. Well, do you suppose Paul's decided he may have a vocation in the Church and wants to meet Mike's father to talk about it?'

Will gave me the kind of look that people give to someone whom they've just discovered to be mentally under-equipped.

'No,' I said quickly. 'Well, perhaps not. It was just a thought.'

Will shrugged. 'No more unlikely than anything else we might think of.' There was a second's thoughtful silence.

'Maybe David will know what's going on,' I suggested. 'He seems to be quite close to Paul at the moment.'

Will's eyebrows went up. 'I wonder why that might be?'

We worked a five-day week. But the airline operated seven days a week. It would hardly have been in business if it hadn't. From time to time we would get a full weekend off, but those were at a premium. More often than not we got two separate days off at odd times during the week. Sometimes my days and weekends off coincided with Will's or Mike's, sometimes they didn't.

This particular weekend Will and I both had the Saturday off, while Mike was free for the whole weekend. Paul too, evidently. Will and I said goodbye to them both in the car park as they got into Mike's Anglia together on the Friday at four o'clock. It was a surreal experience.

'Well, that's that,' said Will as we stopped waving at them when the car turned the corner by the little bridge.

'For the moment. Tomorrow we have my mother to face.'

Will laughed. 'You mean you've got your mother to face. No. Only joking. I'll be there to give you all the support you want.'

'Thank you, darling,' I said.

'I'll drive us home,' Will said. 'Leave your bike chained up. You won't need it tomorrow. Sunday we're both in late. Come in with me.' I repeated my thanks.

It was fun in bed that night. Will and me. Just the two of us. We fucked each other gently, lovingly, and when we settled down to sleep there was plenty of space.

I met my mother off the train at twelve o'clock. Will had very sweetly lent me the Mini, sacrificing his own freedom for a couple of hours in the process. My mother was impressed. Not just by the mode of transport but also, I think, by the fact that I'd found a friend who cared enough for me to lend me it. I drove us to The George and we had a good lunch there while I gave my mother a very censored account of what I'd been up to since she'd seen me last.

Then I drove her to the airport. I had learnt from talking to other people that when you got your first job your mother would be intrigued by the idea of the place where you worked and would be dying to see it. It was certainly so in my own mother's case. I felt awkward and embarrassed walking round the terminal building with her, constantly running into people I knew and having to explain to them who I was with. But eventually the guided tour was over. Out of the frying-pan, though. I now had the guided tour of Will's bungalow to give.

Will was wonderful. He charmed my mother, made tea, found an unopened packet of biscuits and was generally gracious. But there was still the bedrooms issue to face. I wondered optimistically if my mother might have forgotten Mike's existence but I wasn't in luck.

'I thought you said you all had a bedroom each,' my mother said when the tour of inspection was complete.

'Did I?' I lied. 'Well, yes and no. Mike's not here all that much. I have his room when he's not. When he is…'

'He shares my room,' Will came to my rescue smoothly and quickly. I could have smothered him in kisses. Later I would. Obviously my mother wasn't going to ask to see the inside of Will's room and the door to it was shut.

'Oh, I see,' said my mother, sounding like the Queen when taken by surprise by an inappropriate remark from one of her subjects.

'Well, that's the grand tour,' I said, shutting the door to Mike's room and, in my hopeful imagination, closing my mother's mind to further speculation on the subject.

On the way to the station in the Mini my mother said, 'You're lucky to have a friend like Will. I thought him very nice. He's also very good looking, though you may not be aware of that. He has wonderful blue eyes. When he starts looking for a wife he won't have many problems. He'll be considered quite a catch.'

'Yes,' I said. 'I can imagine he would.'

'If the other musketeer is half as nice… What's his name again? Mike?'

'Mike,' I confirmed. 'He's also very nice.'

'Perhaps I'll meet him next time I come down,' my mother said. 'Though I am a bit surprised you don't have a room each.'

'It's a small bungalow,' I said. 'As I told you, it's a sort of present from Will's parents.' Smugly I added, remembering my recent conversation with Captain Wimbush, 'One doesn't look a gift horse in the mouth.'

'Indeed,' my mother agreed. 'But all the same…'

Mercifully she didn't find an appropriate set of words to conclude the sentence with and, equally mercifully, we had now arrived at the station. I braked to a halt in the small car park. 'Right,' I said. 'Three minutes to your train. I'll see you onto the platform.' When we got onto the platform all other thoughts were banished from my mother's mind by the sight and deafening sound of a Superfreighter leaving the runway just a couple of fields away and climbing out, a huge blue-banded silver box on wings, almost above our heads.

When I got back to the bungalow I gave Will the shower of kisses I'd earmarked for him earlier. Then we rapidly tore all our clothes off and leapt into bed.

In the early evening we drove to the beach and went into the Pilot Inn. To our surprise we saw someone we knew standing at the counter with a pint and chatting with the barmaid. It was David. Dressed very casually and youthfully in plimsolls, white T-shirt and khaki shorts. And sunglasses of course.

He smiled happily when he saw us, delved into his pocket and set us up with a pint each. 'I hoped you might come in,' he said. 'Jilly's at her mother's. I'm on my own this evening.'

'You could have come round,' I said. 'You know where we live.' I felt rather than saw Will turn to look at me in surprise. I hadn't told him that David had been inside his bungalow in his absence.

But it was Will who asked the civilized question that had to come next. 'What are you doing about eating?'

'Don't know,' David said. 'I might get some fish and chips later.'

'We could all do that,' said Will. 'Eat them round at our place.'

'I had a big lunch,' I said. But I said it as a matter of form only and the others ignored it. We all knew that wasn't going to put me off fish and chips.

In the meantime we found a table by one of the big windows and installed ourselves there with our pints. We looked out across the beach and the Channel's great blue horizontal paint-splash. 'Hey,' said Will, 'you can see the hump.'

'I've seen it twelve times today,' said David in a world-weary voice. 'Six times going over and six coming back.'

'Will hasn't,' I felt obliged to point out. 'Though that might be all about to change.' I stopped. 'Sorry, Will. Perhaps I shouldn't have said that.'

'It's all right,' Will said. 'Though might-be is still all it is.'

'Ah,' said David. 'Is this anything to do with…? There was some top-secret invention you weren't allowed to tell me about…'

'Can we tell him?' I asked Will. In a beseeching tone of voice

'I suppose so,' Will said. I easily saw through his pretence of reluctance. He was as eager to let David know about the Shackle-it as I was. 'In a week or so everyone will know anyway. Whichever way it goes.'

'It'll go fine,' I told Will. 'You know that. You're not going to lose on this.'

'I hope you are going to tell me,' said David. 'Now we've come this far I'll be very pissed off if you don't.'

Will laughed. Then he and I told David the story together, Will being very over-modest about the thing and me constantly building him and his achievement up. I hardly need to write that David was enormously impressed.

'What time are you in tomorrow?' I asked David.

'Not till two o'clock.'

'Same here,' I said.

'I know that,' David said. 'We're flying to Ostend together. Didn't you know that? Didn't you look?'

'I did,' I said. 'I did know but it slipped my mind. My mother came to lunch.'

David nodded understandingly. 'I can see that might have had that effect.'

'I'm in at nine,' said Will.

'Aaaah,' said David in a falling cadence. The universal expression of mock pathos. But I saw him drop a hand beneath the table and for an unhurried second rub Will's leg with it. I saw Will twinkle a smile back at him. And I realised with a degree of pleasure as well as surprise how the evening was going to turn out.

TWENTY-FOUR

We ate the fish and chips in the kitchen. It was still light outside but the garden had cooled down somewhat. I noticed David's right knee was vibrating up and down as he sat at the table and ate. I read in it an unconscious expression of his tension and excitement. Will had noticed it too, evidently. 'You've left one of your engines running,' he said and we all snickered at that.

When Will and I had sex with Mike it all went very smoothly. Mike was always gently in charge of things – though so gently that you were hardly aware of the fact. But now it was different, because it was David. When I flew with a different Captain everything was somehow exactly the same yet oddly different. Different Captains landed slightly differently, and their take-offs were like individuals' unique autographs. They had different ways of carrying out the S-turns required to join the Decca straight-line routes between the beacons. But tonight, with David joining Will and me for the first time it was more than just having a new Captain. It was like having a Captain who had only just joined the fleet. More than that. We were in a situation that would have been unthinkable in any aircraft: it wasn't actually clear that David would be the Captain of the operations that were to follow; none of us was sure who the Captain was.

Will stood up from the table first. He screwed up our empty chip-wrappings and binned them, and quickly took the empty tea mugs over to the sink. Then he came back and, standing beside his chair, wrapped an arm round David's shoulder. Will was clearly the Captain of the moment. It made sense. We were in his house and he was the master of it.

David read the signal easily. He stood up and put one of his arms round Will, while holding the other out towards me, inviting me to join in their embrace. I was already out of my chair by then. Within a second we were in a three-way clinch. Indiscriminately kissing cheeks and lips. Nuzzling heads and stroking backs. Then after a moment or two, pressing hard cocks against one another's through our shorts.

Then David said to Will, 'I'm sure you know I've got a black eye. Walked into a cupboard and it looks awful.'

'You should see the state of the cupboard,' I said facetiously. The others took no notice.

'Are you OK if I take the glasses off?' David asked.

'Yes,' said Will softly. David removed them and laid them on the table beside him without turning his head away from Will and myself. 'You look fine,' Will told David. Unexpected, it had been an intimate and telling moment.

Then I was aware of Will feeling David's stiff cock through his shorts. I said, 'You won't need to compare them. You're both the same size exactly. Though there is one difference.'

'What's that?' they both asked at once.

'You'll see in a minute,' I told them. And within that minute, by which time we had moved into Will's bedroom and were tearing one another's clothes off, they had.

'You're cut,' Will said.

'And you're not,' said David. The three of us laughed and we tumbled together naked onto the bed.

'What did you two do in Calais?' Will asked.

David said, 'Looked at the sea. Had a beer at the Café de Paris…'

Will said, 'In bed, you twat,' and David laughed.

I said, 'David fucked me. It was very nice.'

'Then perhaps he'll fuck me now,' Will said.

I felt rather than heard David's nervous intake of breath. 'Perhaps you'd like to fuck me first, Will. I've never… You know. And Jack's a bit big.'

'Not that big,' I qualified. 'You should see Mike's.'

'Next time perhaps,' David said and rolled round onto his front.

Will said, 'I want to do it front to front,' and started to try to turn him back.

'My eye,' David explained.

'I'll look into the other one,' Will said. 'It's blue enough for both.'

That was true. Between the two of them Will and David had the brightest collection of blue eyes I'd ever seen. (Mike's, as already noted, and Paul's too, were a lustrous brown. Mine, for the sake of completeness, were hazel. And still are.)

There was going to be a problem here, I saw. A problem for me, that was. With Will and David locked together face to face there wasn't going to be an easy way for me to get involved. I might have athletically mounted Will from behind and experimentally tried to fuck him while he fucked David but I doubted that I was enough of a gymnast to manage it, and I was quite sure that Will would not welcome it.

David resolved my difficulty. He didn't actually say, 'I have control,' but he became Captain of the moment. He reached his hand towards me as I lay on my side next to the two of them and said, 'Come here, Jack. I need your cock.'

I pushed it towards him and at the same moment Will, having made his preparations with a finger, started to enter David. I couldn't see this very clearly but it was evident from David's startled grunts. So David found himself suddenly the Captain of two cocks at once: mine in his fingers and Will's in his arse.

Will came unusually quickly, and that set me off. ('That's gone bloody everywhere,' David said.) Then Will sat up on his haunches, still plugged into David, and between us he and I brought David off. It was the first time I'd seen David ejaculate, as opposed to feeling him doing it inside me. He didn't shoot a great distance the way Mike and Will and I did. Instead it poured rapidly out of him like ketchup from a squeezy bottle: a great quantity that turned his belly into a shining lake.

We got under the sheets together once we'd cleaned ourselves up and snuggled together for a bit. But it was barely dusk outside and far too soon to go to sleep for the night.

'Will your wife be phoning to check you're all right?' Will asked David.

'I thought of that,' David said. 'I phoned her myself. To check she'd arrived all right. I told her I'd be going out and might meet up with mates. She'd interpret that as meaning I'd be out late.'

'It's not late yet,' I pointed out. 'We're not flying till tomorrow afternoon. We could go to the pub for a final pint.'

'The Pilot?' Will queried doubtfully.

'I thought the Railway Hotel,' I said. Then to David, 'Do they know you there?'

David said, 'Not yet,' so we got out of bed and put our clothes back on and headed out in Will's Mini with me driving it. Rather recklessly I must admit.

We had our pints, sitting together round a small table in the linoleum-floored public bar, and found that we couldn't help giggling each time we caught one another's eyes. (As no-one knew him in here David hadn't bothered with the sunglasses.) The joke was that nobody among the considerable number in the Railway Hotel this Sunday night would have dreamed in a million years what the three of us had got up to in bed together just before coming out.

When we arrived back at the bungalow David said it was a shame he had to drive home on his own after he'd had such a good time with us. That was Will's cue to ask him to share a bed with us for the rest of the night and David accepted the offer without the smallest show of reticence.

It was good to be back in bed again together, the three of us. We all gently wanked one another off again and then went to sleep.

In the morning Will had to get up early and go to work. He gave his blessing to David and me in almost the same words he'd used the morning after he and Mike and I had spent our first night together. 'Now you two can have a lie-in together and a wank. No fucking, mind, or I'll be jealous. I'll be thinking of you in the car. See you at work.' Then he leaned down across the bed and kissed us both. After he'd gone David and I carried out his instructions to the letter.

We got up late and slowly. We sat about in the garden in our shorts and drank coffee and talked. Eventually it was time for David to go back to his house in order, as he put it, 'to clean the teeth and get into uniform.' He'd done the rest of his ablutions at our place. I remembered, luckily, that my bike was still chained up in the airport car park, and David said he'd call in on his way back and pick me up. 'Providing that won't cause a problem with Mike,' he added.

'Shouldn't do,' I said. 'Anyway, he said he'd drive straight into work when he got back from Hampshire.' And that was exactly what he did. Quite by chance David and I found ourselves following his car along the access road. We parked next to each other in the car park. Paul got out through the passenger door of Mike's car at the same time I emerged from David's. We all greeted one another with cheery smiles and how-are-yous. Any awkwardness was kept well out of sight, hidden beneath the surface.

Any awkwardness? I couldn't speak for the others at that point. But for me at any rate there was a hell of a lot of it.

But now there was work to be done. I had to fly six trips to Le Touquet and back with Captain Wimbush before nine o'clock tonight, David was on the Calais run – with Paul! – while Mike was also doing the Le Tooks run, with somebody else as co-pilot.

When I finally finished Mike was waiting for me in the crew room. 'Thought you might like a lift home,' he said. 'Unless you particularly want to ride your bike…'

'I'd love a lift,' I said. If Mike wanted to raise difficult issues with me in the car, like who had slept with whom over the weekend, then so be it. But he didn't. And I certainly did not.

But I did put my hand on his thigh as he drove (it was a far easier reach than in a Superfreighter cockpit) and, since he seemed perfectly happy with that, I went on and wedged it in between his legs, lightly tickling his balls and cock through the fabric of his trousers.

'I love you,' Mike said simply. 'My little Jack.'

'I love you too,' I said. I hesitated for a second before adding the next bit but then I said it anyway. 'My little Mike.' He didn't reply to that, but a tiny noise of contentment escaped his half closed lips and I was more than happy about that. Least said, soonest mended is a truism that doesn't always fit the case. But in this instance it did. Back at the bungalow a similar rapprochement occurred between Will and Mike. Then we sat down and ate the late supper Will had shopped for earlier: an omelette with ham and cheese in it, and new bread. Undeterred by the cheese and new bread we went to bed soon after we'd washed up, and masturbated one another to contented climaxes before dropping off to sleep, the three of us together in Mike's bed.

Two days later I was offered another unusual assignment. I told the others about it. 'It involves a night away,' I said. 'Take it,' they both said. More doubtfully I added, 'In a hotel with David.' There was a moment's pause. Then Will said, 'Just do it.' And immediately after he'd spoken Mike echoed the advice. 'Yes, do it.' But I thought I detected some complex feelings lurking in his voice.

The job was a similar deal to the cheese run from Le Touquet, except this one involved Ostend, not Le Tooks, and instead of cheese, race horses. We would fly an empty plane out to Ostend at the end of the evening's work. The plane would already be fitted with a removable wooden floor which was kept in the hangar stores especially for the purpose, and then the floor would be covered with straw – several bales of which had been ordered in specially. A night in a hotel … then David and I would fly two priceless Arab stallions back to Lydd. A groom would travel in the hold with them, keeping them calm but not himself strapped in or harnessed. We were told he would fly standing up. We promised to be extra gentle with the landing and take-off.

On the day of the flight out David and I met in the crew room. We'd both done a few flights during the day but not together. This was the first time we'd been teamed up since… Well, we'd shared a bed more recently than we'd shared a cockpit.

'Weather's all right,' David told me as I walked in. He looked up from the chart. We were the only two people in the room.

'You've dispensed with the sunglasses,' I said.

'I thought it was time,' said David. 'It doesn't look too bad now, does it?' he asked.

'No it doesn't.' It didn't look *too* bad, that was true. If a few dark crayon-like streaks of purple and a general hue of yellow ochre surrounding the eye-socket could be considered not too bad. But it still looked bad enough. I didn't tell David that. 'How did you really do it?' I asked instead.

'Oh God.' David looked around him. We were still alone together. 'It's too embarrassing…'

'You can tell me,' I said. 'I've already made my own wild guess.'

'OK. But I haven't told anybody else.'

'No,' I said. 'And I won't. Not even Will or Mike…. Or Paul,' I added as an afterthought.

David looked at the door again, then said, 'It was after we'd flown to Blackbushe together and you'd told me about Will and Mike. And you and I had … touched each other in the cockpit. Afterwards – I have to admit – I felt quite … sexed up … isn't that the expression? Maybe. Anyway … I did something I'd never done before. I stopped off on the way home on the edge of the recreation ground…'

'By the public toilets,' I helped him out.

'You guessed.' His face now wore a resigned look. It seemed to say: telling you this is going to embarrass me horribly but so be it. 'Well, to put it briefly, I stood next to someone who looked nice – and also encouraging if you understand what I mean.' I gave him a nod to show that I did. 'I stood back a pace in order to… Oh fuck, this is embarrassing…'

'No, I understand,' I said.

'I'd misread him, of course. He took a swipe at my face. It wasn't too bad; he wasn't a hard hitter. I didn't end up on the floor and the skin didn't break. The chap zipped himself up quickly and fled.'

'Oh God, I'm sorry.' I wanted to take hold of him and give him a quick cuddle but in the place we were in I dared not. 'What did you tell your wife?' I asked instead.

'She wasn't home when I got in, thank God. I had time to compose myself. I told her the cupboard door story, same as I told everybody else.'

'Did she believe you?'

David shrugged and looked quickly at the door again.

'She didn't have much choice.'

'No, I suppose not.' I asked, 'When's she due back?'

'Five more days. I think I told you she was going to be away for over a week.'

I did a rough calculation based on other people's experience. 'I think you'll be looking fine by then,' I said.

'Looking fine.' He said it in a particular way that was meant to imply: but perhaps not feeling it. I nodded sympathetically to indicate that I'd heard the unspoken end of the sentence. Then someone came in and David returned smoothly to the weather forecast. 'Bit of a sea fret coming and going on the North Sea coast.'

Ostend lies on the North Sea, not the Channel. It's a fact we ignore in ordinary conversation. But there is an actual line drawn on marine charts. It runs from the north end of St Margaret's Bay, about four miles north-east of Dover, to the Walde lighthouse four miles east of Calais. So Calais, Boulogne, Le Tooks, Lydd, Folkestone and Dover are Channel towns and Channel ports. Deal, Sandwich, Ramsgate, Dunkirk and Ostend are not. They are, strictly speaking, North Sea ports or coastal towns instead.

'Right,' I said. 'Fog on the North Sea coast.'

It was a beautiful late afternoon when we set off. Dover cliffs and Cap Gris Nez came into sight almost as soon as we'd levelled off. When we were lined up on the Decca heading for Ostend I reached out and laid my hand on David's leg. It had become a habit. I did it when I flew with David, I did it when I flew with Mike. I had to make a conscious effort not to do it when flying with

Wimbush or one of the others. God knows what would have been the outcome if I had!

But a moment later I took my hand away. I'd been struck by a new thought. 'Can I drive for a bit?' I asked. The way an eager teenager asks a parent. I added, 'Mike sometimes lets me,' as an afterthought.

'Well, if Mike says yes then who am I to refuse you? Permission to take control granted.'

'I have control,' I said immediately and applied both my hands to the yoke.

'Scylla and Charybdis,' I said when, five minutes later, I flew us between the two white capes.

'Scylla and Charybdis,' David echoed. Neither of us added anything. We didn't need to delve through the many layers of subtext.

I flew us past Calais docks and past the airport, clearly visible today a couple of miles to the right. Then David called up the Ostend control tower. He reported our position and asked about the fog. Through my own headphones I heard their response. It wasn't too bad, they said, but unpredictable. The runway would be completely clear for ten minutes, then the mist would roll in from the sea again and visibility would be poor for the next ten minutes. By now we could see the nearer edge of the fog bank ahead of us. It lay over the sea like a white quilt whose edge has been heavily chewed by dogs, but it ended almost immediately at the coast. However, that frayed coastal edge was far from tidy. In places it strayed inland a mile or more. And Ostend's runway lay less than half a mile from the beach.

I saw David peering thoughtfully through the windscreen. I knew what he was going to say as soon as he spoke. 'Would you be very offended if I asked you to give me the aircraft back? It's just that...'

'Of course, of course,' I said. 'Mike would have said the same. You have control.'

'I have control,' David said. I relinquished the yoke. I didn't return my hand to David's leg. Some serious flying lay ahead of us and we both needed to concentrate.

By the time we were two miles from Ostend we were already flying over the fog. This was the moment to leave the straight-line track and turn onto the downwind leg, travelling two miles beyond the airport, then turning back to land upwind from the east. We could still see where we were on the Decca's handy rolling map, and the altimeters told us our height. But we couldn't actually touch down unless the runway was in sight.

Suddenly it was. Just as we were passing the runway, flying parallel to it on our downwind leg, the fog rolled back and gave me a clear view of it directly to my right. 'I'm visual,' I told David. 'Runway two miles off on right. Three o'clock.'

'Tell tower that,' David said. 'Tell them we're visual and will land in three minutes. If we have to go around we'll make a second attempt. If that fails we'll go back to Calais.' I relayed all that to the tower and they acknowledged it. By now the runway had disappeared behind us.

David began the turn a minute later and a minute after that we were lined up. We began to descend from our thousand feet. The runway lay directly ahead of us but there was no sign of it, although the inland countryside was tantalisingly visible – clear and green – less than a mile away on the left.

We continued to descend but the fog refused to give way as we approached; it clung as if by its fingertips to the ground ahead of us. I heard David breathe out. 'Prepare for go around,' he said. I could hear the tension of the moment in his voice.

Maybe five seconds passed in silence as we surrendered our precious altitude foot by foot. They were some of the longest seconds of my life, but at the end of them the white quilt below us was still opaque and thick. 'Go around!' David called loudly, suddenly, and in unison we pulled hard back on our yokes.

The roar of the engines grew deafening in our ears, but slowly, oh so slowly, when we longed for the sound to rise even more rapidly in pitch. But the seconds passed and the nose went up and at last the forty thousand horsepower of our two Bristol Hercules engines tugged us upwards, away from the seething foggy softness and the unforgiving ground beneath.

David and I heaved the largest, longest sighs I'd ever heard from either of us, then David got on the radio to the tower himself. 'You have control,' he told me. 'Head out to sea. Level at a thousand feet.'

The tower cleared us for a second approach. They suggested that this time we flew a longer downwind leg to give the sea-fret time to roll back in our absence. There was no traffic at our level within twenty miles going east, they said. David said, 'Over and out,' then spoke to me. 'I have control,' he said. In the calmest voice. I took an invisible hat off.

'Now where shall I take you for the next ten minutes or so?' he asked as he turned the plane, by now over the sea, back to the downwind heading towards the east. 'I know. I'll show you Bruges,' he said. 'Fifteen miles downwind will take us there. Circuit the town then fly back. If we can't get down this time we'll continue on and land at Calais.' He chuckled. 'Another night at the Georges Cinq'. And I chuckled too, despite my recent frightening encounter with the fog and its tentacles, and my apprehension about the next one – which was due in about twelve minutes.

David adjusted our heading to a few degrees south of east and within a minute we were over the land and clear of the fog. Then I saw it. It was on the right so I saw it first. Bruges lay flat on the flat landscape like a bejewelled pendant. It hung suspended from the North Sea fog by its Sea Canal as if on a silver wire thread. A lozenge-shaped frame of canals encased it, and smaller canals threaded their way through it, like the silver partitions in cloisonné enamel-work. We crossed the big Sea Canal and David began his cartwheel circuit, making the town revolve beneath us. And as we came round it and the sun swung round behind us the silver water changed like magic into blue. The precious jewel was now enclosed in sapphire; sapphires threaded it, and it hung out of the fog on a ribbon of blue water. No medieval alchemist could have conjured such magic.

We were close enough to see church spires and belfries, market squares and old red rooftops. 'It's wonderful,' I said childishly. I felt myself welling up inside the way I'd done when David had flown me around my home village. Mercifully I spilled no tears on this occasion. I wanted to say, 'Take me there, David. I want to see it.' But I didn't. I just said thank you. Though David got the message. In a way, of course, it was he who'd sent it.

By now we were heading back towards Ostend. We left the fairytale little city behind us. I announced our imminent landing to the control tower. They told us the fog had cleared a bit.

Within a minute or two, during which we re-did our pre-landing checks, we could see the fog again ahead of us. But this time there was a gap in its ragged landward edge and after a moment's careful looking for it we saw the airport runway appear in the gap blearily, like someone coming to a window when they've just woken up.

'Stay there, runway,' I heard David say. 'Fog, don't move. All the same,' this was addressed to me, 'stand by for go around.'

'Standing by,' I said.

We lined up neatly, or rather David did, and pushed forward into our final descent. The runway stayed in sight, though it seemed to slither among foggy tentacles, and we went on down towards it, hearts in mouths. But neither of us felt the need to call Go Around and at last our wheels smacked lightly but reassuringly onto the tarmac. 'Well done, Captain,' I said soberly as soon as our landing roll was finished.

'Well done yourself,' David said.

'I didn't do anything.' I heard the conversation turning into a repeat of the one we'd had in Calais after the engine failure.

'Yes you did.'

TWENTY-FIVE

The airport manager and our Ostend handling agent were quite blasé about our encounter with the foggy element. Unlike us they had not been up there. They hadn't lived through it. They had other news for us. The racehorses would not be ready in the morning.

'It's all been taken care of,' the handling agent assured us. 'The plane stays here. You'll be taking off the day after tomorrow, late morning. In the meantime you get two nights in a hotel, plus all expenses. Paid for by the owner.'

'The owner?' I queried.

'Of the racehorses.'

'I wonder,' said David in his most Captain-like tone, 'if they'd stretch to letting us stay in Bruges for the two nights. Since we've got a whole day to kill before we fly back.'

The handling agent didn't blink. 'I'm sure that'll be fine, gentlemen,' he said

'It needn't be two separate rooms,' David went on smoothly, outrageously. 'We won't mind sharing. Will we, Jack?'

'How did you know I was longing to go to Bruges?' I asked as soon as we'd dismissed ourselves and were heading off to look for the taxi that had been ordered for us.

'I read your mind these days my darling,' David answered.

'That makes three of you, then' I said. 'Because Mike and Will do too.'

The taxi took us to Ostend's station and there we caught a train to Bruges. We spoke English at the ticket office and were understood easily. Fortunately. David told me the inhabitants of this northern half of Belgium didn't like to be addressed in French, and neither of us – in common with most of humanity – spoke a word of Flemish Dutch.

We travelled through a countryside that gave the Romney Marsh a run for its money for flatness. Haymaking was over and the corn was ripening, and the only perpendiculars were poplars. Until we came in sight of our destination; then spires and bell towers pierced up through the landscape.

The Hotel de Londres, our billet for the next two nights was almost next to the station. We checked in. They didn't ask us if we would prefer a double or a twin room. They gave us a double as a matter of course.

What do you do when you check into a hotel room when you're a newish couple? You roll on the bed together and have a cuddle. Mike and I had done that in Le Touquet. David and I had done it in Calais. We did it again now. Only this time we took all our clothes off.

On leaving our grand hotel a little later we stepped across a bridge… It straddled the canal we'd seen from the air: the oval frame that had first appeared silver and then turned blue; the frame that encased the town. We stepped across the little bridge … and within seconds were in a different world and a different century.

There were hardly any cars, though there were bicycles. We walked in the stillness and quiet of a vanished age. Among buildings that were seldom tall; built of narrow Flemish bricks and centuries old. Windows with Gothic arches peered narrowly at us from every wall; there were ancient wooden doors. Every corner we turned among the disorienting crooked streets brought us to the bank of another silver-thread canal and another impossibly picturesque view. And on every stretch of water, however meagre, sailed a swan.

We navigated by keeping eyes open for the Belfort, the nearly three-hundred-foot belfry tower. It appeared helpfully from time to time at the ends of streets or between the roof-line's crow-step gables. We reached it eventually but it had closed for the evening. 'Climb that tomorrow?' David asked as we stood in the wide space that was the Great Market.

'I should say so,' I answered. I wasn't too happy about climbing narrow spiral stairs but with David I knew I would go anywhere. But for now it was time to return to our hotel and dine.

Although it was a hot summer evening we feasted on a stew of beef and dark local beer. Then raspberries with meringue and cream.

'I show you a nice bar after,' a voice beside our table said. 'Where you can try some good beer.' I looked round, slightly alarmed. An attractive blond young man of about my age stood there. When he saw the expression on my face he grinned. 'It is all right. I am the son of the hotel. My name is Dierick.'

David and I were about to get to our feet anyway. We did so now and introduced ourselves. Dierick asked conversationally, 'Are you two boyfriends?'

We hid our confusion in splutters of laughter. Quite apart from the complicated nature of our actual relationship we were still in pilots' uniforms. But we looked at each other and nodded. We'd been to the bank at the airport and changed some money into Belgian francs. Enough for a few beers at least. Tomorrow would have to take care of itself. David said to Dierick, 'Lead the way, amigo.'

We returned across the canal to the old centre and were once again enfolded by the Middle Ages. Dierick took us to the oldest bar in town. The Café Vlissinghe went back five hundred years. With beamed ceilings and dark wainscoted walls, oak chairs and refectory tables it looked as it might have done in Shakespeare's day. Or in Rubens's. Dierick told us how Rubens had painted a picture of a coin on a table here in payment for an evening's beer and then fled. A moment later we were greeting, being greeted by, sitting down among, a cohort of Dierick's friends and acquaintances.

The evening became a blur of conversation – in perfect English – and Belgian beer. I remember that one of Dierick's friends was known as Beastie, on account of his long black ponytail. Some of the gang were homosexual, I guessed. But if so the fact seemed to be of no importance among such a relaxed and convivial drinking group.

David and I pulled away eventually and meandered back to our hotel through winding ways half lit by street-lights. There was a moment when we seemed completely lost, but then the sound of a late train drew us back to our intended route.

It must have been that moment of uncertainty (lost in the sixteenth century darkness) that made David say, 'There's something about what happened to us this afternoon... You know, being up there and wishing you were down here and not sure how you're going to do it...'

'I know,' I said.

'When you're with someone ... with someone who means something to you...'

'I know,' I said.

'Um...' David sounded as though another difficult confession was coming out. But it wasn't quite like that. Or in a way perhaps it was. He went on, a bit awkwardly, 'I actually brought something I wanted to read to you. On that very subject. Written by Saint Exupéry. You know who I mean?'

'Yes,' I said. 'French aviator pioneer before the War.'

'He wrote about his experiences creating the air routes across the Sahara. In a book called Terre des Hommes. We studied it at school. I ... er ... made my own translation of a passage that ... that spoke to me.' Then in an even more diffident voice he asked, 'May I read it to you?'

'Of course,' I said. To my surprise he fished a flimsy piece of paper out of his pocket there and then and started to open it up. We stopped beneath a street-lamp.

David unfolded the paper carefully. 'When I brought this with me I didn't know what was going to happen this afternoon. So it's... Well anyway.

'Exupéry was flying along the West-African coast with a co-pilot called Néri. They were running late and it got dark and they got lost. Looking for an airstrip called Cisneros. But the only lights they could see turned out to be rising stars. He calls the lights *hameçons*, which means silver lures or fishing hooks. He radios the airstrip at Cisneros and tells them to turn their lights off and on three times. They do this, but none of the lights that the pilots can see stop shining continuously. Néri and Exupéry have the feeling of being lost forever among the stars.'

David straightened the paper and positioned himself beneath the lamp in the corner of the crooked alleyway. 'Sorry about the translation,' he said. 'It's just schoolboy...'

'Read it,' I said. 'It's OK.'

And David read as follows:

'From then on we felt as though we were lost in interplanetary space, among these inaccessible planets, searching for the only true planet, our own one, the one which alone contained our familiar landscapes, our friendly homes and all we held dear.

'The one which alone held... I'll tell you the picture that came to my mind, and which may to you appear

puerile. But in the midst of danger we still have human needs and I was thirsty, I was hungry. If we made it to Cisneros we would go on with the journey once we had refuelled, and land at Casablanca in the cool of dawn. Job done! Néri and I would go into town. You can find some little bistros there that are already open at daybreak... Néri and I would sit down at a table, feeling nice and safe, and laugh about the night just gone, over the hot croissants and white coffee. We would celebrate this morning gift of life. Just as an old peasant woman can only connect with her God by means of a painted picture, a simple pendant or a rosary: we have to be spoken to in simple terms if we are to understand.'

At that point David's voice cracked and he had to stop. I reached out and touched the knuckles of one of his hands; it was clenched tightly on his paper scrap. 'Go on,' I said quietly. And after a moment, though with difficulty, he did.

'So it was that the joys of life would gather themselves all together for me in this first heady, steaming mouthful, in this assembly of milk and coffee and corn, with which we make communion with quiet pastures, with distant plantations, and with harvest-time; with which we make communion with all the earth. Among all those stars there was only one, just one, where might be found within the reach of our hands this fragrant dawn breakfast bowl.

'But unbridgeable distances were multiplying between our craft and that peopled earth. All the riches of the world were housed in a single grain of dust, lost among the constellations. And the navigator, Néri, who was trying to pick it out, continued to beseech the stars...

I stopped David with a kiss planted firmly on his mouth. I heard the paper he'd been reading from crackle between our chests. We stayed where we were for some time. Then we were standing, mouths just far enough to speak with, clasping hands. The crumpled paper David had been reading from was sandwiched between his fingers and mine.

'It's difficult…' I heard David try to say.

'I know,' I said. 'More for you… But also for me…'

'I know that too.'

'You read that beautifully. A beautiful translation…' I too was having trouble with my words.

I felt David's arms and his whole body shake. He said, 'I love you.'

'I love you too,' I answered. Then we took each other in a tight embrace that prevented us both from saying more. David's piece of paper, his schoolboy translation slipped to the ground. We would pick it up when we were ready for it.

The next morning I drank my steaming fragrant bowl of coffee and chicory in the hotel dining room and dunked my croissants into it, sitting opposite David across a white linen tablecloth while the sun streamed towards us through the big windows…

When David was born – when Mike was born, a couple of months later in the same year – nobody had ever flown the Atlantic in winter time. The air routes around the empires of the great powers were still being mapped out by grand brave men like Saint Exupéry. When the Atlantic finally had to be tackled in the winter it was because of the dreadful exigencies of War. And among the first men to fly that corridor of winter seas and fog and cold – between Newfoundland and Ireland – was the founder of our own company, Silver City, Taffy Powell. Even to think of him and of Saint Exupéry and the other great pilots of their generation humbled me. Flying a freighter across the Channel or North Sea was nothing in comparison. I was a pygmy who merely rode on the shoulders of great men, of giants.

The sun shone so brightly on the vapour arising from my coffee that I could make out the individual droplets of the steam. The sun brought me the warm and homely fragrance of the fresh croissants on the table. I was not surprised that Saint Exupéry, when lost in the dark sky above Africa and wondering if he would live beyond the next few hours, should think about his breakfast in terms that were so existential, sacramental.

While opposite me sat David, rather silent this morning just as I was, and wondering what the future held for us. It had been wonderful to tell each other we loved each other, wonderful to hear those words *I love you* on each other's lips. It had been magical to finish our short walk back to the hotel walking through the night-lit streets hand in hand. To share our double bed with its pristine linen sheets. To make avid love between them and render them less pristine.

To say *I love you,* though, was all very well. But David loved his wife and would soon be in love with, enraptured with, his as yet unborn child. While I loved Will and Mike and had told them so. I thought again of Saint Exupéry. Of him and his navigator Néri heading through the vast emptiness of night towards one star after another in the hope that one might turn out to be an airfield light – the one true landing ground. It had worked out all right in the end for Saint Exupéry and Néri that night. The lights of the Cisneros airstrip had been veiled in mist. At last the mist had rolled back and the airstrip lights had revealed themselves, shining towards them from the left, many miles away. Just as the airport of Ostend had shown itself to David and me through the mist yesterday…

But now. This morning my heart was flying without compass or other guidance, without any idea where it could find a safe landing ground, towards star after beautiful star.

Across the table I heard David sigh. I looked at him and he smiled. 'This morning I still love you, Jack. But it's difficult, isn't it?'

'Who's ever said love was easy?' I answered equally fatuously.

'Amen,' said David. I looked again at the breakfast bowls and the croissants and thought again of Saint Exupéry and his metaphor of a holy communion with all that spoke of life and living and humanity. 'It's all right,' said David gently. 'No need to cry.'

We spent the day in the heart of the little city, enveloped in the Middle Ages and the glories of a vanished time as if we were flies inside a beautiful piece of amber. We toured the great cathedral and studied the swans. We walked among the gingerbread houses of the nunnish Beguinage. Then we climbed the Belfort beside the Grote Markt, squeezing up the ever narrowing scary stairs. I teetered on the edge of panic as we climbed towards the unseen exit at the top. But I refused to fall. I'd landed through a thick fog blanket yesterday. I'd ridden down to Calais on one engine. The founder of the company I worked for had been among the first to confront the terrors of the winter Atlantic in a fragile 1930s aeroplane... I had David with me.

At last we stood upon the pinnacle, eye level with falcons and looking down on cathedral spires. The whole of Belgium lay spread beneath us. A dull gleam, a horizontal graphite-pencil line, marked the position of the distant North Sea. The fog had cleared. And I had David with me.

In the evening we met up again with Dierick and his friends. They proudly took us round from bar to bar. We learnt to navigate the lengthy lists of Belgian beers. Beers in small bright glasses, a differently shaped goblet for every brand. Beers that shone brightly, copper, amber and gold. Glasses that twinkled, and beckoned us like the stars.

We returned the next day to Ostend airport. By train, then taxi. And then at eleven o'clock we picked up our plane. We met the stable-lad, a handsome boy, and helped him load the two racehorses. Told him to hold tightly to the cockpit ladder on take-off and landing. Promised that as it was his first time we'd be gentle with him. Then we flew up into a cloudless, fog-free sky.

After we'd landed we said goodbye to our thoroughbred cargo, and to the groom. He thanked us for giving him a smooth ride. 'Any time,' David told him – with what I thought a rather flirtatious grin.

Then David and I parted company. David had an afternoon of flights to Calais and back to work through. With Paul. While I was on the Le Touquet run. With none other than Captain Evans.

There was no sign of either Mike or Will when I finished. Nor were their cars in the car park. I unchained my bicycle and cycled home.

Both my official lovers were in the garden when I got back, relaxed and in shorts and drinking tea. But they stiffened up rather when they saw me – I'm talking about their demeanour, not their dicks, here. However they both smiled at me and got up from their chairs. I got a hug from each of them. We did that in the garden these days; we'd ceased to worry about what neighbours might think or say. Will said, 'I'll make a fresh pot of tea,' and went inside. That left Mike and me.

'You had a good time then,' Mike said. We were still standing close, still touching hands.

'Yes. Once we'd pulled ourselves together after our fright in the fog. David and I…'

'Yes,' said Mike, smiling. 'I understand.' Then he paused and looked slightly uncomfortable. 'We had Paul round while you were away.'

'Oh,' I said. 'Well, that was nice. Did he stay?'

'Yes.'

'Which night?' I asked conversationally.

'Both,' Mike said. Then he must have seen my face fall though I'd tried not to let it do that. 'Does that make it worse or better?' he enquired gently.

Miserably I answered, 'I don't know.'

Anthony McDonald

TWENTY-SIX

We didn't mention the Paul thing during the rest of that evening. It was actually a very convivial, very nice evening. It was Mike's turn to cook, and he had done the newly fashionable Italian dish that was called Spaghetti Bolognese. He served it with grated cheddar on top and it was a spectacular success.

Yet when it came to bedtime I discovered that I didn't feel like romping with the other two or even snuggling up with them for the night. 'I'm not feeling my best,' I said. 'Do you mind if I don't join you in bed? I can sleep on the sofa if you like.'

'Don't be ridiculous,' said Mike. 'You're not sleeping on the sofa. You get some shut-eye in my bed if you're out of sorts. I'll sleep with Will. We don't need three separate beds!'

'We never will do,' said Will, which I thought was wonderfully sweet of him.

Then Mike said, 'Any physical symptoms? Do you need anything from the medicine chest? Aspirin? Beecham's powder? Alka-seltzer?'

'No. I'm just a bit shattered after the episode in Belgium. I mean the fog landing,' I added hastily. 'Too much adrenalin all at once.'

'I understand that,' said Mike. 'You get a quiet night's sleep. You'll be fine tomorrow.'

'We'll have an extra one on your behalf,' said Will, grinning cheekily.

'Thanks pal,' I said and grinned back.

But when I'd got into Mike's bed on my own I found myself lying awake and trying to make sense of what I felt and thought. I loved David and seemed to be falling in love with him. But I couldn't bear the thought of splitting up with Will and Mike. Supposing I left them and that that departure of mine should then break them up? I couldn't bear to think about that. I loved them both too dearly. Yes, I was deeply in love with them both.

As for David, what could the future hold for a relationship with him when he already had a wife – who would be back home in a few days? And an unborn son or daughter, who would dispense with their unborn status a few months later. The truth was that I didn't know what I wanted. I decided I needed to focus on that and to try and find out just what I did want. A little thought tapped at the back door of my mind: namely that I wasn't giving any consideration to what the other people involved might want. But that would have made the issue far too complicated. I left that little thought shut out.

The next day we all finished early and met up in the Wingspan Club. When I say all of us I mean Mike and Will, David and Paul and myself. There were other people there of course. There was much talk about the imminent arrival of the first Carvair. It would be flying in from Blackbushe tomorrow afternoon, ready for its first flight – it was known in the business as a 'proving' flight – to Geneva and back the day after that. Again I found myself hoping I might get picked for training to fly the Carvairs during the winter and so keep my job. David and Paul were already members of the permanent complement of pilots. Mike had heard just two days ago that he was going to be kept on over the winter at least. I had heard nothing yet. I was the only one whose future with the company was still in doubt.

Well actually, not quite the only one. In a different way that applied to Will also. The board meeting that would decide his fate lay just about four days away I thought. Although Davies had assured Will that the matter was pretty well sewn up I knew that nothing was fixed until it was fixed. The opera wasn't over till the fat lady sang… I'd heard that expression and it had made me laugh. But there was a great truth in it. Will might be going to flying school at Biggin Hill. He might be among the forty or so pilots who would work out of Lydd next summer… Or he might not.

'Why don't we all go out and eat?' My ears pricked up. That had been Mike's voice. I looked round to see who 'we all' meant. Mike had been addressing David, evidently, and Paul was at David's side. I couldn't imagine that Will and I would not be included. Presumably then, 'we all' meant the five of us. Unless Mike had in mind an even bigger party than that. At that moment Mike turned to me and Will and repeated the suggestion. He made it clear that he did mean the five of us.

We had one more pint each, then drove off in convoy, taking care with the dog's-leg twist in the access road over the little bridge. We went to the George in the High Street. We'd all been earning good money this month – long hours and extra flights to deal with the passenger numbers of high summer – and were feeling temporarily flush.

We all had steaks, after prawn cocktail appetisers, and shared a bottle of hock. That was at Paul's insistence. Most of us would have preferred a bottle of red. I had the feeling that hock wasn't an ideal accompaniment to steak. However we all drank it down happily and it was perfectly all right.

The atmosphere at that cosy table in the George, beneath the beams and the wall-bracket lights, was as pleasant as could be imagined. None of us allowed our communal cheer to be shadowed by complicated thoughts about sex or love. Or if those thoughts did cross some of our minds we made a very good job of not showing it.

I surprised myself as much as any of the others at the end of the meal by inviting both David and Paul back to the bungalow for a nightcap. Though no-one was so surprised as to suggest that wasn't a good idea, I noticed. Everybody seemed equally to want it. And as none of us was flying again till the following afternoon we didn't have to worry about the twelve-hour gap between bottle and throttle.

David insisted on calling in at the off-licence on the way back to get a new bottle of whisky. If Paul had been talking to him about events at the bungalow while he'd been with me in Belgium he was probably aware (David, that is) that there wasn't much left of the old one.

By the time the five of us were sitting around the living room, whisky glasses in hand and laughing boisterously at everything that was said by anyone, no matter how silly or inconsequential, it must have been obvious to everyone what was about to happen. The feeling was like the way you felt at the foot of the runway when the engines were spooling up to take-off power and the whole airframe was shuddering, raring to go, held to the ground only for another minute by the pressure of your foot on the pedal of the wheel brakes. You were keyed up and excited. Adrenalin was flowing. You were also, always and inevitably, a tad nervous.

Paul was, I'd discovered, the youngest of us. Younger by a month than even I was. If we were drinking together in company – that usually meant in the Wingspan Club – it would be he who showed the effects of the alcohol we were imbibing sooner than the rest of us. He always showed those effects most charmingly, though. He was at his cutest and sexiest when he was slightly tipsy. And very entertaining.

Will put the Please Please Me LP on the gramophone. And immediately the first track started Paul got up out of his chair, came over to mine and hauled me out of it. 'Shall we dance?' he asked facetiously.

I laughed, but I joined in the game. For a few seconds we stomped about the small space in a parody of dancing. The others laughed at us and shouted, 'Whoa!' and 'You'll have the table over!' and hastily grabbed their drinks away from it and our erratic orbit of it. Then we came to a stop and I saw that David had got up out of his chair. He moved close to Paul and me and put one hand on my shoulder and the other on Paul's. He said, 'May I have the pleasure of the next one?'

Neither of us answered. But Paul reached out to David's tie – except for Will we were all still in uniform – and started to un-knot it. Then David copied him, except that it was my tie that he started un-knotting. Not to be outdone I reached down and undid Paul's uniform trousers. First the waistband clip and then the zip-fastener.

It kicked off then. Will and Mike were soon all over the three of us, and within a minute all five of us were naked. I already knew what Mike and Will and David looked like without a stitch of clothing. I'd had sex with all of them and found their bodies beautiful and arousing. The only new sight – apart from the sheer wonderful novelty of it being the whole five of us – was Paul without his clothing. And, Jesus, was that something!

Paul was the quietest out of all of us, as well as the youngest. He was taller than David, Will and me, though not as tall as Mike was. But he was also wand-slender, unlike the chunkily muscled rest of us. Now, without his clothes on, he was also the most beautiful, elfin figured and, except for crotch and armpits, nearly hairless. His skin was olive toned and his cock – now outrageously extended – was the longest among all of ours. It wasn't particularly thick, but beautifully proportioned and, like David's, had been circumcised. His balls were cute and tight and almost teen-like.

Paul was the quietest out of all of us? Not now that he'd got a few drinks inside him. Three minutes ago he'd whisked me onto my feet for a boisterous cod-dance. Now he was standing on the coffee table like a naked statue of Peter Pan or Eros on a plinth. We others were taking it in turns to suck his beautiful dick. While fondling and groping one another as well, of course.

There was much talk in the early sixties of orgies. I'd never had experience of one, and nor, I was quite sure, had any of the rest of us. But now I wondered if perhaps we were in the middle of one, plunged into the heart of one almost by accident. If this was what orgies were like, then I thought I couldn't get enough of them. I was thoroughly enjoying this.

We migrated into Will's room. It was fractionally bigger than Mike's. The bed was the same size, though. And even though it was a generous size for two, and accommodated three reasonably comfortably on a nearly nightly basis, it was more than a little difficult to pile our five energetically squirming bodies onto it. Even so we somehow managed it.

It was impossible to know who, at any given moment, had a hand on my penis, or was stroking my back. I couldn't know whose hand was exploring my buttock cleft. As for whose arms and legs and erections I was exploring with my own hands, I didn't have much idea about that either. Sometimes I thought my hand had identified Mike's or Will's or David's balls or penis. But then I was uncertain. It was like trying to learn Braille, or playing Kim's Game.

I was falling for Paul, for the sheer wonderfulness of his physical form and of what I inferred to be his essence. I wanted to be all over him and into him and him in me but it was very difficult to tell in the melee which of the samples of warm and soft or soft-hard flesh that I was embracing or were embracing me belonged to him and which did not. Besides, I had the impression that when it came to falling in love with Paul's physical beauty the others, and particularly David, were experiencing the same emotions as I was and thinking the same thoughts.

'I'm going to come,' I heard David say suddenly. Breathily, urgently. I wondered if it was my own hand, busy at work on somebody's hard penis, that was about to bring him off. And then, within the space of a minute, all five of us had climaxed. None of us had fucked another of us although, with a little burrowing and some contortions, we'd managed to suck one another a bit. It ended up being mainly a massive multiple mutual hand-job, with some rubbing of cocks against thighs and bellies. When we were all emptied out we lay together, collapsed quietly into a tangled pile of ourselves, breathing rather noisily and very conscious of our wetness; none of us was talking; we were all busy wondering, I think, how it was that we'd come this far so quickly. That and what on earth we were going to do next.

Somehow we got up off the bed. It was like disentangling a box of assorted paper clips. We jostled into the bathroom and washed ourselves down a bit. Then we moved on to the stage of passing towels around among us and helping one another dry up. It was a nice example of mutual grooming. Very friendly and intimate. In the middle of that Mike said, touching both David and Paul on the naked shoulder, 'You're both very welcome to stay the night.'

I'm not sure what answer he expected. But it came immediately and we were all astonished by it. We were astonished less by what was said than by who it was that came out with it.

'I'd like to sleep with David.' No, it wasn't me that said it. Nor was it Will or Mike. It was young Paul.

Will said, managing to sound matter of fact about it, 'Fine by me, if that's what David would like.'

'Fine by me too,' said Mike. He had slightly les success than Will in concealing his astonishment.

I looked at David and David looked at me. It was a deep and difficult moment for both of us. For a moment I felt a physical pain at the bottom of my chest: in the place where I reckoned my diaphragm was. But then it passed. I looked into David's blue eyes. They were looking at me like those of an animal that fears it's about to be hit. I looked for signs of his recent shiner but the evidence had melted away. I said, 'It's OK.' Very quietly. 'If it's what you both want.'

Paul's nod of the head was so minimal that you wouldn't have known it had happened unless you were looking for it, waiting for it, and a part of your future – small or great – depended on it. David's nod was even more infinitesimal. He didn't even move his head. He nodded bashfully with only his eyelids.

I pulled David towards me and we fell into an embrace. It was an embrace that spoke of mutual comfort rather than of sex. 'It's OK, David,' I repeated gently.

'Are you sure *you* are?' David said.

'I'm OK,' I said. 'I still love you, though. I always will. You know that.'

'You know it'll always be the same for me,' said David.

Our voices had gone down to whispers. Mike and Will had left the bathroom. Only the naked and beautiful Paul remained in there with us. I couldn't quite believe I was having this conversation. It seemed a very grownup sort of exchange to be having. And we were having it just days after saying we loved each other. I wondered if the shortness of the timescale somehow cheapened the whole thing. Or if I'd misunderstood everything I thought I knew about love. I was suddenly conscious of the extreme fragility of everything human. Human love. Human emotion. Human understanding. Human people.

I sought refuge, as I'd done so often during the past months, in physical contact. I reached out with both my hands and took Paul's cock gently in one of them and David's in the other. They had both been semi-flaccid a moment earlier. They began to stiffen up again at my touch. I tugged them both for a moment. Briefly. Flirtatiously. I said, 'Enjoy your night together, both of you.' Then I found myself adding pompously, 'The future's a different country. There's no knowing what's going to happen in it.' I thought about David's wife, due home in just a few days from now. And David gave my own cock a tweak, while Paul briefly caressed my bollocks.

Paul said, 'Will you be…?'

I said, 'I'll sleep with Mike and Will. As usual.'

David said, 'Jack, you're wonderful.' Then he caressed my cheek lightly with the backs of his fingers. 'We can talk in the morning…'

'Yes, of course.' I thought, but didn't say, *if we need to.* I added only, 'Sleep tight, both of you.' Then Paul kissed me, and I kissed him and then David and I kissed each other. Then I left them both in the bathroom.

I went out into the hall. The door to Mike's room was open and the light was on. A bit diffidently I walked into the doorway and stood there naked. Mike and Will were tucked up in bed together. I said,' Is it OK if I join you?'

For answer Mike pulled the covers slowly aside from Will and part of himself and I saw their two naked bodies coming into sight like speeded-up film of flowers opening.

I

TWENTY-SEVEN

David and I did not talk in the morning. Except in the normal friendly way of house guests who meet on the way to the bathroom and sit around the kitchen table together at breakfast. There was actually nothing to be discussed between David and me, nothing that needed going through or teasing out between us. We'd agreed we loved each other and always would do, but our affair, if that was what it had been, was clearly ended. Without hard feelings.

There might be a lot that needed saying, needed dealing with, between Paul and David, but that was hardly the business of that morning's breakfast. Tea and Corn Flakes. It wasn't quite the same as Exupéry's steaming croissant and bowl of coffee, but nevertheless – and despite the lightness of the general mood and the absence of any heavy conversation – it was a pretty resonant moment for all of us. We couldn't fail to feel it.

After breakfast David and Paul drove off together. Their respective toothbrushes and razors were at separate addresses in the neighbourhood and they needed to take a bit of a tour in order to catch up with them. Will, Mike and I bade them au revoir beside David's car and said, 'See you at work,' or 'See you later.'

And then, now that we were again just the three of us, and despite the momentous things that seemed to have been happening, we didn't discuss anything major either. Perhaps it was just too much for all of us. Too big for us to handle. We didn't have big enough words for it. Instead we tidied the bungalow and went shopping and then we went into work around midday. I spent that day's shift, and the next day's, flying to Le Tooks and back with Captain Wimbush and his Panatellas, while Mike flew with another young FO called Alan. David, however, was roster-paired with Paul both days... Was

Michelle somehow second-sighted? I met David and Paul only in the canteen. Among other people. Our greetings, though, were always friendly.

On the second day after our epic five-some the first of the Carvairs – the First of the Three – arrived from Blackbushe. It looked like... Well, it looked like a perfectly normal Douglas DC-4 except for its bulbous forward end, where, as in the case of the Bristol Freighters and Superfreighters, the cockpit was perched up high to make room for the cars below it. I wrote at the beginning of the book that our planes had the look of dogs or wolves about their eyes, or more prosaically their two-paned windscreens. If the Bristol Superfreighters could be said to have the faces of wolves, then the Douglas Dakotas wore more friendly aspects: they more resembled (if you wanted to be fanciful) the puppies of Labradors or spaniels. The same could be said of the Dakotas' younger, bigger, brothers, the regular DC-4s. But the conversion of those aircraft into Carvairs had wrought a change upon their features. Their 'faces' had more of a look of giant poodles about them and seemed to express surprise that they found themselves so tall and that their fringes had been cut the way they had been. At least that was my impression on seeing my first Carvair that afternoon after returning from Le Touquet.

The two Carvair-trained pilots joined the company that day. We all met them in the Wingspan Club after the day's work was done. We questioned them about the craft, and they told us about the route they would be using to go to Geneva. It would take about two hours and forty minutes, they told us. They were already familiar with the way there from Southend, flying for Freddie Laker.

That night I think David went back to Paul's digs and stayed there. What Paul's landlady thought, God alone knew. But Will and Mike and I went home together and after we'd eaten nestled happily, the three of us, in Mike's bed – which was technically also mine. We were lucky, we three. We had a gift, collectively, for letting recent upsets in our three-way relationship pass behind us. Such things were seen by us as water under the bridge and each time we would get on with the business of living our unusual life together to the full. So we made love one way and another, and fell asleep contentedly. If I was still in love with David... If Mike or Will or both of them were still in love with Paul... For the moment we left those momentous matters aside and concentrated on the wonderful now.

It happened rarely but it happened the next day: Mike and Will and I were all free. David and Paul had the day off too. But in spite of that we'd all agreed that we'd look in at Ferryfield early in the morning, to see the first Carvair take off en route for Geneva and wave her on her way. There wasn't going to be a ceremony as such, but the Mayor of Lydd was expected to look in, and the local press would be there, from Ashford, Maidstone and Canterbury. That was hardly the front page of the Times or Telegraph, but it was something all the same.

The three of us drove together in Mike's car. We barely had time to notice that David's car was already in the car park when we arrived. We could already see that something was badly wrong at the airport.

The Carvair was not looking across the roof of the terminal at us from the departure apron. Instead it was standing on the maintenance apron next to the hangar, regarding us with a pained look in its giant poodle eyes. Part of the cowling had been removed from one of its engines. Ladders were propped against it and mechanics stood on the ladders while yet more stood on the ground below them. 'Oh dear,' said Mike as we got out of the car. I thought that would probably be remembered as the understatement of the day.

Feeling very unsure of our welcome we trooped inside the terminal. The place was abuzz with news. From the reception desk to the coffee bar, from the check-in desks to the crew room we heard the same story. They couldn't start the plane. 'Bloody pre-War engines.' 'The Wing-Commander's beside himself.' 'There's engineers on their way from Blackbushe, apparently.' How many of these details were true hardly mattered. The message was clear. While other flights came and went as usual there would be no 'proving' flight to Geneva today. Five car-loads of passengers were stranded at Ferryfield and the company's face had egg all over it.

We had quickly met up with David and Paul. They seemed none the worse for their night in Paul's digs together and at last David's shiner was fading from obvious view. Now it was David who proposed the crazy idea. 'We could take them in a Super.'

'Not five cars, we couldn't' said Paul. And Mike actually rumpled David's blond hair as he laughed and said, 'You're mad, David.'

Unruffled except as to his hair Paul said, 'We could take two.'

Will came in behind him. 'We've two Skips and two FOs.'

'OK,' said Mike. I guessed he was suddenly determined not to be upstaged by David. 'Let's tell Davies at least. He can only laugh at us or just say no.'

We made a move towards the stairs to the offices and control tower. At least we four pilots did. I saw Will hanging back uncertainly. 'You come too please,' I told him. 'Moral support, you know. Remember with Michelle?'

We didn't get as far as the stairs. Davies was coming down them. 'Sir…' David began.

'Not now,' said the Wing-Commander curtly.

Mike said very quickly before he could be stopped again, 'We could take them in two Supers. We're all free.'

That did stop Davies in his tracks. 'You're joking,' he said, but I could see the idea had hit home.

'We're deadly serious, sir,' said Paul.

Davies looked us up and down. I could see him clock the fact that none of us was in uniform. After a tense second he said, 'Come into the crew room.' Again Will hung back uncertainly beside the open door. I grabbed him by his bare forearm and pulled him through the doorway.

The next hour was one of the more extraordinary that I'd ever lived through. It was ascertained that there were two fit, free Superfreighters ready to go. Whiskey Foxtrot (City of Edinburgh) and Whiskey Mike (City of Aberdeen). It was agreed that David and Paul would fly Whiskey Fox while I went with Mike in his Whiskey namesake. There wasn't time for us all to go home and change into uniform. Michelle was despatched by car with a driver to fetch spare ones from the store in the hangar.

Issues arose by the dozen. One was that there was only one stewardess ready to fly out in the Carvair and now we needed two of them. I said it; it seemed obvious, there he was, standing there. In shorts and T-shirt. 'Will?' Will was too surprised to say no. He nodded, and the Wing Commander accepted his offer.

Silver City employed no male cabin staff at that time, so someone telephoned over to the hangar to ask Michelle to bring an extra uniform back with her. If possible, one without a Captain's or First Officer's stripes on it. Michelle returned a few minutes later. We put them on, standing with everyone else in the crew room. The ones that were handed to Mike, David, Paul and me fitted appallingly. Amazingly Will's fitted him perfectly. It had brass buttons, as ours all did, and a single gold-braid stripe at cuff and epaulette. That was the insignia of a Third Officer. There weren't any Third Officers at Lydd, or even Second Officers. Until this moment. Will was suddenly, by accident, an honorary Third Officer. Michelle had found black shoes for all of us, including Will. Standing proudly in his new finery, including white shirt and navy tie, Will looked amazing.

The one bona fide stewardess we did have was Marianne, with whom David and I had spent a night at the George Cinq in Calais. She had come on duty expecting to have her first experience in charge of the Carvair cabin. Now she found she would be working, as usual, on one of our Superfreighters. She whisked Will away to try and teach him in half an hour everything she'd learned years ago in the course of a somewhat longer training.

Then we heard from outside that, almost absurdly, a sixth car-load of passengers had turned up, on the off-chance of getting to Geneva that day. The Carvair had already been booked to its capacity of five. But in the new situation – two planes with capacity each for three… Tickets were sold. That would go some way towards the cost of crewing and sending out two aircraft.

The Carvair pilots arrived. The pair we'd met in the Wingspan Club yesterday but who today, despite their well-fitting uniforms, would not be going anywhere. They took us through the route at the chart table. There were beacon codes to key into the Decca system, radio frequencies to tune into along the way.

The upper airways of Europe were by now way-marked with modern VOR beacons (that's VHF omnidirectional radio range: be thankful for acronyms) which were located at distances of between fifty and a hundred miles apart. Modern high-flying passenger planes flew from one to the next and then on to the next one, as if following a trail of crumbs. The VOR beacons were easy to use, safe and reliable at night and in cloud. But you needed a VOR receiving set in your aeroplane and our short-hop Superfreighters were not equipped with them. We would have to make do with the older, less powerful beacons that were dotted around the countryside at small airfields, such as the ones we used to find our way to Le Tooks, Ostend and Calais. Between us all we plotted a course, zigzagging a little, that would take us across to the French coast at the Somme estuary, then down towards Beauvais and Paris, which we would pass by twenty miles to the east. We would head on into Burgundy, skirting the mountains of Morvan, to Dijon and Beaune, then turn towards the Jura Mountains. All being well we would discover Geneva hiding next to its famous lake on the other side of them. We filed a flight plan in which we would travel at three thousand feet, rising to five thousand for the final fifty miles as the terrain rose higher towards the Jura and the Alps that lay beyond them.

'You might want the heaters on,' said Davies, who had remained with us throughout most of the briefing.

The Carvair could cruise at over two hundred miles an hour. Our Superfreighters did a hundred and sixty-five. A little more with a following wind. The trip was scheduled to take about two hours and forty minutes. Somebody helpfully got a slide-rule out from a drawer in the map table. It was reckoned that in our makeshift mode of transport it would take us three and a half hours or more. 'What if we need a pee?' asked Paul.

'Take a milk bottle in the cockpit,' said Mike. 'Like they did in the War.'

'Quart bottles with wide necks,' I said and Paul and David sniggered. 'They have them in the canteen. I'm serious.'

'What about the passengers?' Paul persisted. He had a point. Our planes were configured for flights lasting no more than half an hour, not for slow lumbering journeys of four hundred miles.

Davies said laconically, 'Stick a bucket in the nose doors. Strap it in.' He probably spoke from experience, I thought. The foot-passengers' luggage was regularly stowed in the nose doors. For that reason there were indeed straps there.

Will rejoined us suddenly, now looking a tad self-conscious in his borrowed finery. I went up close to him and, hoping nobody would notice, whispered in his ear, 'You look gorgeous.'

'I think I'm ready,' he said to all of us. 'Champagne's on board. Marianne's asking what happens if someone needs a pee?'

Except for the pee question I hadn't given any thought to the major differences between the flight we were embarking on and the cross-Channel hops I'd been doing for nearly two months. On the Le Touquet and Calais trips and even the Ostend run the passengers travelled as if on a country bus. Cooped up for over three hours, though, they would get thirsty and even hungry. Marianne and Will had plundered the stores that were intended to go aboard the Carvair. They had loaded packets of crisps, chocolate biscuit snacks, soft drinks and beer. The champagne had been added by order of the Wing Commander – or perhaps even the board. To celebrate the opening of the route. And now also, to compensate the passengers in some measure for the hour's delay before boarding, the additional length of the flight and the degree of comfort, or lack of it, in the planes we were about to take them in.

And then at last we were walking out to the two side-by-side planes. We were to fly in convoy to avoid getting lost, and had been ordered to keep in radio contact all the way. Mike and I, and David and Paul, parted from one another with friendly waves. In a few minutes Will and Marianne would emerge from the terminal with their respective duckling broods of passengers. Marianne would join David's flight; Will would escort his charges in through the passenger door of ours. We wouldn't be in contact with him till, God willing, we all arrived in Geneva in a little under four hours. At around two o'clock Geneva time. Then there would be an hour to unwind and get a meal before returning to Ferryfield while the July sun was still in the sky.

The wind was a light northerly today, though the sky was clear, and we had been promised it would remain so all the way. So we took off on the north-easterly runway 03, David first then Mike and I a minute later, buffeting a little in David's wake turbulence. David took a wide sweep around the turn at Greatstone so that we could catch him up off the coast; and then we headed south for Abbeville, some twenty miles down the coast from le Tooks, at the mouth of the Somme.

I was keyed up by the novelty of it all: the new route, the path-finding job of locating all the beacons and the unusual sight of David and Paul in the sky beside us, half a mile away. I felt we were on an adventure; like questing knights in medieval times, our lances going before us at the tilt, our pennants flying.

It was easy to find the Somme. That west-facing coast of north-east France has three wide gashes in it. The Canache estuary at Le Touquet that we knew so well, a little south of it the mouth of the River Authie – we sometimes glimpsed it when going in to Le Tooks on a clear day – and south of that the huge estuary of the Somme with the town of Abbeville at the landward end of it. We crossed the French coast there, and soon had left the estuary and Abbeville behind us. After that we were in a bucolic countryside of brown-roofed villages and church spires, golden fields and dark green forests, and dependant for our course on the compass, and the beacons whose co-ordinates we fed one by one into Decca.

We had charts, and we had regular maps as well, to help us with landmarks on the ground. Thanks to those we were able a little later to pick out the sprawling city of Amiens. Paul even made out its immense cathedral, or so he told us over the radio, but neither Mike nor I could spot it. But then David's plane was nearly a mile nearer to it than we were.

I wanted to talk to Mike. It seemed ages since we'd had a proper chat, just the two of us. For a moment, in defiance of instructions, I switched off the radio channel that connected us with David. I came to the point quickly. I asked, 'Are you glad it's me?'

'I'm more than glad it's you,' Mike said. 'Are you glad it's me?'

'Of course I am.' I leaned across and tweaked his knee.

'And David?' Mike queried gently. It was more than reasonable that he'd want to know this.

'I love David, as you know,' I said carefully. 'As I think you do too. But when it comes to loving and wanting to live with… Well, then it's you and Will.'

'I love you, Angel,' Mike said with great feeling. 'But we'd better have the radio back on for a bit.' I clicked the switch, and we communed both with David and the control tower at Beauvais airport. Then I switched it back off again. By that time we'd both filled up with more things we wanted to say to each other.

'You said wanting to live with...' Mike said immediately. 'You mean live with me ... continually? Continuously? Whichever's the right word.'

'Yes. Is that too much for me to say?'

'What about Will?'

'Oh dear,' I said. 'Am I one day going to have to choose between Will and you?'

'I don't know,' said Mike. He sounded pained, or even frightened.

'I don't want to have to choose,' I said boldly. 'I want to live with both of you. For ever. I mean, till one of us dies.' I'd said too much this time. I was sure I had. I waited for the roof to fall in.

Mike said gravely, 'That's what I want too. I wasn't sure I dared to say it.'

My heart flew up like a bird. 'We want the same thing.' I was full of wonder at the way the conversation had gone. Then my spirits came down to earth again. 'But what about Will? Usually it takes two to tango, but in our case it needs the agreement of three. What if, for the long term, he wants me more than he wants you? Or the other way round.'

Mike sighed. 'I know. We can only ask him, though. On the way home. Meanwhile – please – radio.'

I switched it on. But for a moment there was no sound from Paul or David. I wondered briefly whether they too had switched the channel off; whether they too were having a private conversation they didn't want us to overhear. Then it crackled back to life. 'Passing Montdidier to port, three miles,' we heard David say in his most Captainly accent.

We continued to clatter through the sky. I wondered how Will was getting on with the passengers. Had he opened the champagne yet? Thinking of him, fondly in this way, brought an involuntary smile. A while later it was my turn to identify a landmark. Paris was off to my right. Well, we could hardly miss that; its eastern suburbs filled the view and bled away into a smoggy brown haze in the distance. But I managed to be more specific. 'The town of Meaux,' I said. 'Right beneath us. Almost encircled by a meander of the Marne.'

'Where the brie is made,' Paul crackled in my headphones.

Mike was not to be outdone. 'And the mustard,' I heard him say. 'You know. The stuff in earthenware pots with the whole grains in.'

David said, 'Coulommiers visual to port.' Mike thanked him. Coulommiers was one of our way-point beacons. I switched our friends in the other plane off again.

'Why did you take Paul home with you that weekend?' I asked boldly.

I saw Mike start and stiffen as though he'd received a blow. 'Not that much happened. We stopped in a lay-by on the way and wanked each other off across the gear lever. On the way back we did the same again.'

'Same lay-by?'

'There's one at the same place on the other side of the road. At my parents' we were given separate rooms. It's a big house, as I once told you.'

'The rectory, I've heard.'

'Oh, so you know.'

'Will told me. Anyway, yes, but why?'

I heard Mike breathe out. Then he said, like a twelve-year-old child, 'If you must know, I was hurt. Will sleeping with Paul. Then you flirting with David, then sleeping with him in Calais.'

'You didn't say you were hurt,' I objected. 'You behaved as though that was all par for the course. That that was what we did. You being so understanding about

Will and Paul… It kind of gave me the green light with David.'

'I don't always show when I'm hurt,' Mike said huffily. 'OK, I took Paul home to get even with you both. If you like, to spite you.'

I was astonished. That was exactly what Will and I had ruled out as a possibility. We thought our Boy's Own hero Mike would have been above such meanness. But now I made another discovery. That I loved Mike all the more keenly because he wasn't. I was ready to cast myself at his clay feet. 'Oh Mike,' I said. I couldn't throw myself at his feet. We were in a cramped cockpit and I was wearing a safety harness. I did the next best thing. I leaned as far as I could towards him, reached down into his crotch and, after a bit of fumbling among the folds of his uniform trousers, found the small tough softness of his cock and squeezed it between my thumb and first two fingers.

I was conscious of the fragility, the delicacy, of Mike's flaccid penis. The vulnerability of it. I was learning little by little that the same thing went for everything and everybody that was human. My big strong Mike, my Captain and Will's Captain, had been hurt by our behaviour. Wounded deeply. I realised for the first time in my life that whatever kind of human being you were, even if you had the intellect of a Plato or an Einstein, the sensibility of a Michelangelo or a Beethoven, the courage and boldness of an Alexander or the sheer brass balls of a Churchill, you were still tossed around by life's currents like a soap bubble; you were just as fragile, just as uncomprehending of your destiny, and just as vulnerable to a puncture that would send you to oblivion and erase you from history.

'Well there we are,' said Mike, tight-lipped and ignoring my gesture, 'I've admitted it.'

'And I love you all the more for it.'

'Christ, I love you, Jack,' he said with heavy emphasis.

'I'd better put the radio back on.' I did. Then I asked like a youngster, 'Can I drive for a bit?'

Mike smiled slowly. Very sweetly. He nodded and said, 'Yes, Jack.'

I flew us all the way to Dijon. I hadn't realised how near Burgundy was to Paris. We were already well south of the champagne towns of Reims and Epernay; we didn't see them, they were too far to the east. But now all of a sudden we were over Chablis, and the low chain of hills that form the Côte d'Or lay ahead. A gently rolling countryside unfolded beneath us. Green rows of vines marched over nearly all of it, except where brown-roofed villages of golden stone were planted in the fertile soil or a crag of bare rock pierced upward through it.

When we arrived overhead the town of Dijon we were just over eighty miles from Geneva airport. I returned control of the plane to Mike and he adjusted our course leftward towards it. Within a minute the round-topped Jura Mountains had come into view directly ahead. They stood like a gently curved wall, sixty miles long, protecting the city of Geneva and its banana-shaped Great Lake from the north and west. We would have to divert from our crow's-flight path towards the airport some twenty miles before we got there in order to skirt the mountains' southern edge and turn back up the lake valley to make our descent into the airport.

Mike said unexpectedly, as we watched the soft-contoured mountain chain grow closer, 'What do you say to going straight over the top?'

'What?' I said. 'The Jura rise to over five thousand.'

'So?' Mike shrugged. 'We can do that.'

'If you say so, Mike. You're the Captain.' Secretly I was, like a child, thrilled to bits. 'But you'd better break the news to David.' For there he was, still just outside the window, still like us at three thousand feet in the clear sky, a mile to the left of us.

Mike spoke to him on the radio. 'We're going to race you there. Straight in over the top.'

I thought David would say something scathing to that but he did not. To my astonishment he said, 'Well if you are, then we are too. Paul and I've already talked about doing just that.'

'We won't make the Carvair schedule, but we should shave ten minutes off,' Mike said. And then we got down to details. We were already cleared to five thousand feet. Six thousand was for traffic coming the other way, and seven thousand might have been a struggle, and cold and uncomfortable for the passengers. We agreed we'd climb to five and a half. I studied the ground map. 'There's a mountain pass,' I said. 'The Col de la Faucille. The road climbs to four thousand three hundred and forty-one feet. Just a couple of miles to the left of the direct-line route…'

We peered ahead. We thought we could already make out the Col de la Faucille. A notch in the high skyline. A loophole through the battlemented mountains ahead of us. I conferred with Paul. We agreed the route. And the queuing order. David and Paul would go ahead. They were slightly nearer to the pass after all than we were. Then Geneva radar would see us coming one behind the other as we emerged from their mountain blind spot and would know to land David first. David cut in on the conversation. 'Put the heater back on if you can. Passengers. Five thousand feet…'

'Good thinking,' I said. Then to Mike, 'Got a match?'

The heating system in our freighters was primitive. A petrol flame in the vehicle hold (!) drove warm air round the passenger cabin through a duct. The War had only finished seventeen years earlier, and the gung-ho, must-do approach to safety issues that its exigencies had forced on people still persisted in everyday life. We normally ran our petrol-driven blowtorch, during these summer months, during the first flights out in the morning only, then switched it off. The aircraft were as poorly insulated as biscuit tins; they got hot in the sunshine, but would quickly chill down at any height. Mike fished a box of matches from a crevice among the chart pockets and handed it to me. I took my harness off and went down the ladder.

I had just lit the flame-thrower contraption when I saw and heard the door to the passenger cabin open and Will come through it. He squeezed past the cars and came up to me. 'I heard the noise…'

'Just putting the heating on,' I said. 'We're going straight over the top.'

'Crikey!' said Will. 'David too?'

'Yes,' I said. 'It's OK. There's a mountain pass.'

'You'd better bloody find it.' He added, 'Actually I thought you'd come down to use the bucket.' Then he grinned and gave me a quick kiss. 'Better get back.'

I said, 'See you on the ground in twenty minutes,' as he squirmed his way back alongside the cars and their wing mirrors.

By the time I got back to the cockpit the engines were roaring fit to burst and the altimeters were showing four thousand feet. The mountains were coming alarmingly close. Wisps of cloud clung like pennants to their loaf-top summits. The other plane with David and Paul inside it, Whiskey Foxtrot, looked pathetically small ahead of us; pathetically low against the huge horizon rearing rapidly ahead of it. I strapped myself back into my seat.

Four and a half thousand. At this height we would clear the roofs of the lorries on the pass by a few feet. Or might just. Mike addressed our plane encouragingly. 'Climb like a homesick angel,' he said. It sounded

American somehow and quite untypical of Mike. He'd got it from a film, I guessed.

For what seemed ages the plane ahead of us was a grey shape against the mountain wall ahead of it. Too low, too low, I thought. I felt the hair rise on the back of my neck. And then suddenly Whiskey Fox was a silhouette against the blue cup of sky above. It had ridden higher than the pass.

I looked back at the altimeters. 'Five thousand,' I called to Mike. 'Still going up.' Below us now I could see the road and the traffic on it, winding its laborious way through a nest of hairpins that looked impossibly tight and close together. Then we flew quite suddenly into thick cloud and I felt a second's-worth of rising panic. I was conscious of Mike holding onto the column, still pulling it back to maintain climb attitude, holding it with a vice-like grasp. Then we were out of the cloud. We were right overhead the pass. On either side of us mountains were rising even higher than we had. Rocky bird-haunted summits, sparse green vegetation, and little see-through clouds that spun like white candyfloss around the peaks in broken spirals. Then suddenly the ground dropped sharply away beneath us. We'd climbed the gentler, lee slope of the Jura Range. Now we were sailing out like eagles above the scarp slope. There in front of us, like a promised land, lay Switzerland. Below, with filmy cloud obscuring just a few slivers of it, was the valley in which Geneva lay beside its lake. Then the lake itself, shining silver, running from one end of our windscreen to the other. Beyond, the silver-capped summer Alps crowded the southern horizon.

'Descending to three thousand,' Mike said. 'Call Geneva tower. Check we're still going in from the north east.'

We were. Five more miles took us to the lake and then we made a steep right turn over the water. As we banked our runway swung into view like magic, five final miles ahead of us. There was a light breeze from the south west. Two miles in front of us Whiskey Fox, a little lower in the sky than we were, showed us her white back, brilliant as a seagull in the sunshine.

'Well done, Mike,' I said to my Captain when we'd rolled to a stop. 'I'm very impressed.'

'Good,' said Mike. 'I did it to impress you. I didn't want David to be the only one who could dazzle you in the cockpit.'

'Thanks, Mike.' I reached out and stroked his leg across the throttles.

'Three hours twenty-five minutes,' Mike said, glancing at the cockpit stopwatch.

'I'm even more impressed,' I said. Meanwhile I had passed another milestone. I was in Switzerland. My third new foreign country. I'd notched up another first.

TWENTY-EIGHT

'Did anybody need the bucket in the end?' I asked Will as we met on the way into the terminal.

'No. Everybody was far too interested in the flight over the mountains to even think about their bladders. What about you?'

'Ditto,' I said. Mike had put an empty quart bottle into his flight bag as recommended, but neither of us had given it a thought afterwards. But now we were suddenly at crew passport control and having to give a thought to that little potential obstacle. Marianne had her passport with her; she had been scheduled to fly today unlike the rest of us. Surprisingly both Paul and David also had their passports with them. Happily Will, Mike and I all had our driving licences and after a second's discussion among themselves the border police decided that was good enough. After all, we were only going to be in Switzerland for an hour, and we wouldn't be going further than the terminal building.

The airport manager, however, was less happy with us. Mike and David, Paul and I, were summoned to his office.

'You flew a non-standard approach,' he said. He was a bespectacled man with iron grey hair and he kept us standing while he sat behind his desk. 'Without authorisation.'

'Sorry,' said David very quickly. 'We got a bit lost.'

'We had no idea it wasn't standard,' Mike added. 'It's our first time here. Emergency cover and all that.'

'Well don't do it again,' the manager said. 'You caused a hazard to traffic on the pass.' Well, only if we'd fallen out of the sky on top of the climbing lorries, I thought. I didn't tell the manager that. 'I shall be reporting this to your company as a matter of course.

This is the first flight here by Silver City. Not a good first impression.'

'Sorry,' said Paul.

'Sorry,' I echoed.

The manager nodded a tepid acknowledgement. He finished, 'Make sure to follow the route carefully on your way out. VFR.' That stood for visual flight rules. The day was still clear and in any case our planes were not equipped with the latest instruments.

'Yes sir,' said Paul.

'Yes sir,' said Mike. We all filed out of the office and went quickly to join Will and Marianne in the canteen. It took a minute of searching out but then there it was. Will and Marianne were seated at a white-clothed table already eating.

'They've got a wonderful thing called *rösti*,' Will said, showing us what was left of the crisp potato cake on his plate. We four pilots took his tip and made sure to ask for it too, alongside our breaded veal cutlets.

We had brought six cars to Switzerland, but there were no cars waiting to be brought back. More Britons went south for their holidays than did French or Swiss tourists head north. Most of our returning traffic on the cross-Channel routes consisted of British passengers whom we'd already flown out. But Wing Commander Davies was not a man to let a plane fly home empty if it could be avoided, so he had arranged to bring a freight payload back.

I wish that I could write that we filled the holds of Whiskey Fox and Whiskey Mike with cuckoo clocks. But that wasn't the case. What we did load, up and down on the scissor lifts, was pallet after pallet of ripe cherries in trays and punnets. 'Better not bounce that lot around too much,' David said as we watched the loading process going on from inside the crew room.

The weather update was encouraging. Clear skies and a gentle northerly breeze all the way to the Paris area. Clear skies, most probably, afterwards also, though the wind would be a bit different, backing west, then south-west. There were some thunderstorms building up over Normandy in the afternoon heat, but they were not expected to move as far eastward as our homeward route until later tonight. Will took as much interest in the briefing as we four pilots did. After all, he too was a pilot. He was surplus to requirements on the return flight. So was Marianne. They would occupy the spare third seats in the two cockpits: Marianne with David and Paul, Will with Mike and myself.

We set off. Mike and I went first this time, Whiskey Fox a minute and a half behind us. We were cleared for an altitude of four thousand feet till we were well past Dijon. Then we would drop down to two thousand in the Paris area and stay at that for the remainder of the flight. Four thousand didn't actually mean a particularly big initial climb-out. Geneva airport already had an elevation of one and a half thousand feet.

We flew westward to where the Jura Mountains abruptly ended some dozen miles from Geneva's outskirts. The loops and coils of the River Rhone lay beneath us. Once we had left the mountain wall behind us we were free to turn north, taking a bearing on a beacon near Tournus that in turn would bring us within range of Dijon, the next way-point on our road north.

Mike turned wide at the turning point, allowing David to catch us up. Soon he was in sight alongside us, just a mile a way on the right. I lent Will my headphones for a moment, handing them behind me over the seat-back, and he and David and Paul greeted one another over the radio with a laugh.

Then I decided it was now or never. Here were Mike, Will and myself together in an aircraft cockpit. It seemed the right moment. 'Will,' I said. 'Mike and I were having a chat on the way down. Rather a serious one, actually. About the three of us.'

'Oh?' said Will.

'You're making it sound a bit heavy, Jack,' Mike warned me.

'Perhaps because it is heavy,' I said. I went on before either of the others could stop me. 'We talked about how we saw the future. Remember when I first came to live with you both, we somehow agreed we'd live like a household of three people for as long as…'

'Yes,' said Will. I could almost hear him wondering what was coming next. Mike turned the radio off.

I went on, 'Mike and I thought it would be wonderful if the three of us could go on being the three of us – but exclusively, you know. Only the three of us…' I found I was talking rapidly, nervously. I couldn't have coped with being interrupted before I finished. Not least because I wasn't sure how I was going to finish. 'It goes wrong when there's more than three of us or we get involved with other people. Paul, David, any others. Like… You know, when two people get married they say *forsaking all others,* and Mike and I thought that would be a wonderful thing … for the three of us … I mean, to think about trying to keep it that way for ever, to stay together, the three of us … but we didn't know if you'd want that.'

'Christ,' said Will. He sounded very taken aback. 'You make it sound like a proposal of… Well, like an engagement between the three of us.'

'Yes,' I said, in a very unconfident voice. By now I thought I'd said far too much and desperately wished I hadn't.

But Mike chimed in – bless him. He said, in a much stronger, more positive voice than I'd managed, 'Yes, we do mean that. Jack and I. We both mean that.'

There was a moment's silence while Will thought about this and the din of the engines sounded deafening. Then Will said, 'It sounds mad, and crazy. But it's also what I'd like. I don't know if it's been done before...'

'I suppose it must have,' said Mike. 'At some point in human history.'

'It's just that we haven't heard about it,' I said.

'Three men, though?' said Will. Now his voice sounded uncertain. He seemed to be about to backtrack.

'Let's just do it,' I heard Mike say. 'No ceremony. No written words. We're practically there already anyway, for God's sake. We just have to agree not to sleep with – or to have sex with – every fucking person we like.'

'Because when we do we all get hurt,' I said tritely.

'Do we all get hurt?' said Will. 'I thought we agreed we didn't get hurt.'

'I got hurt,' I said. 'I pretended otherwise. Mike said it was the same for him. We talked about it on the way down.'

'All right,' said Will. 'Maybe I got hurt too. Though I didn't think I had.' He went quiet for a moment, presumably putting his feelings briefly into analysis. Then, 'I hadn't noticed... And yet, perhaps... Yeah. Perhaps you're both right.'

'Remember in the canteen at Lydd?' I said to him. 'That day when I told you about me and David...?'

I couldn't see Will's reaction to that because he was sitting behind me. But I felt him place his fingers on the muscle above my shoulder blade and squeeze it. 'Yep. Yes, you're right.'

'Well,' said Mike. It seems as though we've just got engaged, the three of us. Is there any of that champagne left from this morning?'

'We can't drink it now!' I said in astonishment.

'I meant when we get back,' said Mike.

'We can't anyway,' said Will. 'The passengers finished it. Mind you, they did insist I had a tiny slurp.' He stretched out both his arms along the seat-backs and grasped both Mike and me, one shoulder belonging to each of us. Mike brought the radio back to life.

We passed Dijon and followed our beacon breadcrumb trail back the way we'd come this morning. We seemed to be getting home more quickly than we'd travelled on the way out. I'd often noticed that about return journeys. I discovered that I didn't want the trip to end. I was so much enjoying flying this scenic journey, almost hedge-hopping over Burgundy and northern France. Sharing a cockpit not just with Mike but with Will and Mike. If I'd had to die that afternoon, well, the company would have been perfect.

We got a new weather update from Coulommiers as we skirted the eastern outskirts of Paris. Planes ahead of us were reporting unexpected thunderstorms between Beauvais and the Channel coast. The storm track had moved further east than predicted. 'Ah well,' I said to the other two. 'In for a penny, in for a pound.' It was easy to be light-hearted while blue skies and sunshine were all you could see for miles around you.

Mike spoke to David. To make sure he'd heard the same storm warning message.

We sailed on, clattering through the blue like a thousand high-speed football rattles. We made contact with Beauvais, halfway between Paris and the Channel coast. They too warned us about thunderstorms ahead. We told them we already knew about that. We said thank you and goodbye to Beauvais as we left it behind us.

The clouds seemed to come from nowhere. One moment there was a clear horizon, the next the sun was shining on a distant long line of cauliflower-like thunderheads, approaching like an army from the north-west.

The cumulo-nimbus didn't stay distant. Ten minutes later they were looming like mountains beside us. Mike and David had a quick discussion over the radio about tactics. It was decided we would try to thread our way between them. There was no chance of going up over them. The two Captains agreed they probably towered twenty thousand feet above us.

The plan worked well at first. We agreed that David would go ahead a little way. Flying side by side, even a mile apart, was not a good idea when you were pursuing an improvised zigzag course. So we hung back a little and saw David accelerate ahead. Up to a point we followed his zigzags between the piling, boiling cloud mountains, but then they began to change shape more quickly and we had to create our own zigzagging course. The white clouds had filled our view with majesty and brilliance, but now as they grew closer and closer together the air grew dark around us. David's plane disappeared from sight ahead of us, though we continued to keep in radio contact. The sun's light was at last extinguished and we flew through a realm that was night dark. Light came from a point in front of us though. A purple flash, and then another, diffused through the fog.

Then the lightning was all around us. 'We've lost the beacon,' Mike said.

'We'll find another one in a minute,' I said in a voice that sounded confident. I wouldn't come to harm, I thought. I was with Will and Mike.

The flashes grew closer together, both in time and space. They were no longer all in front of us but surrounded us.

One enormous crack, one vivid flash, engulfed us. It made the aircraft bang and shake, and it frightened the three of us half to death. The compass did a somersault.

When the needle came back to rest it wasn't in the same place. 'Shit,' said Mike. And then the radio cut out.

Suddenly we were flying through water, as if through a cataract. The windscreen had wipers like a car's; we used them when taxiing in rain, or even on landing, and even up to the moment of take-off, but they were of no use in full-speed flight. We had to accept quite simply that we couldn't see anything except water ahead of us. Then a warning light came on. It told us that the Decca system had stopped working.

'One of those lightning strikes must have clobbered us,' I said.

'Will,' said Mike tensely, 'what's your dead-reckoning like?'

'I learnt it in the RAF...' Will said uncertainly.

'Then now's your chance to find out what you learnt,' Mike said. 'Jack, hand him the computer.' I did as I was told. Plus the relevant air chart. The air computer was not what most people understand today by the word computer. It was a slide-rule in a circular shape. Will presumably set it on his lap. 'Heading three sixteen,' I told him. 'At least it was before the lightning hit.'

'Windspeed?' Will asked.

'Fuck knows,' Mike said. 'Beauvais told us fifteen knots.'

'Feels more like thirty,' I said, feeling a sudden gust buffet us like a rhinoceros.

'Go for twenty-five,' said Mike.

Will set to and worked out his wind triangle. The wind continued to buffet us and the lightning flashed like fire around us, embracing us with electric flames that filled windscreen and side windows alike. Flame didn't usually appear in cascading water, but now it was doing just that. The rattle of hailstones against our roof and windows even managed to drown the racket of our engines out. 'It's difficult to see the figures with all this shaking,' Will said.

'Be patient,' said Mike. 'You'll get it right.' And at last, in between shocks and shakings Will got his numbers to line up. 'We're on course for Boulogne. I mean, approximately.'

'We'll hold the heading,' Mike told us. 'I'll be as happy to see Boulogne beneath the wing-tip as anywhere else. Just pray the compass is right.'

I might have been worried by now about the condition of the cherries in their trays beneath us; we'd been told to treat them gently. But I'm afraid I didn't give our precious cargo a single thought. I was too worried for myself. Sometimes a really bad electric storm could tear a plane out of the sky and dash it to the earth beneath. I knew that we were all thinking that. And that none of us would say it. The bangs and flashes grew ever more violent. I'd never experienced anything like this. I found myself suddenly praying to a God I'd stopped believing in as a teenager. I wondered about Mike, the son of a vicar. Was he still religious? We'd never talked about this. I wondered what was going through his head and heart.

There was a famous saying among pilots. 'Better to be down here wishing you were up there than up there wishing you were down here.' I had never wished I was down there more than I did right now. I'd thought I'd be happy to die a hero's death with Mike and Will beside me. I now realised I'd been wrong about that. I didn't care who was or was not beside me. I didn't want to die a hero's death. I discovered now that there was nothing remotely heroic about me. I wanted to shout out, 'Help me,' in panic. But I knew that I wouldn't shout. And that nobody could help.

I felt Will's hand then on my neck. Somehow he nuzzled his head against the side of mine for a moment, and then he did the same to Mike. I heard myself say, 'We're going to be OK.' Something inside me had taken it upon itself to try and reassure the others. I could hardly believe it was my voice that had said that.

'We're OK,' I heard Will agree with me. 'For ever. OK. The three of us.'

'We'll be the other side of this in no time,' I heard Mike say. But I did hear his voice shake slightly as he said it.

I thought suddenly of the champagne that Mike had imagined drinking on our return. To celebrate the success of our day's adventure. To celebrate being the three of us. Right now to celebrate being alive seemed quite enough. I remembered Antoine de Saint Exupéry, and how his thoughts had turned in extremis to a bowl of coffee and a warm croissant to dunk in it. I remembered that breakfast that David and I had shared in the Hotel de Londres the morning after we'd told each other we loved each other. That coffee and chicory. Those heaven-scented croissants. I thought now about David. And Paul. How were they getting on, plunging, bucking and rearing through the storm ahead of us? Were they the other side of it yet? Had they...? I could hardly bear to frame the thought. Had they made it? Or had they already come to grief? As we too might. We too. We three. 'We're going to be OK,' I heard Will say, but as he spoke another great flash of light - blue? pink? white? invaded our prison-cockpit, and the bang that accompanied it nearly shattered our eardrums, and his voice too became tremulous with fright.

Will gripped my shoulder hard. With his other hand he gripped Mike's. 'Love you both,' he said.

Mike said, 'Love you both,' and at the same moment I said, 'Love you both.'

Mike and I were both gripping our yokes with both hands but at that moment Mike's right hand left the yoke and moved towards me through the air between us. My own hand left the yoke at the same moment and in the interstellar space between us they met halfway and our fingertips touched for an instant. Another blinding lightning flash and deafening crack that seemed to cleave the heavens sealed the three of us.

'Us three,' said Will.

'We three,' said Mike.

'Us three,' I said. Mike was usually our oracle in matters of grammar but right now the grammar didn't seem to matter very much. I might not be much of a hero but I knew that I was with the two people I wanted to be alive with.

And then quite suddenly the ordeal by rain and hailstones ceased. The flashing was banished to a distance. The cracking of the firmament stopped. Nothing worse was happening to us than that we were flying through a dense fog. But my terror had not abated yet. I found a refuge from it in my immediate task. I checked the compass. 'Heading three forty,' I said.

'We'll stick with it,' said Mike. 'No real point doing anything else.'

But then the compass needle made a sudden jerk. 'Sorry,' I said. 'Heading is now zero nine.' The Decca began to move, although a bit weirdly. I wasn't sure that we could trust it yet. Then the radio came back to life with a small pop. Mike and I looked at each other; I even turned for a second and looked at Will over my shoulder. The expressions on their two faces were unreadable. Could we believe, dared we hope, that the emergency was over? After a minute of calm and level flying we began to believe it was. We could hear one another's sighs of relief. We were out of danger. We were alive and flying. We were riding home in triumph: knights errant returning jubilantly from the quest. Punching the air. We were the three of us. The only problem was that we didn't know where the hell we were. If asked to give our position we would be unable to say anything more precise than, 'Somewhere over northern France, heading north-north-east.'

I tried to contact Whiskey Foxtrot on the radio but nothing came back, and that silence from David and Paul hit me like a stone in the stomach. Then I had a go at tuning into Le Touquet because I knew the frequency by heart. But nothing came of that either. Though the probable explanation for that was an easier one to think about. We simply weren't near enough to them yet. Will, behind me, said to Mike, now in a normal, un-frightened voice, 'Do you want me to try for a position fix?'

'May as well,' Mike said. 'You've still got the air computer?'

Will made a noise that indicated yes and I fished among the 'library' on the clipboard in front of me for a pencil and graph paper. I passed them back to him. 'Good luck, mate.'

Between us Mike and I fed him the groundspeed, the time elapsed since our last real position fix back at Beauvais, our current heading and – guessing wildly – an estimate of the average speed of the wind from the south west.

I heard Will exhale with concentration behind me. Then came Mike's excited voice. 'Alleluia! Gap in the cloud. I caught a glimpse of coast ahead.'

Over the next few minutes the cloud began to break up more and more. At last we could all see the coast ahead of us. The only question was: which bit of coast?

'Will, you can stop doing arithmetic now,' Mike said. 'Concentrate on the ground map.' We pooled our thoughts. We knew every inch of the coastline between the Bay of the Somme and Ostend. That was nearly a hundred miles of coast. It was unlikely that we could have strayed beyond that range in the time since we'd lost our instruments. Even if we'd accidentally turned in a circle, which we didn't think we had, we'd still ended up pointing roughly north. If we didn't recognise the coast... Well, we knew that to the east of our well-trodden beat lay the marshy inlets and polders of eastern Belgium and Holland, while to the west were Normandy's white rocky cliffs. If we found ourselves crossing a chalky shore we would need to turn right; if we found ourselves over dyke-veined marshes we would turn left. It was as simple as that.

'I see a town on the right,' I said. 'Beside an estuary. We're about five miles to the west of it.'

Will held on to my shoulder as, map in hand, he craned past my head. 'It's Abbeville. There's the River Somme and the Bay. Turn right at the coast and in ten minutes we'll be at Le Tooks.' At that moment we probably would have cracked open the champagne had there been any. We knew where we were. And we'd only strayed five miles from our intended course.

We didn't even have to fly all the way to Le Touquet. Halfway up the coastal strip Mike spotted Dungeness Point emerging from the haze on the left and turned towards it. A minute later I made contact with Lydd tower and gave them a position report. They told us the wind direction and cleared us to land on runway two-two, approaching from the north-east. It all seemed absurdly normal. Our colleagues on the ground at Ferryfield could have had no idea what had just happened to us.

Colleagues. Paul. David. What had happened to them? We'd tried them on the radio again and again since it had returned to consciousness but with no success. I asked Lydd if they'd heard from David. They had not. I relayed that gloomy news to Mike and Will and it cast a pall of despondency over all of us.

I hunted for David in the sky, ahead and to the right of us. Mike and Will – Will leaning past Mike's head – looked for him on the left. But there was no sign of him anywhere near us.

Dungeness Point grew nearer and the lighthouse came into sight. One of our sister aircraft passed a thousand feet beneath us, outbound for Le Tooks. The normality of everything was breathtaking. It was Exupéry's morning bowl of coffee and croissant. But it still wasn't really normal. Because there was no David.

Suddenly I heard myself saying, 'Can I do the landing, Mike?' And he told me I could. It was time to turn away from the lighthouse and head downwind up the coast. 'I have control,' I said and I carried the turn out.

A minute later we passed the airport, though I could hardly see it. It was on the left and I was on the right, with only the sea in sight. 'Romney church tower,' Mike reported. That was my signal to turn left and cross the coast over Greatstone. Then Will said,

'Give me the binos.' Mike handed them back to him. Again he craned past Mike's head. Will said, 'It's just that I can see a plane landing. I wondered... Yes! Yes, it is. I can read it! Whiskey Fox!' David and Paul had made it. They were dropping gently, unperturbed, towards the runway at Lydd. If our mood had been despondent for the past few minutes it now soared again. Our jubilation filled the cockpit and it seemed as though its power and energy would burst it. From below us the scent of ripe cherries suddenly wafted up.

TWENTY-NINE

'Our radio was knocked out,' said David calmly when we met in the crew room a few minutes later. Only his face, a sort of greyish white, hinted at what he was feeling.

'So was ours for a time,' said Mike equally conversationally. 'And the compass went a bit wild for a bit.' In his case too, only his skin colour spoke the truth.

'We lost the Decca,' Will added. 'I don't think it's properly come back even now.'

'All in a day's work,' said Paul, and he grinned at us from a whey-coloured face.

The Wing Commander came into the crew room at that moment, peering around then heading over to us. 'Well done, chaps,' he said, sounding serious about it. 'You got back in good time. You got us off a rather nasty hook.' He paused for a second; his face remained serious. 'You made it to Geneva very quickly too, I hear.' He paused again, waiting for someone to reply. I looked at Mike.

'We had the wind behind us,' Mike said, standing up so straight that I could see his calves tautening he backs of his uniform trouser legs.

Davies didn't smile at that. 'I gather you took a route right over the mountains. The airport manager over there referred to it as a non-standard approach. He's filed a formal complaint about it.'

David came to Mike's defence. 'It was our first time there. Perhaps we weren't quite aware of...'

Davies cut him off. 'The Swiss didn't fight their way to victory in two World Wars. Clinging to survival by their fingertips.' He stopped for a second and we all tried to work out where he was going with this. None of us was going to ask. Davies continued. 'They take a different approach to things from the one that perhaps we do. However...' He looked down at our shoes for a moment. Then he looked back up. 'I've been requested to speak to you about the matter.' There was a moment during which he stared at us all with eyes like drill bits. Then, 'All right. Consider yourselves spoken to.' There came another short pause that none of us dared to do anything with. At last Davies's formidable frame relaxed and he said, 'I'm surprised those old buses made it over the mountains like that. Well done, lads, for trying it. The British spirit and all that. You can be proud of yourselves. That's unofficial, though.'

'Thank you, sir,' Mike and David mumbled jointly in a sort of schoolboy or junior officer chorus. They spoke for all of us. Will, Paul and I were not expected to add anything on our own behalves. We nodded our heads minutely instead.

Be proud of Mike, I thought to myself. It had been his idea to shoot the mountain pass. My Captain. My Mike. Will's Captain. Will's Mike. Our Mike.

Davies looked directly at Will at that point. 'Ready for this evening, young man?'

'This evening?' Will said.

'Board meeting,' Davies told him. 'Your presentation of your prototype.'

'I thought that was tomorrow,' Will said.

'You may have thought that,' said Davies brusquely, 'but it cuts no ice. It's tonight. Here, at six o'clock.' He looked at his watch. 'That's in ... thirty minutes.'

'I'll be there, sir,' Will said. 'Here, I mean.' Then, 'I don't know how I should dress...'

The Wing-Commander looked Will up and down, took in the fact that he was clad in what was obviously a Third Officer's uniform with its single stripe. He appeared to pause for a moment's thought. Then, 'Come as you are,' he said. 'That should do fine.' His mouth twitched up at the corners in the beginning of a smile. Then he turned round smartly and headed for the door.

'Right,' said Mike in his Captain voice. 'That gives us just enough time to get home, rinse our arm-pits and get the Shackle-it.'

The champagne came later. In the Wingspan Club. It wasn't just in honour of Will's success at the board meeting. It wasn't just in celebration of our Valkyrie ride across the mountains and through thunderstorms. It wasn't just because they'd found the problem with the Carvair's engine and corrected it, and the aircraft would be able to fly to Geneva tomorrow at the appointed time of ten o'clock. It seemed to be a sort of thanksgiving for all those things and everything besides. We were celebrating the busiest early summer in the company's history. And we were celebrating the summer itself. For Will and Mike and me it was also a celebration of the fact of *us*, although that was a detail we kept hidden. Except of course from David and Paul, who were also having their own private celebration. They too were evidently celebrating *us,* to judge from the way they looked at and spoke to each other, and the way their bodies behaved whenever they were doing that, although their *us* was a different *us* from our *us*.

Mike and I, David and Paul, hadn't attended the board meeting, obviously. We'd had to wait till afterwards to hear about it. From Will and from others. The news was all good, though. Will had risen to the occasion wonderfully, board members said. He'd done his demonstration of the Shackle-it inside the belly of Whisky Kilo, and had actually knocked three extra seconds off our best trial timings. Not having to worry about ripping garden forks out of the ground probably helped him a bit.

It was Captain Evans actually who first reported Will's success to Mike and myself. I hadn't realised he was a member of the board. Perhaps I should have. 'We heard about your exploits today,' Evans then told us. 'Sounds like you had some fun. Wish I could have come myself, but I'd already gone off on the Calais run by the time the trouble with the Carvair came to light. And Wimbush is on his hols of course. And you went in over the mountains…'

'That was Mike's idea,' I said.

'Whoever had the idea, I'm impressed,' Evans said. Nothing had been said by any one about the fact that we'd nearly died when our aircraft was struck repeatedly by lightning in a major thunderstorm. But, I supposed, when you'd engaged Stukas and Messerschmitts in high-altitude gunfights you didn't give much thought to minor incidents of that sort.

Evans moved off and Will joined us, pushing past the fronds of a small indoor palm plant. I hadn't remembered there being potted palm trees in the Wingspan Club. Perhaps they spent most of their time out on the terrace during the summer months. Will had his champagne glass in one hand and the edge of a precariously teetering tray of canapés in the other. 'Have some of these,' he said. 'There's smoked salmon. Lumpfish roe…'

'Bloody hell,' I said, as Mike and I each grabbed a handful from the aluminium dish. 'They are pushing the boat out.'

Will said, 'David's taking Paul to the George for the night.'

'Wow,' I said. At least it wasn't the Georges Cinq in Calais. 'That's a bit close to home.' The phrase *shitting on your own doorstep* plopped into my mind but, quickly remembering stones and glass houses, I didn't come out with it.

Mike said, 'When's David's wife due back?'

'Tomorrow night,' I said.

'Make hay while the cat's away,' said Will. 'Can someone hold this while I help myself to a sandwich?'

I found myself rubbing shoulders with other high-powered board members. Even the Chairman himself. He was yet another highly decorated Wartime flying ace; he now also sat on the board of our parent company Britavia. During the War he must have been a petite and dapper chap. These days he was short and plump. 'How long are you staying with us?' he asked me conversationally.

'Just till the end of the summer,' I said. 'That's all I know for the moment. I'd like to stay on of course, but they can't keep all of us.'

'No, of course,' said the Chairman. He screwed up his eyes a bit as he thought. 'Winter traffic's less than a quarter of what it is in summer. Though of course you already know that... You say you're waiting to hear if you're staying.'

I said, 'Yes, sort of.'

'Hmm,' he said. 'Not really fair to keep you guessing. If they don't want you – I mean if they can't keep you – it's time they told you that. Give you a chance to look elsewhere. By the way, I did hear about your feat of derring-do today... We all heard about it. Very impressive.'

'It wasn't me,' I explained hurriedly. 'I was simply one of the co-pilots.'

'Don't put yourself down,' said the Chairman. He looked me in the eye quite searchingly. 'Most of the great feats in aviation have depended on the courage and resourcefulness of co-pilots. I never underestimate co-pilots. First Officers. Second Officers.' He glanced over to where Will was standing talking with another group, still wearing his pilot's uniform with its single stripe.

'Third Officers. What good flying comes down to, in a nutshell, is teamwork.'

'Yes sir,' I said. 'I do agree with that. It's teamwork.' The Chairman couldn't have guessed the reason why I sounded so fervent as I was saying that.

Then the Chairman caught sight of someone else who was walking in our direction. It was the Wing-Commander. The Chairman beckoned him. 'Alastair, come here a moment.' And the Wing-Commander meekly did so.

'I've been talking to this young man, Alastair. One of the heroes of today's adventure. Rescuing the company from ignominy and ridicule in the local press.'

'Yes,' said Davies. He had the look of someone who has been waylaid while on his way to talk to someone else. He acknowledged me with a tight smile.

'He's hoping to stay on through the winter,' the Chairman told Davies baldly. 'In fact he'd like to stay for ever, I think. But he doesn't know yet if you want him.'

'I see,' said Davies, looking slightly wrong-footed. 'Well,' and he looked at me, 'it isn't decided yet. But if you're seriously interested…'

'All my friends are staying,' I blurted out childishly.

Davies gave a grin of surprise but not, I thought, an unsympathetic one. 'In that case, we'll have to see what we can do,' he said. 'I'll speak to Michelle in the morning.' He moved away, returning to his intended path towards whoever it was he'd been going to speak to.

The Chairman gave me a smile that was almost gloating. 'That means yes,' he said. 'You can safely tell your friends that.'

We were at the beach. The three of us. The sun was just going down behind us and the sea was melting from blue to turquoise. The air was still warm, still scented with iodine and sea salt. We'd just been running races on the shingle... Have you ever run races on shingle? It's the funniest thing... But even when you race on shingle someone wins. Someone has to. Among us it was always Mike. Well, he was the tallest out of the three of us – by three inches at least – and he had the longest legs. By now in the shortest shorts.

Breathless we collapsed laughing, or trying to, on the still warm stones. 'Are we a little drunk, do you suppose?' Will asked as he tumbled down on top of Mike and me.

'Perish the thought,' said Mike, and giggled.

A serious thought came to me. 'David's wife's back tomorrow. What's going to happen then to him and Paul?'

'God knows,' said Mike. 'But it'll sort itself out. Somehow. Life always does do in the end.'

'But in their case,' I said, 'I don't see how. The three of them...'

'Four,' said Will. 'Don't forget the unborn kid.'

'It's going to be messy,' I said. 'And I don't mean the kid. Someone's going to get hurt.'

'They all are,' said Mike. A bit sententiously, I thought. 'That's what life does to us. There's no life without pain. And there's no living without compromise.'

We disentangled ourselves and lay back, still and separate for a moment, as we digested Mike's pronouncements. They sounded a bit serious for such a celebratory moment in our lives. In our life.

'Listen,' Will and I heard Mike resume. 'It's up to them what happens. Up to David and Paul, I mean. We can love them but we can't live them.'

'Can't live them?' queried Will.

'Can't live their lives for them,' Mike clarified.

Will and I made murmurs of agreement. Then Will reached over and started to tickle Mike's belly. To stop him taking himself too seriously. And I joined in.

But we three had changes to deal with too. Will would soon be leaving Ferryfield for half a year. In the autumn, when his training at Biggin Hill began. Admittedly he would only be leaving Mike and me for a few days at a time. He'd be lodging with my parents during the week but returning to us and to his bungalow at weekends. It would still change the dynamic of our set-up somewhat. But we'd deal with that when the time came. Somehow.

We'd deal with it. We were strong now. The three of us. Tested by ordeal of water and fire. Annealed and hardened, tempered and quenched like the swords of legend in the forges, on the anvils, of the gods. We couldn't guess what the future might hold; we could only hope there'd be plenty of it. And that we'd explore it together. The three of us. We musketeers.

We lay back again, separately on the stones. 'One day I really will bring you both down here to fish,' said Will.

'Yes,' I said. 'Come down here at night and fish for sea-bass and plaice, and Dover sole…'

'Promises,' Mike said.

I looked up at the empty sky. It was like looking at a theatre curtain in the expectant moment when the house lights were going down. There would be a few minutes' hiatus now, and then the stars would appear. 'No planes now,' I said.

Mike chuckled. 'No stars to steer them by.'

I said, *'The one true star … our own one, the one which alone contains our familiar landscapes, our friendly homes and all we hold dear.'*

'What the fuck…?' asked Will.

'It's a quote,' I said. 'From a beautiful book. By Antoine de Saint Exupéry. *'Among all those stars there was only one, just one, where might be found within the*

reach of our hands this fragrant dawn breakfast bowl.
Coffee and a croissant. Or coffee and a baguette. I forget
which. David read it to me. His own translation.'

'And you remembered it?'

'Yes.'

Mike was evidently aware of the significance of that.
After a second's thought he said, 'He's a clever chap,
David. And lovely with it.' He paused again. Then,
'Jack...?'

'Mmm?'

'Are you sure you're OK?'

I thought for a moment. Then I said, 'Yes, I think so.
Yes, I am now.'

Will, lying on his back on the pebbles, eyes shut,
murmured, 'We'll come and fish for sea bass, sole and
plaice.'

I sat up. 'You're talking balls, Will.' I slapped his bare
leg.

That made Will sit up, and Mike sat up too. We were
sitting facing each other, cross-legged on the stones. I
found myself admiring Will's chunky thighs. And the
considerable mound of his crotch in his shorts. Mike's
too. The light sank towards the west behind The Pilot.
Eastward the sea became a sheet of glass between us and
France. On the darkening 'hump' the tiny light of a car
or lorry appeared, seeming tentative as it made its way
across the lonely top of that distant hill. I wanted to
reach out and touch Will's hand. So I did. As he had
touched mine, across the table in the Railway Hotel two
months ago. I wanted to reach out and touch Mike's
hand too. So I did that as well. And Mike's hand met
mine half way. In the mysterious infinities of time and
interstellar space.

****

I had indeed loved David and I always would do. I'd even got briefly excited about Paul. But the trouble with having a multiplicity of partners – and one of the reasons that most societies today frown on it – is that the heart finds itself saying *I love you* to more people than it can successfully accommodate. Three's company, four or five's a crowd. I know that for most people two is company and three doesn't work. But for the three of us that summer, somehow it did. Even if it required a bit of an effort from all of us. Perhaps we were unusual people. Perhaps we were simply lucky. We had the wind behind us. We had a will to make it work. And we were young.

No, that won't do. We still are young. Young in the heart anyway. Which is the only place that matters. The only place where it's important to be young. But back then we were very young…

THE END

****

Author's Note

Silver City was a real airline. Though it was named not after Las Vegas but the mining town of Broken Hill in Australia, where the idea for the company was originally floated. It grew into one of Britain's most important independent airlines during the 1950s and early '60s. Lydd Ferryfield airport was for some of that time a busier place than London's Heathrow.

However, the book you've been reading is a work of fiction. Although I have tried to give a reasonably accurate account of Silver City's routes, routines and procedures, I have not been writing a text book. I have taken some liberties with the time line. For example, Silver City merged with Freddie Laker's Channel Air Bridge in 1962. By the time of this story's setting in 1963 the fleet was wearing the livery of the now merged entity, British United Airways. And all the characters and the individual adventures in the book are fictitious. I would be very surprised indeed if there were as many as five gay men among the company's complement of about forty pilots.

I have, though, made use of one event that is not fictitious. That is the story of the 'Shacklip', the device for securing cars in the hold quickly enough to reduce the turnaround time to eleven minutes. The inventor of this was a Mr (later Captain) Bert Hayes. A Hurricane pilot during the Second World War, he nevertheless found himself under-qualified when it came to flying commercial aircraft. Like the fictional Will he worked for Silver City as a driver. And he, having come up with his invention, bargained with the board, who in return for the use of the idea, agreed to pay for him to be trained as a commercial pilot. He returned to work in this capacity for Silver City and later moved to British Caledonian Airways, captaining BAC 1-11 jets.

In researching for this story I have used a number of sources. I am indebted to two books in particular. *Ferryman*, by Air Commodore 'Taffy' Powell (Airlife Publishing Ltd. 1982) and *Silver City Airways, Pioneers of the Skies,* by Keith J. Dagwell (The History Press 2010).

I am particularly grateful to Peter (former First Officer) Wareham who has supplied me with many wonderful nuggets of information about the company's operations, remembered from his time flying out of Lydd in the 1950s. His patient responses to my many detailed questions have been much appreciated.

I am also grateful to Charles Coussens for reading the manuscript.

I have quoted at some length from Antoine de Saint Exupéry. The extract comes from his wonderful autobiographical book, Terre des Hommes. An English translation of the book exists under the title: Wind, Sand and Stars. However the translation I have quoted from was David's own.

Finally, yes, The Fourteenth of July / Le Quatorze Juillet, G-ANWK, was a real aeroplane, as were the others whose names and registration numbers I have quoted. I remember watching Le Quatorze Juillet, Whiskey Kilo, take off and land at Lydd as a child. As a twelve-year-old I bought and made up the Airfix kit model of it. The kit is still just about available on the internet.

Anthony McDonald

Anthony McDonald is the author of more than twenty novels. He studied modern history at Durham University, then worked briefly as a musical instrument maker and as a farmhand before moving into the theatre, where he has worked in every capacity except director and electrician. He has also spent several years teaching English in Paris and London. He now lives in rural East Sussex.

If you have enjoyed the flying episodes in this novel you may also enjoy **Along the Stars** by the same author.

Other novels by Anthony McDonald

THE DOG IN THE CHAPEL
TOM & CHRISTOPHER AND THEIR KIND
DOG ROSES
THE RAVEN AND THE JACKDAW
RALPH: DIARY OF A GAY TEEN
IVOR'S GHOSTS
ADAM
BLUE SKY ADAM
GETTING ORLANDO
ORANGE BITTER, ORANGE SWEET
ALONG THE STARS
WOODCOCK FLIGHT

MATCHES IN THE DARK:13 Tales of Gay Men
(Short story collection)

Gay Romance Series:

Sweet Nineteen
Gay Romance on Garda
Gay Romance in Majorca
The Paris Novel
Cocker and I
Cam Cox
The Van Gogh Window
Gay Tartan
Tibidabo
Spring Sonata
Touching Fifty
Romance on the Orient Express

All titles are available as Kindle ebooks and as paperbacks from Amazon.

www.anthonymcdonald.co.uk

16775563R00169